//////// NASCAR

SECRETS and LEGENDS

FORBIDDEN ATTRACTION
by Marisa Carroll

From the opening green flag at Daytona to the final checkered flag at Homestead, the competition will be fierce for the NASCAR Sprint Cup Series championship.

The **Grosso** family practically has engine oil in their veins. For them racing represents not just a way of life but a tradition that goes back to NASCAR's inception. Like all families, they also have a few skeletons to hide. What happens when someone peeks inside the closet becomes a matter that threatens to destroy them.

The **Murphys** have been supporting drivers in the pits for generations, despite a vendetta with the Grossos that's almost as old as NASCAR itself! But the Murphys have their own secrets... and a few indiscretions that could cost them everything.

The **Branches** are newcomers, and some would say upstarts. But as this affluent Texas family is further enmeshed in the world of NASCAR, they become just as embroiled in the intrigues on and off the track.

The **Motor Media Group** are the PR people responsible for the positive public perception of NASCAR's stars. They are the glue that repairs the damage. And more than anything, they feel the brunt of the backlash....

These NASCAR families have secrets to hide, and reputations to protect. This season will test them all.

Dear Reader,

Welcome to the world of NASCAR: SECRETS AND LEGENDS. The stories in this continuity series combine two of our favorite elements—family dynamics and stock car racing.

We grew up in a small town in northwestern Ohio, far from the superspeedways of Daytona and Talladega, but we were privileged to know a man who was familiar with all we weren't. His tales of competing with the great drivers of his era were fascinating for two teenage girls. But in those days his stories were about the only contact we had with the sport.

Now all that has changed. We are a short hour-and-a-half drive from Michigan International Speedway, and with satellite TV and radio hookups we can watch each race of the season, and we do. But some of our best times are still spent listening to the retelling of those great stories from back in the day....

We hope you enjoy Justin and Sophia's story as much as we enjoyed writing it.

Carol and Marian

//////NASCAR

FORBIDDEN ATTRACTION

Marisa Carroll

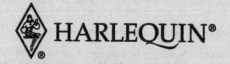

HARLEQUIN®

TORONTO • NEW YORK • LONDON
AMSTERDAM • PARIS • SYDNEY • HAMBURG
STOCKHOLM • ATHENS • TOKYO • MILAN • MADRID
PRAGUE • WARSAW • BUDAPEST • AUCKLAND

ISBN-13: 978-0-373-21785-4
ISBN-10:   0-373-21785-4

FORBIDDEN ATTRACTION

MARISA CARROLL

is the pen name of sisters Carol Wagner and Marian Franz. The team has been writing bestselling books for almost twenty-five years. During that time they have published over forty titles, most for the Harlequin Superromance line, and are the recipients of several industry awards, including a Lifetime Achievement Award from *Romantic Times BOOKreviews* and a RITA® Award nomination from Romance Writers of America. Their books have been featured on the *USA TODAY*, Waldenbooks and B.Dalton bestseller lists. The sisters live near each other in northwestern Ohio, surrounded by children, grandchildren, brothers, sisters, aunts, uncles, cousins and old and dear friends.

The generations-old Grosso-Murphy feud worsened when driver Kent Grosso started receiving blackmail threats—until photographer Tanya Wells proved an incriminating photo was a publicity stunt.... But who was behind it?

CHAPTER ONE

"C'MON, HUGO. I FINISHED fifth not thirty-fifth. A top-five finish at Daytona. The Great American Race." Justin Murphy gave his uncle a feigned clip on the shoulder. "Lighten up. You're acting like I went out there and screwed up the car." The first race of the season had ended two hours earlier but the celebrating inside the Turn-Rite Tools corporate suite was still going strong. Twenty-five or thirty people filled the smallish space, eating, drinking and crowding around Justin and his uncle—and crew chief—Hugo Murphy. "Everyone here's fine with my finish."

"Yeah, well, Dixon Rogers isn't and he still calls the shots at Fulcrum Racing, don't forget. Do you think these suits from Turn-Rite won't ditch you in a heartbeat if Dixon lets it be known he's 'looking to go in a new direction' for next season? Or the other way around. The sponsor didn't drop fifteen million dollars in the kitty not to get their chance at the championship."

Of course he'd thought of that. What driver didn't worry about what his team owner was thinking—or his sponsors, big and small. But hell, he'd run a good race, except for that one blown call, and who could blame him for taking off after Kent Grosso that way? Wasn't he put on this earth to outdrive the Grossos, father and son, and avenge his family's honor?

"Justin, we need another shot of you with our employee of the year." Diane Meeks, his publicity rep from Motorsports Media Group—MMG—elbowed her way through the well-fed and tipsy gaggle of Turn-Rite executives, towing a slightly bewildered-looking man and his young family in her wake.

"Sure," he said, raising his hand to the bill of his orange-and-brown Turn-Rite Tools ball cap to make sure the logo was properly positioned. He smiled and held out his hand to Nick Harris, a guy who appeared to be not much older than he was, a couple years past thirty, maybe, with a pretty wife, two cute kids and another on the way. But inside, Justin wasn't smiling. He'd blown it. He'd been running good the whole race. The car's setup was excellent. The pit crew had been smoking—and he'd let it slip through his fingers just to beat Kent Grosso off pit road.

"Thanks, Justin," the plump, fortysomething PR rep said as the photographer positioned the award winner and his family next to him.

"Glad to oblige," he responded, shifting into sponsor-stroking mode as quickly as he shifted gears on his race car. He flashed Diane his trademark killer smile and she flushed slightly. Not so much because of his unequaled sex appeal; she seemed immune to his charm. But because he knew she was lined up right behind Hugo to rip him a new one for letting himself get carried away chasing down Kent Grosso, when he should have been protecting his chances of a second-place finish.

Now he'd gone and done the right thing in the PR department, so she'd have to hold her tongue for the time being. Diane was a good rep and she never strayed far from her objective, which was marketing one Justin Troy

Murphy as a driver with the potential to be one of NASCAR's greatest. Her biggest problem was that Justin usually failed, if just by a car length, to live up to the hype.

He gave her a two-fingered salute and a wink that told her he knew exactly what she was thinking, then bent to autograph the back of Nick Swan's oldest kid's T-shirt. He was a good driver. But good wasn't enough any more; sponsors didn't pay millions of dollars to back a driver who never made it to Victory Lane. A top-five finish at Daytona was cause for celebration certainly—witness the crowd around him—but it wasn't the same as being in Victory Lane. That's what Turn-Rite Tools was paying the big bucks to see happen.

"You managed to finish fifth," Hugo growled under his breath when they were momentarily left alone in front of the decimated buffet table, not letting Justin off the hook as easily as Diane had. "Because you *coasted* over the finish line just ahead of the pack. You ran out of gas because you pulled out early just to beat Kent Grosso out of the pits."

"I wasn't going to let the SOB get out ahead of me— Hey, what's up, buddy?" Justin interrupted himself as the Harris kid came running up once more.

"Can I have your autograph, too?" the boy asked giving Justin a grin but holding out his fine-tipped permanent marker to Hugo. "Right there on the back beside Justin's." He spun around, presenting his back to Hugo, looking over his shoulder. "Please? My dad said you're the best crew chief in NASCAR. That's why we're sponsoring your team."

"I'm mighty proud to hear that," Hugo said, no trace of the anger that Justin sensed simmering below the surface evident on his uncle's weathered countenance. He signed the back of the boy's T-shirt, then shook hands with the father who had come hurrying up to make sure his son wasn't out of bounds.

"Good racing," Harris said as he shook hands with Justin one more time, then put his arm around his son's shoulder and wandered away. Justin watched them go. He had never walked arm and arm with his father. Troy Murphy had died before Justin was old enough to remember him, and even though he was a grown man now, a small part of him still felt the loss.

The marketing V.P. who was hosting the celebration announced last call. He wanted everyone out bright and early for the filming of Justin's kick-off spot for the Turn-Rite spring advertising blitz. Everyone headed for the bar, except Justin and his uncle. "Good racing, my butt," Hugo muttered under his breath. "You're just lucky you didn't drag the catch-can guy halfway down pit road on national TV when you took off early."

Justin locked his jaw and kept his mouth shut. His impatience and momentary lack of focus had put a team member at risk and he wasn't proud of it. "It was the only way to beat Grosso out of the pits." The excuse sounded as lame to his own ears as it did to his crew chief.

His uncle snorted in disgust. Hugo was a tall man, thick across the neck and shoulders. He had twenty years and twenty pounds on Justin, but his nephew harbored no illusion that the older man couldn't knock him flat on his butt if he put his mind to it.

"I apologized to Eddie. He's okay with what happened." Justin ground out the words between clenched teeth. He'd been wrong and they both knew it. No use wasting breath defending the indefensible. He slid on the mirror-finish wraparound sunglasses that he endorsed and that his cousin, Hugo's adopted daughter, Kim, declared made him look like some warrior angel—but she was always grinning like a fool when she said it—and headed out of the suite to avoid escalating the argument with his uncle.

"Justin," Diane called after him. She didn't add "get your scrawny butt back here," but she might as well have. Justin kept on walking. He knew he should stick around for another round of hand-pumping—hell, he was more than likely contractually obliged to—but he'd had enough.

Hugo was the only father Justin had ever known. Being at odds with the man who'd raised him from a baby wasn't where Justin liked to be, but it seemed it was where he ended up more and more often lately. It wasn't as if he'd just started driving like his dad. Brawn over brains, muscle over finesse, that kind of thing. Hugo shouldn't have been surprised that he'd taken out after Kent Grosso today. It was his style. Besides the fans liked to see flat-out racing, and that's what he'd given them. Even above the roar of all that combined horsepower he could hear the whoops and hollers of approval as he'd crowded onto the race track just a nose ahead of Grosso's car.

Hugo caught up with him at the elevators. "Don't go ditching the sponsors like that again, you hear?" he growled.

"Diane will cover for me."

"They don't pay that woman enough for pulling your chestnuts out of the fire after every damned race," Hugo muttered.

"Look. I'm tired and I want something to eat beside chips and dip," Justin grumbled, knowing he sounded like a petulant child. Pleasing the major sponsor of your car was second only to driving the car in a driver's litany of duties; often it seemed to Justin that it actually was number one.

"You weren't going to starve to death if you took five minutes to say goodbye." Hugo had raced some in his younger days, but he hadn't been a natural at the sport like his Uncle Connor or his older brother, Troy, Justin's father. He'd found early on he'd rather run the behind-the-scenes race strategy and leave the driving to others. And he was damned good at what he did. But so was Justin, if they would just let him race like he wanted to.

"We'll thrash this out back home," Hugo said, his tone just shy of making it a command, not a request. Home was Mooresville, North Carolina, where the Murphys had lived for seven generations. For the past two seasons, Justin had driven the No. 448 Turn-Rite Tools Chevrolet for owner Dixon Rogers's Fulcrum Racing team. He'd finished out of the Chase for the NASCAR Sprint Cup both years. But this season was going to be different. This year he was determined to make it. "What time are you and Dennis pulling out?" Dennis was a distant cousin on his father's side. He was Justin's spotter and he drove Justin's motor home from track to track.

"I'm not leaving tonight," he reminded his uncle. "I'm doing a shoot for a TV spot for Turn-Rite here at the track tomorrow, remember?"

"You're right. I forgot." Hugo took off his own Turn-Rite hat and ran his hand through his hair. "I've got a car to get ready for California next week. I can't always remember your schedule."

"That's my job." Diane broke in, coming up behind them. "I made your excuses in there, Justin," she said, jerking her thumb back over her shoulder. "Now I have to go back and do some more to settle the ruffled feathers."

"I appreciate that, Diane," Justin forced himself to say.

The photographer caught up with them, panting with the effort of shadowing the fast-moving Diane while carrying his heavy equipment. "Seven o'clock sharp. Pit road. The film crew will be set up by then. Makeup shouldn't take too long since they're going to shoot you in full track gear." Ordinarily the No. 448 car would have already been loaded on the hauler on its way back to the shop in Mooresville while a show car, used for public appearances and identical to the one he drove today, would have been its stand-in. But a different setup was required for the Fontana track, so Justin's car was still in the garage and a second Fulcrum Motors hauler would soon be on the road for the grueling twenty-five hundred mile drive from North Carolina to California.

"Seven!" Justin frowned but didn't say what he thought about wearing makeup or getting up that early in the morning.

"Seven," she repeated deadpan. "Sharp."

"Yes, ma'am," he said in his best good ol' boy drawl. "I'll be there with bells on."

"Fine," Diane replied, ignoring his sarcasm. "I'll meet you at the garage in the morning." She said her goodbyes and walked back in the direction they'd come, signaling for the photographer to follow her. He had to jog to keep up once she hit her stride. The woman might be a dozen pounds overweight but she sure could move.

"You'd better be there on time," Hugo warned, letting Justin know he was still angry. "I don't want the Turn-Rite people to have anything else to complain about. Despite the handshakes and back-slapping up there in the suite, they've been hinting that a car that doesn't make the Chase three years running isn't what they had in mind for their fall advertising campaign."

The Chase for the NASCAR Sprint Cup started in September. It was still February. But NASCAR wasn't like other sports, with seasons leading up to the playoffs and championships. The first race of the season was the biggest one of all. Daytona. The Superbowl of stock car racing— and Justin had messed up big time.

"Three times a charm," he said under his breath before Hugo's warning came back to him. *Or three strikes, you're out?*

"I'll see you Tuesday at the shop. We can go over last year's tapes of Fontana before we fly out to California," Hugo said, his mouth still set in a tight, straight, line.

"I'll be there."

He probably wouldn't be in his house in Mooresville long enough to unpack. His plane left for California Tuesday afternoon. Fulcrum Racing owned a corporate jet, as most race teams did, and of course Dixon had his own private Gulfstream, but the retired Hall of Fame baseball manager was also rumored to have the first dollar he ever made. If Justin's schedule differed from the rest of the team, he flew commercial. One day he was going to have to get a plane of his own like that jerk, Kent Grosso. Right now, he wasn't quite that high on the NASCAR food chain. Yet. But one day, in the not too distant future, he intended to be.

When the elevator doors slid open, uncle and nephew parted ways, Hugo heading toward the garage to make sure nothing had been left behind in the hurry to load the hauler, and Justin to his motor home. His backside hurt from sitting for hours in the hard seat of his race car. There was a blister on his heel where the heat of the exhaust pipe running under his feet had seeped through to his skin despite the fire-retardant boots and protective shields he wore over them. He wished he had the nerve to use the bottom of a plain old foam coffee cup to protect his feet like some other drivers did. But that image was not one that either Turn-Rite Tools or MMG approved of, so he never tried it, and now he was suffering the consequences.

Maybe he'd just take a long hot shower, grab a sandwich and call it a night—get his beauty sleep so he'd look good for his close-ups tomorrow. That way if he couldn't cut it as a NASCAR driver, he could make his fortune in the movies. He snorted at the thought and picked up the pace. The security guard at the gate to the private motor-home lot waved him through with a "good race."

The lot was emptying fast. Motor homes, some of them rolling palaces costing over a million dollars, were being buttoned up and moved out, heading for home, or starting on the long cross-country trip to California for the second race of the season. The corners of his mouth turned up in a smile as he regarded his vintage 1947 Spartan Manor travel trailer, dwarfed as it was by the two fifty-footers parked on either side. He couldn't afford one of the big rigs, but even if he could, he didn't want one. For all their top-end furnishings and electronics, they still came off an assembly line. His manor was one of a kind. They didn't make them like this baby any more.

And if the powers-that-be had their way, this one wouldn't be sitting here among the homes-away-from-home of his fellow drivers much longer. More than one track had been less than happy to allow the Manor into the Owners' and Drivers' lot last season. Diane had come to the rescue hinting around that negative publicity, the weeding out of any individuality in the sport, was not a good thing. The suggestion that a rig that a fan might be proud to own wasn't good enough for a NASCAR Sprint Cup Series driver sent them grumbling away. But he had the feeling the Manor's days were numbered. New rules would be written and codified and his trailer would be banned from the tracks for "the good of the sport" and retired to the same hillside overlooking Lake Norman where he'd originally found it.

The glow of the interior lighting reflecting off the mirror-finish of the aluminum shell reminded him he wasn't going to be alone when he shut himself inside. And the person in the motor coach wasn't his cousin Dennis who had "other" plans for the night. "Damn," he muttered under his breath yanking open the high, tight collar of his uniform and dragging down the zipper. *Lucy.* He'd forgotten all about her. *What did that say about their relationship?* he wondered, as he punched in the code for the state-of-the-art security system he'd installed when he'd done the trailer restoration.

Lucy Gunter, his on-again, off-again girlfriend, was sitting on the built-in sofa to the left of the door, her long legs stretched out in front of her, her head propped up on one of the red and gray-patterned throw pillows that matched the forties-style brick-red upholstery on the cushions and complimented the blond finish on the birch cabinetry. Her laptop was open on the fold-down table of the dinette opposite her, but she'd stopped using it long enough ago for the screen saver to kick in. She was watching the plasma-screen TV he'd had mounted into one of the overhead cupboards, but he suspected by the sleepy look in her eyes that he'd caught her napping.

Good, maybe that meant she was as tired as he was and she wouldn't remember he'd promised to take her dancing at a new club she'd heard about from one of her friends.

"Hey," he said leaning down to give her a quick peck on the cheek.

"Hey, yourself." She sat up and ran her fingers through her strawberry-blond hair, making no attempt to prolong the kiss. *Hell,* he thought to himself, *how long had it been since they'd gotten any more romantic than a quick hug and kiss? Weeks? Maybe longer.*

"Do your duty by the sponsor?" she asked as he opened the built-in refrigerator and snagged himself a bottle of water.

"I fulfilled my contractual obligations," he said.

"You drove good today," she said swinging her legs onto the linoleum floor. It really *was* linoleum, the old-fashioned kind and damned expensive flooring, but period appropriate, as the woman at the motor-home restoration place assured him. Up until he came across the Manor sitting among the pine trees above the lake he wouldn't have believed there was such a thing as a vintage-motor-home restoration service.

"Tell Hugo that."

"Well, you drove good about 185 laps," Lucy amended. "I don't suppose he was too happy with you for waving off the gas guy that way just to beat Kent Grosso out of the pits. He wasn't running that well."

"Yeah, but he sure made up for it those last fifteen laps." Grosso had finished second. The spot where Justin had been running for twenty-five of the last forty laps.

"The Grossos have always been able to push all your buttons. You beat him onto pit road by three seconds. Staying in for another gallon of gas would have made the difference."

"I figured I'd get another lap. I guessed wrong." He drove with his heart, not his head. Trouble was, there wasn't room for that kind of racing in today's NASCAR. At least to hear his uncle tell it.

He braced himself for a lecture on listening to his crew chief and the importance of fuel consumption modules, but to his relief Lucy changed the subject. "You want something to eat?"

Since he already had his head in the refrigerator, she hadn't just made a lucky guess. "I could use a sandwich." He usually wasn't hungry right after a race, there was too much adrenaline pumping through his bloodstream to be hungry. But now the adrenaline rush was wearing off and he was ravenous.

"Go take a shower. I'll make you something." She shut down her laptop. "Since we're stuck here until tomorrow, why don't we head out to the new club I told you about?"

Her words were casually spoken but there was a hint of challenge in her voice. He felt another twinge of conscience. He hadn't been around much over the past week. Of course, being a driver's girlfriend she knew that was the way it had to be, especially at Daytona during Speedweeks. But he hadn't been that busy every single hour. She'd used up a week of her vacation time to be with him. He could have taken her out to dinner, someplace nice and quiet, out of the way, where they could have eaten in relative peace, but he hadn't. Dennis kept the refrigerator stocked, and the guys at the hauler outdid themselves most nights with the gas grill and the turkey fryer. But it wasn't the same as a romantic dinner for two.

Lucy was looking at him over the top of the refrigerator door. "We don't have to go if you're tired. I know you have to film that TV spot tomorrow." A slight frown pulled her softly arched brows together over her blue eyes, and he realized her expression mirrored his own.

"Nah, I'm not tired. I'll change and eat my sandwich while you get your dancing shoes on." He glanced at the clock located in a panel above the wraparound windows in the kitchen area at the front of the coach. "We've got plenty of time. The place won't even start rockin' for another couple of hours."

Her frown disappeared and a smile spread across her face. "Great," she said. "Everyone will be there. It's impossible to get in if you're not on the list."

Justin gave her a big cheeky grin. "Does finishing fifth in the Great American Race automatically get your name on that list or do I have to wear my Turn-Rite threads to rate that?" He folded his arms across his chest and struck the pose that stared down at everyone entering a Turn-Rite store throughout the South and the Midwest.

She reddened slightly. "You're making fun of me."

She wasn't in the mood for his teasing tonight it seemed. Come to think of it she took everything he said to heart these days. Were they heading for another breakup? His frown returned. He shut the birch pocket doors he'd installed to separate the kitchen-sitting area from the bedroom and bathroom and undressed.

His relationship with Lucy had been rocky from the start. They'd already called it quits twice, then got back together, vowing to give it one more chance. But he wondered if they'd make it through another rough patch. He wasn't the marrying kind. Not with his family history. A father who everyone pretty much agreed was an A-1 bastard, who some people still liked to say had made his pretty, young wife's life so miserable she'd committed suicide, even though she had two little babies to take care of. What if he turned out to be as bad a husband and father as his dad? The thought as always made him feel as though a cold fist had squeezed itself around his heart. Better not to go there at all.

He cranked up the hot water in the stainless-steel shower and let it pour over him, hoping to ease a few of the aches and pains he'd accumulated through five hundred miles of hot hard racing. His mother had been depressed, Hugo had always told him, not herself when she took the overdose of sleeping pills. Her death had been an accident, pure and simple. They called it postpartum depression now. His dad had been hard to live with, but he hadn't been a monster. Not by a long shot.

But how was Justin to know that? The same blood ran in his veins. And even Hugo, a good man, hadn't been able to keep his own marriage together. Justin wasn't about to invite a woman to share his life when he didn't know for sure he wasn't going to turn out just like his dad. After all someone—driving a *Grosso* pickup—had hated the man enough to run him down and leave him for dead by the side of the road.

CHAPTER TWO

SOPHIA GROSSO CURLED HER fingers around the steering wheel of her Chevy Blazer and peered out the windshield. The dark bulk of the old warehouse loomed over them and she wondered what in heaven's name she was doing here. "Are you sure this is the place?" she asked her friend and coworker, Alicia Perez.

"Positive. I followed Neil's directions to the letter."

Neil Sanchez was her brother Kent's crew chief. Sanchez wasn't exactly Sophia's favorite person in the world, but she kept that fact to herself. Loyalty to the team was drummed into a NASCAR driver's family from early childhood. "It looks deserted."

"Except for the two hundred cars in the parking lot," Alicia observed dryly.

Sophia giggled a little, feeling foolish. "You're right about that." The big, poorly lit parking lot was full of vehicles. Lots of SUVs and sports cars and even a few limousines. More were pulling in behind them. "What did you say this place was called again?" she asked as she switched off the ignition.

"*frenetic.* With no capital F," Alicia said, preparing to climb out of the SUV. "It's the hottest club in town. Lucy Gunter said that John Travolta and Matthew McConaughey were both here last night. Not to mention all the drivers. It's almost impossible to get in unless you know someone who's absolutely on the A list."

"Like my brother?" Sophia asked, jiggling the door handle to be sure it was locked. "The reigning NASCAR Sprint Cup Series Champion because I can guarantee you my name won't be on it." She pushed the button to set the alarm and zipped her keys securely into her purse. She didn't particularly like crowds and she definitely didn't like tromping across big dark parking lots with bad paving in high-heeled sandals.

Alicia laughed. "Hey, we live right next door to each other, right? We've worked together for over two years. I know you don't party with the in crowd. How many Friday nights have we spent doing laundry and watching movies together?"

"Don't remind me," Sophia said, wrinkling her nose. "I'm an old stick-in-the-mud and I know it."

"Yeah, and you're the pokiest driver on earth. All those racing genes in your blood and you drive slower than my Nana Estella."

"Hey, you, watch the sass. It's a long walk back to the condo," Sophia warned.

"I feel like I could dance all the way out to the beach." Alicia tossed her head, sending her mane of shining black hair swinging around her shoulders.

Sophia wished she could do that without feeling like a complete fool. Maybe because she was a blond—although in all honesty an artfully enhanced one—she didn't allow herself to play off the feminine mannerisms that seemed to come so naturally to her fun-loving and outgoing friend.

"How do you find out if we're on the A list or if we have to stand in line with the *hoi polloi?*"

"Hoi polloi? Where do you come up with this stuff?" Alicia asked, linking arms.

"It means—"

"I know what it means. I went to college, remember. I just can't believe you use it in everyday conversation."

"Okay. I'll watch it. If we make it inside I swear I won't use a single word over two syllables."

Alicia giggled. "You already did. *Syllables* has three syllables."

Still giggling, she sauntered up to the muscular Latino manning the velvet rope blocking the entrance into the former warehouse. There were rumbles of consternation from the crowd of people behind them, a few voices raised in question at their jumping the line.

"Hola," Alicia said, batting her long, thick and completely authentic lashes at the man. "I'm Alicia Perez and this is my friend, Sophia Grosso. She's Kent Grosso's sister. The NASCAR champion? He finished second in the race today?"

"I know who he is," the man said, his expression hard as the concrete beneath their feet. "I don't know who you two are. I need to see some ID."

"Sure," Alicia said, producing her driver's license from her tiny purse with a flick of long, red nails. Alicia had had them applied the first day they arrived in Daytona Beach. Normally she kept her nails short and unpolished. She was a registered nurse, as was Sophia, and back in Charlotte they worked together at the same geriatric care and rehabilitation center, Sunny Hills, where Sophia was the director of nursing services. While her friend flirted with the doorkeeper in Spanish, Sophia fumbled in her larger and less fashionable purse for her identification.

"Here," she said, finally locating it in one of the zippered pockets. She handed it over.

The guard gave it a long look. He raised his eyes and smiled for the first time, "Welcome to *frenetic,* Senorita Grosso. Your brother drove a hell of a race today. But I'm one of your dad's biggest fans. Sure was sorry to see him out of the race so early."

"So was I," Sophia answered with a smile. Her father, Dean Grosso, drove the Smoothtone Music Dodge and had been driving stock cars since before she was born.

"Enjoy, ladies." He unhooked the velvet rope for them to pass through.

"Look, they're opening the doors. It's like something out of a sci-fi movie, isn't it?" Alicia murmured excitedly.

Sophia had to agree. A shiver ran down her spine as the huge metal garage doors slid upward revealing a black void beyond, with only a single, narrow corridor of light to guide their way. As soon as they stepped over the threshold, the big doors slid downward again, cutting off their escape, or at least it seemed that way to Sophia.

"C'mon," Alicia said urging her forward. They followed the narrow walkway of light, past a waterfall at least twenty feet high that thundered into a gigantic stainless steel vat, instead of a pool. Lasers arrowed out of the depths of the vat and colored lights played over them, making Sophia slightly dizzy. "Impressive," her friend yelled into her ear. A few steps later, as they entered the vast high-ceilinged club, the noise from the waterfall was replaced by loud music and what seemed like a thousand voices, laughing and shouting.

Other than an awe-inspiring number of lights and lasers, a stage for the trio of DJs and a bar that had to be fifty feet long, the owners of *frenetic* hadn't done much to upgrade the warehouse ambiance. And why should they? Sophia thought, gazing around. In six months or a year at most, this place would be relegated to the long list of clubs that used to be trendy, but were now "so over," as Alicia liked to say.

"I'm going to get something to drink." Alicia pantomimed putting a glass to her lips.

"I'm going to find the emergency exits," Sophia shouted back. "This place is a firetrap."

Alicia rolled her eyes. "Relax. Want a margarita?"

"Designated driver," Sophia yelled, wishing she'd brought ear plugs. This place was almost as loud as the race track—almost.

"Great. In that case I'll drink one for you. And I'll bring you a club soda."

"Thanks."

Sophia didn't even try to find them a table. These kinds of clubs weren't made for sitting and talking. They were for dancing and hooking up and probably all kinds of other dealings that Sophia would rather not think about. She managed to find a spot by a steel girder that helped support the roof lost in the shadows high above her, scoped out the exit signs and the most direct path to them, and then looked around to see if she could spot anyone she recognized.

A few of the younger drivers were probably here, but she knew that a lot of the racing community had either returned to their homes for a day or so, or were already on the road to the next race, all the way across the country in California.

She and Alicia had one more day of vacation at the condo on the beach that her great-grandfather Milo Grosso and his wife, Juliana, owned, and then it was back to the real world for them, too.

Ten minutes later, Alicia was back from the bar with a brimming, salt-encrusted margarita and a glass of sparkling water garnished with a tiny sliver of key lime for Sophia. She nodded her thanks, not even attempting to say the words aloud and turned her attention to the bank of laser lights that surrounded the stage where giant TV screens behind the DJs showcased the everchanging patterns of color and movement on the dance floor. She didn't recognize the music—alternative or cutting-edge rock, or Lord knows what it was called these days—but the visuals were entertaining, so she focused on the screens instead.

She wondered for a moment if she was getting old. This place did nothing for her. She was only here to give Alicia a good time. Sunny Hills wasn't the most exciting place in the world to work. And it was even farther down on the list of places to meet eligible men—at least eligible men who were not contemporaries of her great-granddad.

She smiled as she realized how straightlaced she sounded even to herself. She was only twenty-eight-years-old, not a hundred and twenty-eight. She had to put a little more effort into enjoying herself.

"Hey, look. Isn't that Rafael O'Bryan?" Alicia hollered with her mouth just inches from Sophia's ear.

Sophia looked at the jumbo screen directly over the stage. As far as she could tell, the camera covering that particular screen was shooting down almost directly on the middle of the dance floor. Sure enough, Alicia's ultra-sensitive male-seeking radar had homed in on the hunky winner of the big race.

The handsome driver was surrounded by women and he seemed to be dancing, or maybe gyrating was a better word, with three of them.

"C'mon. Looks like he's taking on all comers. Let's go dance with him."

"No thanks." Sophia wasn't going to go out there and make a spectacle of herself with the heartthrob of NASCAR—as she'd seen him described in *People* magazine. Especially after today, when he'd put her father into the wall. She'd as soon scratch his eyes out as dance with him.

"Spoil sport," Alicia pouted but she stayed by Sophia's side, tapping her foot to the nerve-tingling bass beat of the music. "Wow. There's another one." The camera angle had changed, catching the crowd at the edge of the dance floor. A man in a pale blue dress shirt, open at the throat, the sleeves rolled halfway up his forearms, a leather jacket hooked nonchalantly over his shoulder by one crooked finger, stood scowling down at a petite blond who seemed to be urging him to dance. His brown hair was cut short and laid against his skull like a seal's pelt. There was no way Sophia could tell the color of his eyes in the distorted light of the cavernous space, but she didn't have to see any more clearly to know they were an even darker brown than his hair, or that the seal-sleek hair felt like silk threaded through her fingers.

Justin Murphy.

She'd know those high cheekbones and that aquiline nose anywhere even if she hadn't seen it staring down at her from half a dozen billboards on her way to work each and every morning. And the reason she knew his eyes were brown and his hair smooth as silk was because almost fifteen years before, on her thirteenth birthday, Justin Murphy had had the audacity to back her up behind the pool cabana at the motel where both their families had been staying, and kiss her full on the mouth. Her first kiss—and it had to be the boy she despised most in the world. She'd fully intended for the precocious son of her dad's front-tire changer to be the recipient of that honor.

She'd been mad, she remembered. But she'd liked his kiss, too. And when he'd challenged her to meet him again the next night so that he could teach her how to French kiss, she'd taken the dare. She was scared, not sure she wanted a boy to stick his tongue in her mouth, but she wasn't going to let a Murphy know that.

She hadn't liked it, just as she suspected but he'd only laughed and told her when she grew up she would, then he sauntered away. Leaving her to brood and plot how to get him alone again and show him she could kiss just as good as he could. It had taken several weeks to accomplish her goal. Back then, families didn't travel together that much. Her dad and mom had been one of the first couples to bring their children with them to races on a regular basis. But when she did have the chance she took it, sneaking off with Justin to a little wooded grove near the campground where they were staying for the August Michigan race.

And this time, it had been good. A little like kissing the devil, making her feel scared and tingly all at the same time. Sophia knew she was supposed to hate Justin Murphy with all her heart. Her great-grandpa, Milo, had been telling her that all her life. But it was hard to think badly about someone she liked to be with. Because, believe it or not, they didn't always just kiss. They talked, too, about all kinds of things. She would confide her girlish dreams of being an actress, or maybe an astronaut, or a teacher or nurse, whichever occupation interested her at the time, and he would tell her his goal in life. Hers changed almost weekly, but his was always the same. To be a NASCAR driver. The best NASCAR driver in the world.

Sophia's parents didn't allow her to date, and in those days before drivers traveled with their luxurious motor homes, she didn't go to every race, but for the next two summers whenever they could sneak off and be together, she'd let Justin Murphy lure her into one quiet, secluded spot or another and they would talk and kiss and neck a little. And brother, could he kiss! She got a little overheated just recalling those stolen moments, even all these years later.

But the summer she was fifteen, Justin's kisses had gotten more demanding and his hands had begun to roam a little too intimately. Sophia wasn't a very sophisticated fifteen and she'd become a little frightened of his intensity. She'd scrambled away, running out of the woods with Justin hot on her heels—straight into her brother's arms.

At seventeen, Kent had seemed a grown man to her, especially in his uniform, driving his first NASCAR Bush Series season.

Kent had taken one look at her mussed hair and clothes—and the guilty look on her face—and sent a red-faced and sullen Justin packing, then proceeded to give her the lowdown on the family history once more.

The Murphys and the Grossos had been sworn enemies for two generations, he'd reminded her. She had no business rolling around in the bushes with the son of the man who had sabotaged their father's car and got him accused of cheating—probably lost him the championship that year—and who also made Dean, for a time, the prime suspect in his death when Troy Murphy went and got himself killed by a hit-and-run driver. And even further back in the mists of time, Justin's great-uncle Connor, had cheated to win a race, taking the championship from Milo, before, he too, was killed under mysterious circumstances.

That all these things had happened before Sophia's birth made not one iota of difference. Grossos did not forget. And they did not forgive. She was a Grosso and that was the way it had to be.

Chagrined and ashamed that she'd betrayed her family's honor, she'd agreed.

She hadn't let herself be alone with Justin Murphy ever again. In fact, they'd barely spoken in the dozen years since. The origins of the bad blood between their families might have occurred before she was born, but she was a Grosso and she stayed loyal to her clan.

The camera angle changed again, the scowling countenance of the driver of the No. 448 car disappeared from the screen. The tightness that gripped her chest when she first recognized her old nemesis eased. Sophia managed a deep breath and a swallow of her lukewarm club soda. It had only been a few kisses, well maybe a little more than just kisses, but nothing serious, nothing like—true love. And it was a long time ago. If she was going to get worked up over Justin Murphy here and now, it should be because he'd traded paint with Kent on the race track a few hours ago, not because he'd taught her to French kiss when they were in their teens.

A few more minutes passed. Justin Murphy and his blond companion didn't appear on the dance floor or on any of the other giant screens. She relaxed a little more. Once more, she'd managed to avoid coming face to face with him. And once more, in a small, guarded corner of her heart she was disappointed.

Alicia finished her margarita and, hoping to snag

another, looked around for a waiter but there were none to be seen. "One more for the road," she said wiggling her glass in Sophia's face. "Can I get you a refill?"

Sophia held up her half-full glass and shook her head. "I'm good."

"Come with me anyway. We're never going to meet any guys standing here." At least Sophia assumed that's what Alicia said, since she was tugging her along by the wrist. Black hair swinging, hips swaying, her friend parted the mostly male crowd around the bar with only a smile, Sophia followed reluctantly in her wake. Now only four large men stood between Alicia and her margarita.

They were too deep into race talk, Sophia surmised from their gestures and the fact that two of them were talking even louder than the music was playing, to notice their arrival. Alicia wiggled her way between them. She was smiling, her mouth moving, her red-tipped hands gesturing. Heads swiveled in Sophia's direction and she saw her friend's mouth form the words, "Kent Grosso's sister," with a sinking heart. Two seats at the bar were suddenly vacated.

Alicia slid onto one stool and urged Sophia to take the other. Gingerly, Sophia perched on the edge of the seat and pasted a smile on her face. Maybe it wouldn't be so bad. Five minutes later Alicia was deep into her second, and final, margarita—her friend had a very low tolerance for alcohol—and Sophia was fending off the slurred come-on of one of the inebriated foursome.

"No, I can't get you tickets for the races at Bristol," she said as politely as she could manage. If she had a nickel for every time someone had made that request, she'd be able to afford a suite at the famed Tennessee short track. "I don't even go to those races myself." Which was true.

She didn't go to Bristol or Darlington or any of the other races she could talk her way out of.

Sophia's deep dark secret was that, in a family of danger-loving men and strong, independent women, she was a sniveling coward and had been since she was old enough to realize that her daddy, and then her older brother, risked life and limb on a daily basis. When she did have to watch them race, like today, she was a nervous wreck for days afterward.

"Ah, c'mon, honey, you're a Grosso," the drunk wheedled. "Your dad's been racin' for thirty years. 'The Best Racer Who Never Won The Cup' isn't that what they call him?" Sophia curled her hand into a fist. She hated that phrase with a white-hot passion. Dean Grosso was one of the best drivers in the business. He'd just never had the luck to go with the skill. "Your brother came in second today. He's got a good chance to win it all again this year. I'll bet all you have to do is snap your fingers and, *poof,* tickets appear out of mid-air." What appeared out of mid-air was beer splashing out of the bottle he was waving between them.

Sophia gasped as the cold liquid soaked her to the skin.

"Oh hey, I'm sorry," he said, attempting to swipe at the stain down her front, his hands coming way too close for comfort.

"I'm all right. Don't bother," she said leaping off the padded bar stool and out of range of his pawing.

"Nah, honey. Let me make it up to you. I'm awful sorry," he said, but he was smirking as he stared at the wet, clinging bodice of her sundress. She knew he could see just about everything she'd been blessed with and she didn't like the look in his eyes.

"I'm fine. It's time for me and my friend to go." The guy was on the verge of turning ugly. She didn't want to be anywhere around when that happened.

"Hey, let me give you somethin' for spoilin' your dress. You know. To get it cleaned." He pulled a twenty out of his pocket, attempting to shove it down her bodice.

"Don't even think about it," she said mimicking her mother's most authoritative tone and it worked momentarily, at least, because he jerked his hand back as if he'd been burned. "Alicia, we're out of here." She turned to urge her friend off her bar stool. "Now."

The drunk got his courage back and thrust the twenty at her once more. "I said I want to give you something—"

A large tanned hand clamped around his wrist stopping his fingers from getting closer. "I think you'd better do as the lady says."

Oh great, she thought miserably as she grasped Alicia's hand so they didn't get separated in the crowd. Not another drunk, this one with a knight-in-shining-armor complex, sticking his nose in to save a damsel in distress, one who was capable of making a safe getaway on her own.

She spun around, intending to send her would-be rescuer off with her version of one of her nana's patented put-downs, when she found herself staring into the brown eyes and million-kilowatt smile of Justin Troy Murphy—the object of all her girlhood fantasies and the man every last member of her family despised.

CHAPTER THREE

"SOPHIA?"

It *was* her. The glare from those cornflower-blue eyes was unforgettable. And boy, was she an eyeful! Smooth, straight, sunlight-streaked hair that just brushed the curve of her chin, peaches and cream complexion touched with a sheen of gold from the Florida sun, and curves that would do justice to a world-class road course.

"Um, hello, Justin," she said, not sounding one bit happy to see him.

"Need some help?" He'd glimpsed her once or twice from a distance as he and Lucy bickered over whether to sit at the bar or to try to snag one of the smattering of little tables, or when—or if—he'd ever take her out onto the floor to dance. All that time he'd kept looking out over the crowd toward a pillar where Sophia was standing—tantalizing sightings—never quite certain if he was mistaken or not. Until a couple of minutes ago, when he'd gotten his first clear look at her being towed across the dance floor by a short, shapely brunette, and the punch of adrenaline coursing through his gut put an end to his uncertainty. When was the last time he'd been this close to her without her being surrounded by Grossos or worse yet, media and fans? Five years ago at Darlington. He remembered the encounter like it was yesterday.

He'd just moved from the NASCAR Craftsman Truck Series to the NASCAR Busch series, driving Dixon Rogers's second car, a piece of junk, but hell, he'd have driven a donkey cart to make it into the Show. He was damned glad to be where he was. Sophia, NASCAR princess, as he'd called her back when they were kids, was there to cheer on her brother as he made his first start in the Vittle Farms car, a ride that got Kent Grosso within inches of Raybestos Rookie of the Year honors.

By then it had been years since they'd kissed, but he hadn't forgotten what it felt like. He would have kissed her again—if he could have gotten her alone. But both Kent and Dean had been hanging around the hauler and all he'd managed was a, "Hi, how are you? Long time, no see," accompanied by a wink and a grin that had her blushing like a teenager.

She wasn't blushing now. Or looking like she wanted to be kissed. Her pretty mouth firmed into a straight line. "It's okay, Murphy. An accident, that's all. He just picked the wrong way to apologize. My friend and I are leaving."

His name must have set a few synapses firing in the brain of the guy who'd spilled beer all over Sophia's white dress. He swiveled his head toward Justin. "Hey, aren't you Justin Murphy?"

"Yeah, that's me." Justin said, snapping out of the pleasant fog of memories and into the nasty situation in front of him. There wasn't much use denying who he was. He wasn't Kent Grosso, or Rafael O'Bryan, but he wasn't a nobody either. He'd been interviewed on every TV station in town over the past ten days.

"Well, I'll be damned," the drunk said. "I'm an O'Bryan fan myself, but hey, a NASCAR driver's a NASCAR driver.

How about your autograph? Might be worth somethin' someday." He thrust a napkin at Justin and began fumbling in his shirt pocket for a pen.

He couldn't find one and Justin wasn't carrying one either. At the race track he usually had one with him. All the drivers did. It cut way down on the time it took to sign autographs.

"Here." Sophia shoved a pen into his hand. "Sign it so we can get out of here."

"Do it," Lucy urged from behind him. "I don't like the looks of that guy's friends."

Justin didn't argue with either woman. He shoved his new leather bomber jacket into Lucy's hands and took the pen from Sophia, scribbled his name and handed the napkin back to the drunk. From the corner of his eye, he could see the guy's friends muttering among themselves. From the dirty looks they were shooting him, he wasn't going to have to sign any bar napkins for them.

He took Lucy by the hand and started backing away from the bar. He locked gazes with Sophia Grosso for a few moments willing her to follow him to the door. Not counting on her to read his mind, he barked, "Follow me."

"Don't worry about us. We can get ourselves out of here."

Yep, it was Sophia all right. The most stubborn girl he had ever met. In that respect, at least, she hadn't changed a bit.

A shadow fell over him. "Hey, you. Murphy. You cost me a bundle of money today. What the hell were you doing blowin' off yer crew chief, pullin' out of your pit early?" This guy was even bigger than his buddy, and not an ounce of it was fat. Justin had to tilt his head to meet his bleary-eyed gaze. His heart rate accelerated a couple of beats. He could hold his own in a fight, but not against a guy who outweighed him by fifty pounds.

"Just racin'," he said letting his North Carolina drawl thicken to the consistency of blackstrap molasses. "Just racin'." He held up one hand palm out, in a gesture of peace.

"You cost me five hundred bucks today with that stupid move. I had you picked to finish in the top three," the mammoth drunk said, getting angrier with each word.

"Alicia, stay with me," Sophia spoke quietly, but Justin could hear every word even above the din. Sophia began urging her friend away from the bar, moving to her left until the two of them were almost beside him, beyond both the drunks' reaches. Others had begun to take notice of the raised voices and people began to inch away, forming a ring around them. Justin racked his brain for a way to defuse the situation but nothing came to mind beyond the urge to punch the jerk in the mouth.

"Damned crazed driver, just like the rest of the Murphys. Only one that had the juice was Connor, and he drove his Harley off the side of a mountain." His great-uncle hadn't *driven* off the side of a mountain. He'd been forced off the road and fallen to his death—according to family legend. To this day Hugo still thought Milo Grosso had had something to do with the accident that occurred twenty years before his birth. The beginning of the feud that threatened to outlast the Hatfields and McCoys.

"I drove the best race I could," Justin said holding on to his temper with both hands. "Sorry I couldn't get the win for you, buddy."

"Tell that to my ex. That was her alimony money I bet on you, loser. You Cup drivers all make money hand over fist. Five hundred bucks is chump change to you guys. Why don't you just give me a handful of C-notes and we'll all leave here friends."

Justin shook his head, the easy, practiced smile he'd kept anchored on his face with a direct effort of will, hardening into a grimace. "No can do, buddy."

"I think you can." The drunk must have been in bar fights before. He swung the beer bottle in a short arc, connecting with the edge of the granite bar. Shards of glass flew like shrapnel, beer sprayed his face in a parody of a Victory Lane celebration. Justin went into a slight defensive crouch as the broken neck of the beer bottle flashed back and forth in front of him. He heard Lucy gasp and the brunette with Sophia Grosso let out a yelp, but Sophia never made a peep.

Justin took a step to his right trying to keep the three women behind him as the drunk lurched forward. "You pretty boys are all alike. Am I right, honey?"

"That's enough, Kurt." One of his friends made a grab for the arm holding the beer bottle but the drunk fended him off. His friends held on to his free arm.

Justin reached behind him to grab Lucy by the wrist. He was as brave as the next guy but he wasn't stupid enough to take on a drunk waving a broken beer bottle. "Let's get out of here," he growled at Lucy. He could see Sophia and her friend were still beside him. Why hadn't she taken off when she had the chance? Justin backed up a few more inches, never taking his eyes off the bottle. Where in hell was a bouncer when you needed one?

Just then the drunk broke loose from his buddies. Flinging one against the bar, and the other to the floor, he lunged. Justin was backed up against a wall of people who had come to a stop when they reached the edge of the dance floor, and had nowhere to go. He wondered how long it would take him to bleed to death if the drunk went for his throat with the broken bottle. From the look in the guy's eye that was what he was aiming to do. He could hear Lucy sobbing, feel her trying to push her way through the crowd, but no one was moving.

He flexed his knees, thought maybe he could bring the guy down with a diving tackle. The drunk kept coming, the beer bottle swinging in tight, ugly circles. He wished he hadn't given Lucy his jacket. The heavy leather would have afforded him some protection, but it was too late now. Justin turned sideways to present a smaller target, made a grab for the hand holding the beer bottle and felt the jagged edge burn along the length of his forearm. Pain shot up his arm to his shoulder and into his brain. A woman yelled. The drunk hesitated, confused. At the same moment, from out of nowhere a leather purse swung like a mace on a chain and slammed the big man up side the head.

The drunk dropped to his knees. Someone shoved him down onto his stomach and straddled him. Justin stomped on his wrist, not caring if he broke the guy's arm, and the broken bottle went skidding from his grasp as he shrieked in pain, obscenities spewing from his mouth.

Already the crowd had started to gather around them again. Voices rose, yelling questions, hollering encouragement, screaming for someone to call the cops. He could see people getting ready to take pictures with their cell phones. Great. That was all he needed. To end up on the eleven o'clock news. His arm hurt like hell and he could feel blood dripping between his fingers and onto his shirt. His stomach heaved with pain and adrenaline. Time to blow this joint. "Let's get out of here," he hollered to Lucy.

"This way." It was Sophia Grosso—the leather purse that had felled the drunk was slung over her shoulder by a gold chain—motioning him to follow her toward a dimly lighted exit sign. She was towing her friend by the hand, parting the crowd as though she were eight feet tall and five feet wide, not willowy and blond and just an inch or two shy of his own five-ten. Justin gave Lucy a shove and followed in her wake.

Thirty seconds later, they emerged into the parking lot in the shadow of an old loading dock. Sirens sounded in the distance, coming closer with every passing second.

Sophia's friend was sobbing quietly and Lucy's breath was coming in quick short gasps. His head was spinning and his arm burned like fire. He looked down and saw blood running off the ends of his fingers, but nothing spurting, so the bastard hadn't cut an artery. He wiggled his fingers, saw they all worked, and figured he hadn't been hurt too bad.

"We can't stay here," Sophia urged when the big metal door they'd exited through swung open again and a half dozen people burst into the night, looking for them. Probably to take photos for the tabloids. Sirens grew louder and closer. Three police cars arrived with a squeal of tires and soon the strobe effect of blue and red lights bouncing off the dingy brick walls of the old warehouse rivaled the laser show inside.

"My truck's right in the middle of that," Justin said, angling his chin toward the VIP parking area.

"This way. I'm parked on the far side." Sophia was already moving—her high heels beating a tattoo on the asphalt, her hair swinging—still clutching her friend's hand as though she were a child. "We need to take a look at that arm. I have a first aid kit in my car."

"In a rental car?"

"My car," came the short, sharp reply. She didn't even sound winded. He, on the other hand, was beginning to have a hard time catching his breath.

"We drove down," the brunette said on a hiccup. Alicia, he'd heard Sophia call her. "We brought Sophia's great-grandparents. They don't like to fly anymore."

"Are you okay?" Lucy asked, her voice thin with shock as they passed beneath the anemic security light that served to illuminate this whole stretch of parking lot. "You're bleeding pretty bad." She clutched at his uninjured arm. "We should get you to a hospital."

"No."

She recoiled at the vehemence in the single word.

"My sponsors would have my hide hanging from my trailer door by the first lap of practice next week."

"It wasn't your fault."

"Tell that to the tabloids and the TV news guys."

As if on cue, a panel truck pulled in behind the police cars. Even from a distance it wasn't hard to spot the call letters of one of the local cable stations emblazoned on its side.

"How badly are you hurt?" Sophia's voice floated over him.

"I don't know," he answered honestly. "Not too bad. Bleeding like a stuck pig, though."

She stopped before a black SUV and beeped off the security, then looked around. "Most of the action's going on out front. That Hummer will hide the light from my truck." She opened the rear hatch and pulled out a small red tool box, the kind a lot of guys carried in their cars, but not many women. To his surprise when she opened this one, it wasn't filled with jumper cables and wrenches, but bandages and first aid supplies. "Sit," she said, motioning him onto the tailgate while slipping on a pair of latex gloves.

He did as she asked. To tell the truth he was feeling a little shaky.

"Let me see your arm." She hadn't looked directly into his face until that moment. Her blue eyes were dark as the twilight sky. Her hair was more spun silver than gold in the hazy light, lighter than he remembered. His head began to spin, maybe from loss of blood, maybe from the smell of her hair—lemony, but kind of spicy, too. He was doubly glad, now, that he was sitting down.

He dropped his gaze to her mouth. Her lips were thinned into a straight line but he knew from experience that they were warm and soft and full. He had the strongest urge to take her in his arms and kiss her just like he had so many years before. She was a woman now, not a shy, young girl, and he wondered if her kisses would reflect that maturity. He would like very much to compare the two. The out-of-bounds thought jerked him back to reality with a jolt that hurt his arm. What the devil was he doing thinking of kissing Kent Grosso's sister when his girlfriend wasn't two feet away? Not to mention the fact that he might be bleeding to death, for all he knew.

Well, if he *was* bleeding to death, he sure as hell would like to take a few new memories of the taste and feel of Sophia's very kissable lips with him to that big race track in the sky.

"That cut needs stitches," Alicia observed.

"Probably half a dozen," Sophia agreed, her voice and face as calm as Lake Norman on a misty October morning. Her movements were as sure and as confident as her voice. Blood poured down the back of his hand and dripped off his fingers staining the skirt of Sophia's white sundress.

She paid no attention to her ruined dress. Covering the long, ugly cut with a thick square of white gauze she applied pressure to the wound and he winced.

"Ouch."

"Sorry, but we need to stop the bleeding. You really should see a doctor tonight."

"I'm not going to the damned hospital," he growled. "I already said that. And I'm not going back in there to file charges with the police, so don't even go there." He turned his head to make sure Lucy didn't jump into the argument on Sophia's side. She opened her mouth as if to do just that, then shrugged and looked away.

Sophia gave him one more long, assessing stare that made him squirm with more than the pain of his injury. "Okay. You're the one with the cut on his arm. I know you don't want to be hauled in front of NASCAR for this little episode. It wasn't your fault, but that's not how the media will see it. You're right about that. Maybe if you can stay holed up for a couple of days it'll blow over without too much damage. I don't think it's a good idea, but I'll patch you up if you promise to see a doctor as soon as you get back home."

"Deal," he said. He'd see the team doctor when he got back to Mooresville. The guy was good, and better yet, he was discreet. Justin held her gaze, his voice roughened with pain and with the effort it took to offer his gratitude to a Grosso, the family he'd been taught to despise since before he could understand what the word meant. "Thanks. I appreciate what you're doing," he said tightly.

"Don't mention it. But I mean it. You get yourself seen by a doctor you can trust. As soon as possible. I don't want it said that this Grosso was responsible for the death of yet another one of the Murphy clan."

CHAPTER FOUR

SOPHIA REGRETTED HER bitchy remark the moment she said it. He couldn't help what had happened tonight. The bar fight hadn't been his fault. In fact, he'd done his best to talk his way out of it. Even after the drunk made the crack about him pulling out of the pits early.

With Alicia's help, she put three butterfly bandages on the two inches of Justin's arm where the broken beer bottle had sliced the deepest, then proceeded to clean up the rest of the long, jagged cut with alcohol wipes. The sting of the disinfectant made him suck in his breath, but he never flinched or made a sound as she worked.

"You're lucky," she said, cleaning blood from the back of his hand, feeling the ropy tendons of his wrist move beneath her fingers as she worked. His hands were big and strong, his arms well-muscled. Her father and brother both had the same strong hands and upper-body development. A lot of stock car drivers weren't big men, but only someone completely ignorant of what it took to wrestle nearly two tons of steel and raw horsepower around a track for five hundred miles at speeds close to two hundred miles an hour, was stupid enough to declare they weren't real athletes. She knew how many hours in the gym it took to stay in the kind of shape Justin Murphy was in. "The laceration on the back of your wrist isn't very deep. You'd have been in real trouble if he'd severed a tendon or ligament," she said, trying very hard not to think about Justin Murphy's upper-body strength or conjure up the long-repressed memories of being wrapped in a younger version of those arms.

"Why did they serve someone so obviously drunk?" Alicia asked as she stuffed the soiled wipes and gauze into a plastic bag she'd found in the back of the Blazer while Sophia secured the bandage with white tape.

"Even if the bartenders refused to serve him, his buddies probably kept feeding him beer." Sophia stripped off the latex gloves and dropped them in the plastic bag.

"Yeah, right." Alicia looked back over her shoulder. "We shouldn't have come here. The place is a dive." The sounds of dozens of cars starting up in other areas of the parking lot signaled the fact that the police had shut down the club, sending disgruntled party-goers out into the Florida night looking for somewhere else to continue their revelries.

"We should be leaving, too, before the cops start sweeping the parking lot," Justin said.

"He's right. We should get out of here fast. Thanks for patching him up," Lucy said.

"No problem." She'd met Justin's current girlfriend a couple of times through her brother. She was a friend of Tanya Wells, the woman Kent was in love with and who Sophia expected would become her sister-in-law in the not too distant future.

She began putting things back in her first aid kit. It had been a present from her nana when she graduated from college, and she kept it well-stocked. She shut the lid and fumbled a little to secure the snap-down locks. Her hands were trembling and her heartbeat was way too fast, making her feel lightheaded and a little sick to her stomach. Her position at Sunny Hills was administrative, so she wasn't often called on to perform first aid anymore. But as the director of nursing services, she taught a required first aid course for the center's nursing assistants every three months, so she kept up with the basic techniques.

"Is there anything special I should do for him tonight?" Lucy asked.

"I can think of a couple of things," Alicia giggled. Sophia had forgotten how tipsy her friend had become, but now that the emergency was over, Alicia's impairment was becoming obvious once more.

"Quiet," she hissed.

"I don't need any special treatment tonight," Justin growled and Sophia glanced up to see Lucy's face turn red, then drain of color. He swiveled his head toward his girlfriend. "I meant medical stuff," he clarified, holding out his hand in apology. Lucy nodded, but her smile looked forced to Sophia.

"I'd recommend a couple of aspirin, or whatever kind of pain reliever you normally take," Sophia said to break the silence that stretched out between the couple.

"I'll see he gets some."

"I don't take painkillers, you should know that," Justin said stubbornly, and once more Lucy looked as if she couldn't decide whether to cry or slap his face. Sophia felt awkward being caught in the middle of what was obviously a relationship on the skids. Justin slid off the tailgate of her Blazer and she turned to face him. As she did so she glanced down and saw the dark red trails of blood staining the skirt of her dress.

Her eyes snapped shut, but it was too late. Justin's blood. He might have died at the hands of that crazy drunk. Images of the jagged edges of the broken bottle inches from his throat, from his chest, from the veins and arteries of his wrist and arm crowded in on her. Her head began to spin, bile rose in her throat, and the next thing she knew, she was sitting in the exact spot Justin had been sitting just seconds earlier with her head between her knees.

She groaned. "Oh no, did I faint?" She could feel his hand on the back of her neck beneath her hair, steadying her. She closed her eyes again and took a deep, shuddering breath.

"Yes," Alicia warbled. "Just like you did when I got hit in the nose with the softball at the residents' picnic."

"Not quite," Justin interrupted, and even through the ringing in her ears she could hear the smile in his voice. "But close enough."

She straightened up, and he shifted to perch on one hip beside her. She could feel the weight and the warmth of his arm wrapped around her shoulders, steadying her. His good arm, thankfully. She would have lapsed into a coma from embarrassment if he'd had to catch her 130 pounds with his injured arm. "I'm okay," she said wriggling forward until her feet touched the ground again.

"Don't be in such a hurry," Justin warned, the amusement replaced by a thread of steel. "I don't want to have to pick you up off the asphalt again."

She lifted her hand and pushed back a strand of hair. "I won't faint again. I promise. It was just all that blood."

"You were doing fine before."

"I wasn't thinking about it then," she said miserably.

"I thought you were a nurse?"

"I am," she snapped.

"A nurse who faints at the sight of blood? How'd you get through school?"

"I don't always faint. Just when I'm personally involved—I mean when I know the patient. And I'm an administrator now, not an E.R. nurse. I don't see that much blood anymore." She wanted to sink through the pavement. A Master's degree in Nursing Science and she fainted at the sight of blood. But it was Justin's blood. She groaned.

His arm tightened on her shoulder. "You aren't going to be sick, are you?"

Both the steel and the equally sexy teasing note in his voice were gone, pure male horror tinged his words. She managed a grin, regaining her poise and equilibrium.

"No. Honestly, I'm all right." She wriggled off the tailgate and got shakily to her feet. She stepped in a crack in the broken asphalt and nearly went down again.

"Yeah, you're great," Justin said sarcastically. He shot a glance at Alicia, swaying a little where she stood, a tipsy smile on her face as she watched Sophia make a fool of herself in front of one of the hated Murphys. And not just any Murphy, but Justin, her own particular nemesis. For years he'd been the subject of her adolescent Romeo and Juliet fantasies, her daydreams of healing the breach between their families so they could be together forever. "And your friend isn't in too good a shape, either."

"She has zero tolerance for alcohol. The drunk who went after you wasn't the only one they over-served in there tonight."

"How many drinks did she have?" Justin asked, narrowing his eyes.

"One and a half."

He snorted. "One and a half? They were so watered down you could have served them at a daycare center. You weren't kidding about the zero-tolerance thing, huh?"

"Nope." Sophia's knees weren't quite as rubbery as they'd been. She figured she could make it to the driver's side door if she didn't step in another hole. She took a step forward but Justin's lean, strong fingers closed around her waist.

"Oh no, you don't. I'll drive you back. Where are you staying?"

"My family's condo on the beach," she said responding to the ring of command in his tone before she could stop herself.

"Lucy, you drive my truck back to the track, okay?"

Justin's girlfriend didn't respond for a moment. *His girlfriend,* Sophia reminded herself. *Don't forget that.* She moved a little away from his side, or tried to. As soon as she shifted her weight, his fingers tightened with a grip that would have had her struggling inelegantly to break it.

"Let me get this straight," Lucy said in a tight voice. "I'm supposed to drive your truck back to the track and wait for you while you chauffeur her all the way out to the beach?"

"Sophia's in no shape to drive," he repeated before she could defend herself. "And her friend is drunk as a—" He caught himself and amended what he was going to say. "She's over the legal limit. She can't drive."

"We'll call a cab," Sophia finally managed to get a word in edgewise. "Pick up my SUV tomorrow."

"You'll never get a cab to come out here tonight. Not in this mess." Justin jerked his thumb toward the parking lot. "And your Blazer wouldn't last an hour unattended in this neighborhood."

Lucy tossed her head. "Never mind, Sophia. Let him play knight in shining armor. It's a role he doesn't get to fill very often." Her eyes blazed with anger and hurt, and Sophia suspected more than a hint of tears. "I'll go get your truck and drive it back. I'll leave the keys in the trailer after I load up my stuff and find a place to sleep. I'll send you a text message when I'm settled, so you don't spend the rest of the night worrying about me," she finished with a sneer. She spun around and stalked off across the parking lot.

"Lucy, wait," Justin yelled, pushing Sophia, none too gently into the passenger seat of her SUV. Leaning over her he jerked the shoulder belt across her midriff and rammed it into the fastener. "Stay put. I'll be right back."

"Forget it." Lucy, still close enough to overhear, turned around, but kept walking backward. "Tonight was the last straw, Justin. We're through. Don't bother to come looking for me to weasel your way back into my good graces. You're never going to change. You think with your—you know." She waved her hand in the general direction of Justin's lower half. "Can't keep your mind on one woman to save your soul. I've had enough. Like the old saying goes—It's three strikes and you're O-U-T of my life for good."

SOPHIA WAS STRUGGLING TO find the release on her seat belt when Justin stomped back to the Blazer and stuck his head in the passenger side door. "Is your friend buckled in?" he demanded peering over her shoulder, his expression dark and stony. When they were teenagers sneaking off to make out in some secluded spot, she'd thought that scowl was the sexiest thing she'd ever seen. But then he'd been a boy—and now he was a man. The scowl still sent shivers up and down her spine, but for a different reason. This was an alpha male in no mood to be crossed. Sophia stopped fumbling with the catch for a moment and scooted around in her seat.

"Alicia?"

"Hmm?" came the sleepy reply.

"Fasten your seat belt."

"It's fastened. I'm not that drunk, just sleepy. It's been a long day." Alicia's words were replaced by a sigh and a gentle snore.

"She's out for the count," Justin observed disgustedly. He slammed the door to emphasize his words, then rounded the front of the SUV in half a dozen strides and dropped into the driver's seat, slamming that door with only a fraction less vehemence than he had hers. "Where the hell is this condo of old Milo's anyway?"

"Go after Lucy," Sophia said, ignoring his demand for directions. "You can't just let her walk away like that. Alone. In a place like this."

"I am going after her," he said turning the key in the switch. "Not that she'll listen to a word I say." In the near darkness that descended when the overhead lights faded out, his profile looked carved from granite. "But I can't let her go stomping through that crowd of drunks by herself."

He slid the Blazer out of the slot and began to weave his way through the haphazardly parked vehicles left in the lot. They caught up with Lucy just as she was opening the door of a dark-colored Silverado. The cops were concentrated around the club entrance, hauling off the beer-bottle-wielding drunk and his cohorts and paid them no attention.

Justin angled himself out of the SUV and covered the distance to the pickup in half a dozen quick strides. From where she sat, Sophia had no trouble at all reading the hurt and anger in Lucy's body language as she glared down at Justin from the running board. Whatever she said to him was short, sharp and to the point. She barely gave him a chance to withdraw his head from the cab of the truck before she slammed the door on him and drove off, spitting gravel and scattering a few lingering patrons of the late, un-lamented *frenetic*.

"I take it your apology wasn't accepted," Sophia said, nerves and embarrassment loosening her tongue.

"Bingo. I'm still going to follow her back to the track," he said in a challenging tone.

Sophia lifted her hands in surrender. "Fine with me. You can get out there and make up with her."

He shook his head in stubborn denial. "No. I said I'd drive you home and I'm going to drive you home. Look at your hands. You're still shaking like a leaf. You didn't want to be responsible for another dead Murphy. Well, I don't want to be the first Murphy to be responsible for a dead Grosso."

Sophia sat there gasping like a goldfish but couldn't come up with a response to that one.

Alicia stirred. "Are we home yet?" she murmured.

"No," Justin said. "Go back to sleep."

Sophia remained silent until they turned into the main entrance of the speedway complex, heading unerringly in the direction of the gate that led to the Owners' and Drivers' lot. "I admit I was pretty shaken up back there, but I'm perfectly capable of driving this vehicle."

Justin didn't respond. He pulled in behind Lucy as they crossed beneath the track and entered the huge infield. He sat drumming his fingers on the steering wheel until she passed through security. "She'll be okay now." Sophia wasn't surprised to see a fair amount of movement and activity in the lot, even this late at night, as some of the huge motor homes made preparations to break camp and head off for points north or west.

Justin merely grunted, retracing their path back to the highway. "Now. Tell me where are we going?" he said, still in that don't-tread-on-me tone.

Sophia gave up arguing and recited the directions to the beachfront condo her great-grandfather had bought over thirty years before. She might not be the most experienced woman in the world when it came to men but she knew when one was not going to change his mind. She sighed and closed her eyes, breathing deep and slow to help steady her shaky insides, then promptly fell asleep.

"Sophia." His voice wasn't angry any more, but low and just a little rough around the edges. He sounded as exhausted as she suddenly felt. His hand on her arm was warm, his touch light as a feather. "Wake up. We're here. Which one of these condos belongs to old Milo?"

"Oh. We're here already?" She felt color rise in her cheeks as she pointed to the second building in the semi-circle of eight low-rise buildings that composed Silver Sands Resort. "I didn't mean to fall asleep."

"I thought you were just resting your eyes," he said, with that hint of teasing laughter in his voice that she remembered all too well. A man's voice now, just as his body was a man's body, not the slim, angular boy she'd known so long ago. It was a stranger's voice and a stranger's body, but somewhere inside it was still Justin, her first crush, if not her first love—and the thought both intrigued and upset her.

She glanced at the digital readout on the dash. A little before 1 o'clock. "How will you get home?" she asked, as he unfastened his shoulder harness and opened the door, letting in the sounds and scents of the ocean that lay just beyond a small rise of grass-covered sand dunes.

"I'll call a cab."

"It will take forever to get one out here this time of night." She pushed away the memories of old times that swirled closer and closer to the forefront of her thoughts, undid her seat belt and stepped out into the cool, windy darkness after he rounded the front of the Blazer and opened her door.

"Nice place," he said.

"We like it." Some of her happiest childhood memories were of Speedweeks when dozens of friends and extended family members crowded together in the small condo to share the excitement of racing at Daytona. She wondered if she would have gotten over her infatuation with the younger Justin Murphy sooner if their families had traveled to all the races, as many did now, instead of staying in motels at just a few? Would familiarity have spelled doom to their clandestine meetings—or led to a more intimate involvement? It was an intriguing question but one she didn't intend to explore.

"Beddy-by time for you," he said, helping a sleepy Alicia out of the back of the Blazer and half-walked, half-carried her toward the condo.

"I don't suppose you want to tuck me in?" she asked, giggling a little.

"Oh boy. She's still out of it," Sophia apologized for her friend as she unlocked the front door. "She's not that kind of girl."

"I'm not that kind of girl around ordinary guys," Alicia amended with drunken dignity. "Hot stuff here is a bona fide NASCAR driver. That's the difference."

"We all put our fire-retardant underwear on one leg at a time same as the rest of the guys," Justin said, relinquishing Alicia into Sophia's care with obvious relief. "Sleep tight, Alicia."

"Nighty-night," she warbled, tottering off across the living room to the bedroom the women shared. "It was a hoot meetin' you tonight."

"My pleasure."

"Good night, Justin," Sophia said, her hand on the doorknob.

"Good night, Sophia." Justin raised two fingers to his forehead and gave her a little salute. He already had his cell phone out punching in a number on speed dial. She felt odd just leaving him standing on the doorstep, but how could she invite him into her great-grandfather's home? He was an old man, with a history of mini strokes, and he'd been carrying on a blood feud with Justin's family since the very earliest days of NASCAR.

Half a century ago, Justin's great-uncle Connor had died when his motorcycle had been forced off a mountain road. Some said it was Milo's doing, payback for Connor's cheating that had cost Milo that year's championship. And if that wasn't scandal enough, twenty years later, Justin's father was run down by a Grosso pickup whose driver was never identified. A driver who could have been her own father, the rumors insisted. Too much of a coincidence, the wags said. Too many similarities, too much bad blood.

No, she had tempted fate more than enough tonight. Justin Murphy, looking like some kind of warrior refugee from an urban battleground, was not now, and never would be, welcome in her home. The thought caused a surprisingly uncomfortable little pang in the vicinity of her heart.

"Tully?" His call had connected. "This is Justin Murphy. Hey, I need a car to pick me up." He repeated the address she'd given him back at the track. He listened for a moment. "That long?" A frown clamped his dark brows together over his eyes. "Yeah, I'll wait. But tell the driver there's a bonus in it for him if he makes it quicker." He gave her a lopsided grin. "Busy night for the car service the team uses down here. It'll be forty-five minutes before they can get someone out here. Will security roust me out if I crash on the beach 'til he shows up?"

Sophia stiffened her spine. She might be the family coward but she wasn't an ingrate. Connor and Troy Murphy's deaths had happened decades ago. Even the stolen kisses were years in the past. Justin had gotten her and Alicia out of an ugly spot back there at the club. She owed him at least the courtesy of a comfortable place to wait for his ride to appear.

"It's too cold to sit out on the beach," she pronounced. "Have a seat on the lanai." The lattice-covered porch sheltered the backside of the first-level condo. Flowering vines trailed over the roof and draped the sides. A grouping of wicker furniture, including an old-fashioned swing, with soft cushions in tropical prints made it an inviting retreat.

"You don't have to babysit me, Sophia."

"You didn't have to drive me out here but you did. Now I can't leave you sitting out here alone in the cold and damp," she responded, her tone as stubborn as his.

"Fine. I'll wait on the lanai instead. Just shut the door and go to bed. Good night." He turned away.

She shut the door as he'd told her—but moved past him to the swing and sat down, pushing off with one foot. "Please, join me," she said.

He was silent for a minute, his expression hard to read in the restless movement of shadows and moonlight that filtered down through the leaves above them. "Oh, hell," he said, a low rich chuckle that slid over her nerve endings like quicksilver. "You always were the most aggravating girl I ever met. I'm too tired to argue with you. I'll sit."

"You don't have a jacket. Do you want a blanket to put around your shoulders?"

He dropped onto the swing beside her. "Damn. My jacket. I gave it to Lucy back at the club. She must have lost it in the scuffle. It was leather. Brand new, too."

"You can call them in the—"

"You really think it will be there?"

"Probably not. But if you'd been wearing it, it would have been ruined anyway."

"Might have protected me from getting this though," he said, lifting up his arm.

"You're bleeding again." Sophia reached out and touched the bandage where a half-dollar-sized spot of blood had seeped through the dressing. "I should probably rebandage it for you."

"It's okay," he said, jerking his hand back as though her touch burned his skin. She dropped her hands into her lap.

"Sorry," she murmured, lowering her gaze, suddenly miserable and not knowing exactly why.

"I don't want you to faint on me again."

"I told you it's only when I know the patient. I get too stressed," she said. The trouble was, she was also stressed being this close to him again after so long a time apart.

He reached out and lifted her chin with the back of his fist. His expression was serious, his brown eyes dark and unreadable. "I haven't forgotten those kisses we shared back in the day. Not one of them."

"It was a long time ago," she said, a little breathless again, the way she'd been back in the parking lot of the club. "We were kids."

"We aren't kids any longer." He didn't have to tell her that. He was every inch a man, and she was reacting to that maleness with all her female body and soul. "Will you go crying to your daddy like you did back then, if I kiss you tonight?"

Her eyes flew upward and clashed with his. "I did not go crying to my daddy," she said regaining a little of her wits, if not the will to get up off the swing and leave him sitting alone in the dark. "It was Kent. He wanted to protect me." Justin must have sensed what she was thinking because he reached out and curled his long fingers around her wrists, cutting off her escape.

"Well, it worked. Dean cornered me at the track that last night. Came up in the stands in his driving uniform, helmet under his arm. Scared the hell out of me and read me the riot act. First time in my life I ever spoke to the man. Dean Grosso. NASCAR Sprint Cup Series driver." He didn't say "the man who might have run down my father," but she suspected he was thinking it. "Told me to stay the hell away from you if I knew what was good for me."

"You must have listened," she whispered. "I don't think we've said a dozen words to each other since that summer."

"Of course I listened. He's the man my uncle Hugo is convinced ran my father down and killed him." She had been right about the direction of his unspoken thoughts. His voice had deepened, darkened. "I didn't want to be next on the hit list."

Reality came flooding back to Sophia. What had she been thinking, to want to know what it would be like to kiss Justin Murphy, the man, not the boy? She must be losing her mind.

"Let me go, Justin," she said, the words leaving her lips far more reluctantly than they formed in her brain. "This was a bad idea. I shouldn't have suggested it. I have to go inside. Nana is a light sleeper. She mustn't wake up and find you here."

"Of course she can't. I'm one of those damned no-good Murphy's. Can't have one of our kind sniffin' around the NASCAR princess."

"Don't call me that again," she snapped, tugging to be free of his grasp, sudden anger making her bold once more. "And for the record, you didn't make me cry when you kissed me back then. Ever. Even when you kissed me that first time and spoiled my plan to get Bailey Tuttle behind the pool cabana so he could be the first."

"Bailey Tuttle?" Now a car chief on a NASCAR Busch Series team, Bailey was heavyset and the father of three bratty little boys.

"He wasn't as chubby back then," she said defensively.

"Well, I'll be damned." His anger seemed to have disappeared as quickly as it erupted. His voice softened, so she had to lean slightly toward him to hear his next words—a tactical error she regretted immediately as his mouth came close to hers. "I'm glad I got there first. I wasn't lying when I said I haven't forgotten that kiss. Or any of the rest of them, for that matter. I thought it was great at the time, but I've had a lot more practice since then. Wanna check me out?"

"No," she said. "I don't want to kiss you now." The denial sounded unconvincing even to her own ears.

"Well, I want to kiss you," he said, his mouth closing in on hers, "then and now."

And so he did.

And she let him.

For a moment or two, she felt as if time had dropped

away and she was fifteen again, Juliet to his Romeo, before reality came flooding back. She jerked away, breathing hard. She pulled free of his encircling hands and stood up. "This is madness," she said. "I'm going inside. Goodbye, Justin. Thank you for all you did for Alicia and me tonight," she added automatically.

He stood when she did and she noticed he was struggling to keep his breathing even, too. "Don't go, Sophia. I won't kiss you again." His face was shadowed, but she doubted she could read his expression even if they had been standing under a floodlight. "But I do want to see you again."

"No," she blurted out, her gaze darting to the door, afraid she'd awakened her light-sleeping great-grandmother. "Why would you want to do something so foolish?"

"Because we were friends—and maybe a little more— all those years ago. We could be again."

"You're involved with Lucy Gunter. I don't poach other women's men," she said.

"Lucy and I were headed for a breakup long before tonight. And for the record, Lucy doesn't play games. If she said we're though, we're through."

"That doesn't mean I want to pick up where she left off."

"Why? Are you involved with someone?"

"No," she said. "There's no one."

"What happened to that doctor you were going to marry? Two, no, three years ago, wasn't it?"

"Evan?" She was surprised he'd heard about her ill-fated engagement. After all, it had lasted barely two weeks. A lapse of good judgment that rivaled her behavior the last few hours. "He married someone else," she said shortly. "Actually he's married two someone elses since I gave his ring back. And I've heard rumors his second marriage is on the rocks already." She had come to her senses just in time where the two-timing Dr. Thomas was concerned. She would do well to remember that unhappy interlude, so she wouldn't make the same mistake again. "I'm glad you brought up my engagement," she said her chin in the air. "It reminds me how unwise it is to be here alone with you."

"C'mon, Sophia. Don't be as hardheaded as the rest of your clan. There was something between us all those years ago. A spark of it's still left. You feel it, too. Let's give ourselves a chance to see where it might take us."

She brushed past him and opened the door. Her heart was beating like a hammer in her chest because, heaven help her, a part of her wanted to say yes to him. "It would take us to the devil," she said, horrified to hear the regret she was feeling had found its way into her voice. "Goodbye, Justin."

CHAPTER FIVE

THE PHONE RANG WHILE Sophia was pouring pasta into a strainer in the sink. "Get that will you, please," she called over her shoulder to Alicia. It had been their first day back at work after returning from Daytona, and neither of them felt like eating alone, so Sophia had suggested taking a container of Juliana's fabulous marinara sauce out of the freezer to thaw while Alicia ran out for a loaf of crusty Italian bread and a container of mandarin orange and spinach salad from their favorite deli. After that they were going to the basement of the apartment building to do laundry, then call it an early night.

Alicia appeared at her shoulder. "Here you go," she said, handing Sophia the cordless phone. "I'll finish up here."

"Hello?"

"Hey, Sophia."

"Justin?" She shot Alicia a startled glance. "How did you get this number?"

Since her family was famous, Sophia had always had an unlisted number. It was amazing, and at times a little scary, how many people tried to get to her father and brother through her.

"Alicia gave it to me," he said.

She put her hand over the mouthpiece. "You what?" she demanded of her traitorous friend.

"I sent him an e-mail," Alicia said with a bit of a pout, her dark eyes filled with feigned innocence. "You know, thanking him for getting us safely back to the condo. He answered it and asked for your number so he could thank you properly for patching him up. The least you can do is say 'you're welcome.'" She bustled away and stuck her head in the refrigerator, going suddenly and completely deaf.

"I'm pretty conscientious about checking my website e-mail," Justin said. Obviously he had excellent hearing and had overheard their remarks. "Good thing, too. Your number's unlisted and you forgot to give it to me in Daytona."

"I didn't forget. I had no intention of giving it to you there. Or here," she said, giving the back of Alicia's head a hard stare.

"Yeah, well, I won't abuse the privilege."

"There's no reason for you to call again, so that won't be an issue."

"Ouch, that's harsh. Okay, I get the picture. I'll erase it from my phone's memory when I hang up." She got the impression that he was smiling as he said it.

"Thank you, I'd appreciate that," she replied with as much dignity as she could muster. For some reason, her palms were sweaty. Her brain synapses were misfiring, making it hard to concentrate on logical thoughts instead of feelings. She was reacting to the sound of his voice just as she had when she was a moonstruck teenager. She could feel herself blush and turned her back on Alicia and walked the few steps from her tiny kitchen to her living room.

"I called to thank you one more time for taking care of that jerk at the club the other night. He was getting ready to gut me like a fish," Justin continued.

"You don't need to thank me for anything, Justin. I just

reacted to the situation. A reflexive response, I guess you'd call it."

"Damned good reflexes," he responded, and this time there was no laughter in his voice. "Not only did you take out the bad guy—with your *purse*—but you got us out of the building so fast no one really had time to get proof it was me in the middle of it. I haven't heard a peep from NASCAR."

"I'm glad to hear that." She really shouldn't prolong this conversation. Her accelerated pulse rate and the warm fuzzy feeling in her middle were dangerous reminders of just how much charisma Justin Murphy possessed. But instead of saying goodbye, she heard herself ask, "How's your arm?"

"Good. I saw the doctor this morning when I got back to town. It had opened up again so he put a couple stitches in it but he says it shouldn't give me any trouble driving this weekend."

"I'm glad," she said, and she was. She'd been worried about the ugly cut on his arm on the drive back from Florida with her great-grandparents. Afraid he might be too wary of NASCAR hearing of the incident, or just too damned macho to have it properly looked after. "Good luck in California." It was time to end this conversation. It wasn't wise to stay on the line with him any longer.

"Sophia?" he said before she could tell him goodbye.

"Yes?" she responded, wary now.

"I meant it when I said I'd like to see you again."

"I don't think that's a good idea, Justin." She should hang up on him. Immediately, before her traitorous hormones betrayed her.

"Just for a drink or coffee. No frolicking in the bushes, I promise." There it was again, that down-home drawl of his that could melt a stiffer resolve than hers.

"I told you before I don't poach other women's men."

"And *I* told you *Lucy* and I are through. She made that crystal clear when I got back here and found she'd cleared everything of hers out of my house."

"I'm sorry," she said automatically. But deep inside, she was appalled to find she wasn't sorry at all.

"I hope she finds the right guy for her, now that we quit trying to make it work. I'm footloose and fancy free. You wouldn't be poaching if we spent a little time together."

"Justin—"

"Don't say no. Say you'll think about it."

"I—"

"I'll call you when I get back from Fontana."

"You promised to erase my number," she managed.

He chuckled, and her knees went weak and wobbly for a moment or two. "I lied," he said. "Goodbye, Sophia. And thanks again for saving my sorry ass." He broke the connection, and she was left standing with a dead phone in her hand.

"Well?" Alicia asked, hands on hips. "Are you going out with him?"

"No," Sophia said regaining her resolve now that she could no longer hear him breathing softly in her ear. "I am *not* going out with him."

"But you're going to think about it, right?" her friend demanded as she waved Sophia to a seat at her own kitchen table. "He's as hot as a firecracker and a real comer. And he's sweet on you. Go for it."

"Alicia you know how my family feels about his. His dad almost ruined my father's reputation in the sport. His great-uncle did the same thing to my great-grandfather. I can't just go out to the farm and announce to all of them I'm going to start seeing Justin Murphy. No way," she ended fervently, repeating the litany of old animosities for her own sake as much as Alicia's.

"But you're not going to put a block on his calls, right?" Alicia asked, anxiously.

"No, I won't block his calls. But I'm not going to answer, either. I'll let the machine pick up," Sophia said surprising herself. How could she consider going even that far down a road that could lead only to hard feelings and maybe even a broken heart? She must be losing her mind.

Alicia sat down and picked up her fork with a satisfied grin on her face. "Good," she said. "At least it's a start."

"JANICE WANTS ME TO remind you that there's a call for you on line two," Olivia Washington, Sunny Hills' assistant director of nursing services, said as she stuck her head inside the doorway of Sophia's office. "Don't you see the light blinking?" It was Friday, just before lunchtime and Sophia was busy getting all her ducks in a row for the annual state inspection of the facility that was scheduled for the following week.

She looked up from her desk pointedly ignoring the digital readout of the already familiar number on her telephone console. "Yes, I see the light blinking. And Janice knows that I don't take personal calls during working hours," she said primly, referring to her administrative assistant.

Olivia snorted inelegantly, leaning her considerable weight against the doorjamb. Olivia was African-American, a single mother of two teenage boys who had worked her way through nursing school while waiting tables at Denny's. She was a decade older than Sophia and about a century wiser in the ways of the world. She had applied for the job of assistant director when her mother came to live at Sunny Hills a year earlier, and now Sophia didn't know how she'd managed without her.

"Well, I'm going to answer it," she said bluntly. "You're forgetting it comes up on my phone, too, and the blinking is driving me nuts. Talk to the man. It's not like he's stalking you or anything, is it?" Alicia and Olivia were also friends. Alicia had filled the older woman in on every detail of the episode with Justin Murphy and kept her abreast of Justin's ongoing efforts to get Sophia to go out with him.

"Don't you dare pick up that phone," she warned her friend and colleague.

"He's called three times in the last five minutes. Janice said that always before when she told him you didn't accept personal calls at work unless it was an emergency he hung up. I think you should talk to him this time."

"I don't—" Sophia began then changed her mind. "All right. I'll tell him myself."

"Good," Olivia said. She grinned lasciviously and returned to her desk, leaving Sophia staring at thin air.

Reluctantly, she pushed the button on her phone console that connected her with line two. "Sophia Grosso," she said in her best director-of-nursing voice.

"Sophia. Thanks for taking my call." It was Justin. His voice *was* certainly hard to resist, at least for her.

"What do you want, Justin? I'm very busy this morning."

"I have someone I'd like you to meet," he said, and beneath the good-ol'-boy drawl she thought she detected the slightest hint of strain, of uncertainty.

"I don't understand, Justin?" She hadn't spoken to him since Monday, although he'd called her home phone three times that she knew of, and even left his cell-phone number with Janice who had promptly entered it into Sophia's

Rolodex. She had a sneaking suspicion her friends would have put it on her speed dial, too, if they could have gotten their hands on her cell phone.

"I'm at St. Meinrad's Children's Hospital here in California," he said quietly. "I have a fan here I'd like you to meet."

"A fan of yours?" It seemed out of character for him to try and impress her with a sick child. It also disappointed her. Far more than it should.

"His name's Wiley and he's a Kent Grosso fan."

"What?"

His voice had regained its usual cocky tenor. "Yep, he's the number one fan of the 427 car on this floor. When I told him I knew Kent Grosso's sister he didn't believe me. So I called. I hope you've got a minute to talk to him. He's a great kid."

"Of course," she said, surprised again. So she did know him well enough to realize trying to impress her through a sick child's admiration of a NASCAR driver wasn't the way Justin Murphy worked his magic. "Sure, I'd be happy to talk to him. What's his name again? Willie?"

"Wiley," Justin repeated. "Wiley Calverson. I'll give him the phone."

"Hi," came a small, tentative voice.

"Hi, Wiley. My name's Sophia Grosso. Kent Grosso is my big brother."

"You're really his sister?" The small voice grew strong. "You're just not saying that because I've got cancer and you feel sorry for me?"

She chuckled. "No," she said. "Cross my heart. He's my big brother and I've got the scars to prove it."

"He beat up on you?" Wiley sounded incredulous.

Sophia laughed again, losing her nervousness. She had

done a rotation on a pediatric cancer ward when she was in nurse's training. It had been a heartbreaking, but uplifting experience. "No, he didn't beat up on me. But he was bigger than me and sometimes he forgot to be careful when we were playing ball or racing go-karts."

"You raced go-karts?"

"Sure," she said. "But that was a long time ago." Before she'd lost her nerve. Or matured enough to realize how fragile human life really was—or whatever it was that had happened to her to steal her joy of watching her father and brother race.

"What do you do now?"

"I oversee a bunch of nurses who work with elderly people."

"A nursing home," he said wisely. "That's good. Old people need nurses like sick kids do."

"How old are you, Wiley?" she asked, wondering what the child's diagnosis and prognosis were.

"I'm nine. I've been a Kent Grosso fan since I was six. That's when I got sick. I was supposed to go to the race Sunday, but I'm not feeling so good so Justin came here to see me. But I'm a Grosso fan. I had to tell him that right off. It wouldn't be right to lie."

"No, it wouldn't. But Justin's got a lot of fans. I'm sure he doesn't mind that my brother's your favorite driver."

"Yeah, that's what he said. I have a sister, too," Wiley admitted. "Orange is her favorite color so she said she'd be Justin's fan. I'm going to give her the helmet and stuff that Justin brought me," he added heroically.

"That's good of you," Sophia said. "I'll tell you what. When we get done talking I'll call my brother, and I bet I can talk him into getting you a helmet and some other car gear, then you can both be all set to watch the race Sunday."

"Wow! He'd do that for you?"

"Yep, he's my brother and he's a good guy."

"He sure is a good driver. I bet he gets the pole this afternoon. And if he doesn't, I hope it's Justin here that does," he added after just a moment's hesitation.

"Me, too," she said and meant it.

"It's sure been nice talking to you." She could hear fatigue in the boy's voice.

"I liked talking to you, too, Wiley. Goodbye."

"Goodbye, Sophia. And thanks." She could hear him fumbling to hand the phone back to Justin.

"Thanks, Sophia. I appreciate that."

"I was glad to do it. I'll see if Kent will give the boy a call. Can you give me the number there?"

"He'll like that," Justin said, reciting a string of numbers that she scribbled on her desk ledger.

"Will he be strong enough to make the race on Sunday?" she asked, already afraid she knew the answer.

"I don't know," Justin said quietly. She could picture him turning slightly away to shield his answer from listening ears. He didn't have to add any more details. Sophia's memories of her children's-hospital rotation were all too clear.

"I'm sorry," she said.

"Life sucks some days," he replied. "Look." His voice regained its vibrant tone. "Wiley's mom and dad want some pictures and then we're going to meet some more of the kids and staff on the ward. I've got to go."

"Oh. Okay. Talk to you later," she said. Why had she added that? For heaven's sake, couldn't she control her tongue at all around him?

"Promise?" he asked—and before she could respond she was left with only a dial tone buzzing in her ear.

"HI," SHE SAID, AND IT sounded as if she were standing right next to him instead of being almost three thousand miles away.

"Hi, yourself." He'd almost given up hope of hearing from her. The only one of his calls she'd answered was the one from the children's hospital. After that, it was back to square one. Phone rings. Answering machine picks up. No return call. Until now.

"I…I thought I'd call and check on your arm. That was a pretty hard hit you took today. I was afraid, uhm, you might have popped a stitch…or something."

"The arm's fine." It was, too, healing well. He glanced down at the scar, already starting to lose its angry red color in the shallowest areas. "The rest of me feels like I hit a concrete wall at 180 miles an hour." He kept his voice even, ordinary, everyday cool so he didn't scare her off. Slow. Steady, don't make any sudden moves and spook her.

"It wasn't your fault," she said. God, she had a sexy voice, all honey and moonlight and sweet breezes.

"I doubt your dad sees it that way." He leaned against the headboard of the bed. He was sitting in a motel room in Los Angeles wishing he were already halfway back to Mooresville with the rest of the team, but Turn-Rite was angling to break into the West Coast market and he had three store openings to attend in the next forty-eight hours. It would be early Wednesday before he got back to Mooresville. Forty-eight more hours before he could figure out a way to see Sophia face-to-face instead of trying to further his suit on the telephone.

"You couldn't help getting loose that way. It was clean racing. He won't hold a grudge." She sucked in her breath and he knew she was thinking the same thing he was. All the Grossos held a grudge against him and not just for getting sideways on the race track today and taking the Smoothtone Music car out of the race.

The whole week had been a car wreck. He'd had engine problems from the minute they rolled the car off the hauler. He'd qualified thirty-fifth, and today, Sunday, the race itself had topped it all. His back end had gotten loose on the eighty-second lap. He'd overcorrected and slid out in front of Rafael O'Bryan, his own teammate Ron "Shaky" Paulson and what seemed like half the field. Eleven cars got caught up in the wreck. Three of them had to be towed back to the garage, including Dean Grosso's.

"Well, you've got an off week to put it all behind you and get all your aches and bruises healed up before Vegas."

The ache he had for her wasn't going to heal up before Vegas, or any time soon after that. "Yeah, there are a lot of races ahead of us." He folded his arm behind his head and leaned back against the pillow. "Sophia, have you changed your mind? Will you go out with me? We won't have another off week like this for a while."

"I shouldn't," she said. He felt a smile curve the corners of his mouth. She hadn't said no, at least not right away. Slow. Take it slow. He needed to play this very carefully. He sat upright and put his feet on the floor, working to keep his breathing under control.

"Just for a sandwich and a beer, nothing fancy. No strings attached. I owe you two thank-yous now. Let me pay you back."

"Why two thank-yous?"

"Your brother called Wiley at St. Meinrad's even before I left the hospital. That was damned nice of him. He told me at the driver's meeting this morning that he'd sent a helmet and a bunch of T-shirts over to the hospital, too."

"Kent's a good guy." He could hear the pride and love in her voice and he wished all that emotion, that pride and caring, was directed at him. "Did…did Wiley make it to the race?"

"No," Justin said. He had to swallow hard before he could say anything more. "He wasn't feeling too good today. I talked to him though. He said to say hi to you."

"I'm sorry, Justin." He thought he heard a catch in her voice. "Life is so unfair to some people."

"Yeah. But it shouldn't be unfair to little kids."

He heard her suck in her breath and knew he'd let his fatigue and disappointment seep into his voice. He wanted to do something for kids like Wiley. And kids like he and Rachel had been, orphans being raised by an overworked and overextended single uncle. He wanted to build a place for them, and their families and caregivers to go to unwind, let off steam, have fun without thinking of all the problems they'd left behind.

He knew just the place too, the forty acres he and Rachel owned on Lake Norman, back home near Mooresville. He wanted to have the money and the prestige to build a camp for orphaned children, staff it with experts and endow it for the future.

But Justin was never going to make that kind of money, be counted among the top tier of drivers, if he kept having days like today, where he finished so far back in the pack the winner was already on his way to Victory Lane before he crossed the Start/Finish line.

"Justin?" Soft, a hint of laughter sparkling beneath the velvet. "You didn't doze off on me, did you?"

"No, but I'm not at my scintillating conversational best, I guess."

"You need your rest. I'll say goodnight."

"No, wait. You didn't answer my question." He was wide awake now, fully focused. He couldn't let her get away again without giving him an answer.

"Will you go out with me?"

She sighed and he couldn't tell if it was with resignation or anticipation. "Yes," she said. "I believe I will."

CHAPTER SIX

"FAR BE IT FROM ME to meddle in my children's lives. But—"

Sophia sat on the high stool pushed up to the granite countertop in the kitchen of the century-old white farmhouse where her great-grandmother reigned supreme. "Of course you don't, Nana." Sophia, hands folded in front of her, kept her face impassive and swallowed a smile. Juliana Grosso meddled constantly in her middle-aged grandchildren's lives as well as her grown great-grandchildren's lives. It was what she did best.

Or second best, anyway. Sophia's stomach growled as she inhaled the marvelous mélange of smells wafting to her from the simmering pots on the restaurant-sized stove. In fact Juliana's kitchen would be the envy of many four-star chefs. Stainless steel appliances, double work zones, a granite-topped island crowned by wire-mesh framework holding a compliment of gleaming copper pots and pans. It stretched across the length of the big, old house, anchoring Milo's domain, with its fieldstone fireplace, state-of-the-art entertainment center and an assortment of comfortable couches and recliners on one side, and Juliana's staging area on the other—a sunny breakfast nook with floor-to-ceiling windows, and a pine table and chairs that seated twenty if no one minded bumping elbows as they ate. And no one ever did. To be invited to Villa Grosso—or the farm, as everyone called it—was an experience not to be missed.

"What are you cooking tonight, Nana?" Sophia asked. Juliana was technically her step-great-grandmother, but she had always been, and always would be, Sophia's nana, just as Milo was Grandpa, not Great-grandfather. Her father's parents had died very young, leaving Milo to raise her father and his brother, her Uncle Larry, alone. A short time later, he'd married Juliana, a lounge singer fifteen years his junior. The difference in their ages, not to mention Juliana's occupation, had been cause for gossip and a few raised eyebrows, but the marriage had proved a happy one, enduring forty-seven years, and Sophia loved her eccentric and opinionated great-grandparents with all her heart.

"Antipasto, linguini with marinara, fresh grilled asparagus and strawberry shortcake. Wanna stay?"

"I can't," Sophia said before she could stop herself. "I have a date."

"A date? On a Monday night? The only people who make dates on Monday nights are car people. Drivers. You have a date with a driver?" Mondays and Tuesdays were often the only days of the week NASCAR drivers spent in their own homes.

"Other people make dates on Mondays, Nana," Sophia said but she knew she didn't sound convincing.

"Not around here, they don't." Juliana took a taste of her creation, wrinkled her nose, then gave a brief nod. "Not my best effort, but it will do. Your mom and dad are both going to be home tonight, maybe even your brother." Her parents had moved into the big house ten years ago, after she left for college and Milo had suffered a series of mini-strokes.

Her great-grandparents had added a bathroom and bed-sitting room along the back of the house—overlooking a wandering stream and the pastures where Milo's beloved Tennessee Walkers grazed and the beef steers grew fat on the sweet green grass—and turned the entire second floor over to Dean and Patsy. The old house was so big that the remodel still left several guest bedrooms for out-of-town family and friends although they often overflowed into the bunkhouse-like apartment over the multi-car garage whenever the races came to Charlotte.

"Are you sure you and your young man won't join us for dinner? Is this a clubbing date, or a dinner date?" Juliana probed as she moved to the sink in the island where Sophia sat and began cleaning a strainer of early-season strawberries.

"I…I don't know. We haven't exactly set the agenda," Sophia confessed, as Juliana handed her a berry she had dipped in a tiny bowl of confectioner's sugar. "He's got commitments today."

"He *is* a driver," Juliana declared triumphantly. "What's his name?"

Sophia was spared having to answer when the door that separated the kitchen from the formal rooms of the house swung open and her mother entered. Patsy Grosso was dressed in her usual daytime attire of slacks and a button-down shirt, today in a creamy, coral pink that complimented her fair complexion and short-curly brown hair.

"Hi, Mom," Sophia said, leaning over the counter to snitch another strawberry. Juliana gave her a dark look and tapped her knuckles with a wooden spoon. "Save some for the rest of us."

Patsy gravitated to the pots on the big range and lifted

the lids, peeking inside. "Smells heavenly," she declared. "I'm hungry already. Hi, baby," she said moving around the island to give Sophia a hug. "Are you staying for dinner?" She settled onto a stool beside her daughter. Patsy was close to fifty but she looked ten years younger. Sophia shared her mother's fair Irish complexion and bone structure, and she hoped she aged even half as gracefully.

"I can't," Sophia said. "I have too many things to do before the plane leaves tomorrow. By the way, I'm going in to work for half a day so I'll have to go straight to the airport from Sunny Hills." Even though Kent had his own plane, Alan Cargill, her father's team owner, saw to it that Milo and Juliana flew on his private jet to any of the races they cared to attend. Since Las Vegas was one of their favorite haunts, they always took him up on the standing invitation even though, as a rule, the older couple didn't like to fly. Sophia usually went along to keep her great-grandmother company at the quarter slots, and take in a show or two, when Milo was at the track.

"It will be fun to all be there together. We haven't spent any time together lately. I only hear bits and pieces about what you're up to." Sophia hadn't seen her mother for almost two weeks, only talked to her on the telephone. The silence between them had actually been a good sign. If the incident at *frenetic* had seeped out into the NASCAR community Patsy would have confronted her immediately, demanding all the details. She might have imagined it but she swore she saw a look pass between her mom and nana.

Did they know? No, she would have been interrogated by now. Her mom was just being her normal caring self. She hoped.

When she and her brother Kent had been growing up,

Patsy had been a stay-at-home mom, baking cookies and running carpools, traveling to races only during school vacations, so that they could have the same kind of upbringing as their non-racing friends. She also managed Dean's substantial financial investments and, in the course of the last couple of years, she and Sophia's father had invested in a NASCAR Nationwide Series team. Her mother worked hard at every task she undertook and car ownership was no different. Consequently, all three of her drivers were doing well this season. Sophia was proud as she could be of her mother, but sitting alongside these two successful and formidable women, she felt some of her own insecurities rear their ugly heads.

"Alan, dear man, has arranged for us to have one of the team's motor homes. It's brand new. The three of us should be very comfortable," Juliana said.

"Maybe we'll have time for a family dinner next week. It will be like old times." Patsy said, sounding a tad wistful. She looked at her watch. "I'm late. I have to get to the shop."

"You're working too hard," Juliana scolded. "Spending all those hours at the garage when you should be with your husband."

"I see quite enough of my husband," Patsy said. Sophia looked up, startled by the sharp edge to her mother's voice. But when she caught her eye, Patsy smiled, seemingly untroubled, and Sophia decided she'd been mistaken about the undertone of anger and frustration she'd just heard in her mother's words. Patsy rose from her stool and crossed the room to where her purse hung on a hook by the door. She stuffed the computer printouts she carried into her bag and slung the strap over her shoulder. "Since you're not staying for dinner, I'll see you in Vegas, baby. We're flying in with Kent. We'll have plenty of time for some girl talk, stuck out there in the middle of nowhere."

"I've already been in touch with a car service," Juliana interrupted. "We can head for the Strip whenever we want."

"Wonderful. We'll have lunch someplace special and talk, talk, talk."

"Great, Mom. I can't wait," Sophia said. There was one subject she wasn't eager to talk about with her mother—her pending date with Justin Murphy. Sometimes she herself didn't believe she was going through with it. But since their long-distance conversation after the California race, something had changed. Perhaps it had been the hint of vulnerability she'd heard in his voice as they discussed the sick little boy? Perhaps it was the charm offensive he'd conducted by phone this past week? Delicious echoes of that long ago flirtation? She wasn't certain precisely what it was, but he had worn down her defenses until she'd finally given in to his pleadings and agreed to go out with him.

However, once the decision was made, finding a mutually convenient time hadn't been easy. Justin didn't return from California until Wednesday morning. On Thursday and Friday, Fulcrum Racing had tested cars at the Hickory track, keeping him out of town two more nights. Sophia had spent the first half of the week involved with the state inspection of Sunny Hills and on Saturday evening, she'd celebrated its successful completion with friends. Sunday evening she'd promised to help Alicia with her taxes and that brought them to today.

"Fly safe, baby," Patsy said with a wave, unaware of Sophia's wandering attention. "I've got to run. I'm meeting with the crew chiefs in half an hour."

"You make sure Dean and Kent know we're eating at

seven," Juliana called after her as Patsy hurried into the mudroom and out the back door. "And tell that man of mine to get his scrawny carcass back here, pronto. If he doesn't get his nap he'll fall asleep in his linguini."

"I'll do my best," Patsy hollered just before the door banged shut.

"That man is too old to be spending so much time at the shop. He should be here keeping me company," Juliana muttered as she moved to the stove to tend her bubbling pots.

"I've got to be going, too, Nana," Sophia said. Her father—and her brother, if he showed up for dinner—would be discussing the Fontana race, and Dean's DNF. Did Not Finish. Her father had been knocked out of the race because of Justin's mishandling of his car. The last thing she wanted them to know was that she was going to be seeing the man later that evening.

Her misgivings must have shown on her face. Juliana put down her spoon and came around the island, settling onto the stool beside Sophia's. Her silvery hair was teased into a twist that had been out of fashion for forty years, but somehow looked right on her. She was wearing a loose green blouse with sleeves pushed up to her elbows, over a dark gray, broomstick skirt topped off by a chef's apron tied around her ample middle. Gold hoops dangled from her ears, and off to the side of the counter, she'd laid half a dozen gold bracelets and assorted rings.

"Don't think I've forgotten what we were discussing before your mother came into the room. You're not leaving without telling me who you're seeing tonight," she prodded, folding her hands beneath her cleavage. "Is it that handsome devil Rafael O'Bryan?"

"No," Sophia answered truthfully, if evasively.

"I was afraid of that." Leaning forward Juliana rested her hands on her knees. "I have heard rumors about what went on at Daytona after the race," she said, tilting her head to gauge Sophia's response, the way she had always done when she suspected a much younger Sophia of trying to flimflam her. "Was there any truth to the stories?"

"That depends on what you heard." Sophia had never been able to lie to Juliana, even about little things, even when it was better if she didn't tell the truth.

"A friend of a friend told me there was a fight in some tacky bar and that Justin Murphy started it," Juliana responded, eyes sparkling with curiosity. Juliana loved to gossip. "Is that what happened? I listened to the racing call-in shows on radio all last week. They hinted at it. Swore it happened, but there weren't any pictures. Or any police report. And as far as I know, NASCAR hasn't called him into the trailer."

Sophia sighed. She might as well get this over with. Her great-grandmother had sources of her own. She'd been part of the NASCAR scene almost since its beginning. She knew everyone and everyone knew her. And when Juliana demanded someone tell her something, they usually did. Better tell the story her way than have Juliana hear a distorted version from someone else.

"It wasn't a tacky bar," she said. "It was a club and Justin Murphy didn't start the fight. In fact he did his best to talk the guy out of it."

"Then there really was a broken beer bottle and Justin getting cut and everything."

"Yes," Sophia said, her heart sinking.

"And you and Alicia were there?"

Sophia nodded.

Juliana threw up her hands. "Then my source was right."

"Did you tell Mom and Dad?"

"I suppose you don't want me to?"

"Please. And I don't want Grandpa to find out. It would give him another stroke." Milo was spry and alert, but he was also ninety-two years old.

"Milo's a tough old bird, but finding out you're dating Justin Murphy would send his blood pressure through the roof," Juliana agreed.

"I'm going out with him tonight, Nana," Sophia confessed, covering Juliana's hand with her own. "Am I making a mistake?"

"Of course you are," Juliana said bluntly. "No good can come of this, sweetheart."

"It's only a date, Nana."

"But he has a girlfriend. I read about them in one of the celebrity magazines."

"They broke up," she said.

Juliana looked skeptical. "Your father's not going to like this. The young hothead put him out of the race last week. That was a good car he was driving. Now it's scrap."

"It was just racing," Sophia said having no better excuse to offer.

"Bad blood lasts a long time in this part of the country. It lasts even longer in NASCAR racing. Connor Murphy doctored his gasoline and beat your grandfather out of the championship. It doesn't matter that it happened fifty years ago. Milo's never forgotten. Or forgiven. It's a point of honor with him.

"And then Connor went and got himself killed on that damned motorcycle of his and there are still people who believe my Milo did it. That angers him most of all. He was an FBI agent. A decorated veteran. To have people whispering behind his back all these years that he might have caused Connor's death—" She threw her hands in the air. "And that womanizing nephew of his. Your Justin's father—"

"He's not *my* Justin—" But Juliana was on a roll and ignored Sophia's denial.

"He framed your father for cheating and then went and got himself run down and squished like a bug by someone driving one of our pickups. Your momma was pregnant with you and she almost miscarried she was so worried that the police would blame the hit-and-run on your father." She rolled her eyes. "My Lord, I hope never to have to go through that kind of scandal again in my life. Why do you want to go out with him when you know it will only cause trouble in the family and bring you heartache?"

"I don't know," she said truthfully, meeting Juliana's dark gaze. She hadn't been this uncertain of her feelings for a man in a long time, maybe never. When she had ended her engagement to Evan she had been very certain she was doing the right thing. Kind of like Lucy Gunter that night in the parking lot. She'd declared it was over and never looked back. But now Sophia wasn't certain of her feelings at all anymore. "Justin and I barely spent any time together, and when we did it was…" She sighed, at a loss for words. "…*frenetic,*" she said with a crooked little smile. "And in the middle of it all, he broke up with his girlfriend. Or I guess it's more accurate to say she broke up with him—"

"As she should," Juliana said. "And? There's more to this story I'm guessing."

"He kissed me."

Juliana rolled her eyes and shook her head. "It's not the first time that's happened."

"It was different before. Then he was a boy and now he's a man."

"Your father and brother will hunt him down and beat him to a pulp if they find out."

Sophia took a deep breath. "He kissed me. I liked it. He asked if he could call me. I said yes. We've been talking now and then since Daytona. When he asked me to go out with him, I said yes."

"Now it will be your grandfather who will hunt him down. Sophia, are you sure you want to go through with this?"

Sophia looked deep into her grandmother's wise eyes and saw a hint of approval in their depths. Juliana knew how it felt to be an outsider, knew what it was to love unwisely, but to go after the man she wanted despite the obstacles that separated them. Her spirits lifted, and a fraction of her uncertainty drifted away.

"Yes," she said. "I want to see him again. So I am. Tonight."

JUSTIN SPENT THE AFTERNOON going over the results of the speed and engine tests from Hickory. NASCAR only allowed two test sessions per team at tracks where NASCAR Sprint Cup Series races were held. But if the team owner wanted to pay for time at a sanctioned track where Cup races weren't held you could run as often as you could afford to. Dixon Rogers sometimes made Ebenezer Scrooge look like a big spender, but not when it came to his race cars. Then the sky was the limit. They'd tested for two days, and on paper the results looked great.

But in his gut Justin knew the car still wasn't right.

He kept his thoughts to himself, though. His crew chief, his car chief and his engine builder all thought it was fine. First rate. Top notch.

He was only the driver. All he had to go on were his instincts. And in the twenty-first-century NASCAR, that didn't count for much. Not like it had in the old days.

"What ya' doing tonight, little brother?" Rachel asked as she drove him, in a Fulcrum Racing Impala, to her small apartment so he could borrow her truck. Dennis had already left for Las Vegas with the Manor pulled by Justin's 4x4. He really needed to get a second vehicle but he was holding out for a Porsche and he needed more than a fifth place finish at Daytona to justify the expenditure.

He could have borrowed a company vehicle himself, but he didn't want to be seen driving anything with Fulcrum Racing lettering. It was hard enough to stay unrecognized these days without advertising his connection to the race team. But Dennis, a true Murphy, bullheaded through and through, had resisted all his pleadings to loan him his Corvette. Justin suspected, despite Dennis's stable of girlfriends—one in every race city—it seemed, his car was his one true love.

"I have a date," he said. He didn't keep things from Rachel. They'd always been close. Neither of them could remember their parents, although Rachel claimed to have memories of their mother singing her to sleep and showing her the tiny, blue-wrapped bundle that had been his infant self, and telling her to take good care of her baby brother. Since Rachel was just over a year old when he was born, he sometimes wondered if it was a true memory or one her imagination had created so that she could justify trying to boss him around for the rest of his life. If she remembered their father, she never admitted to it, even though he had died less than a year after their mother.

He loved his talented and focused sister, who knew her way around a racing engine better than almost anybody in NASCAR, but she also made him uneasy.

They'd been so alike as kids. Born to NASCAR, born to race. School had been a pain in the neck, a necessary evil that kept them away from the garage and the cars. They didn't play hooky, Hugo would have had their hides if they did; but they only took the courses they had to and skated by with barely passing grades so they could get back out on the track and drive. Go-karts, late models, trucks—anything with four wheels and an engine.

But somewhere along the way, Rachel had found her true calling and cleaned up her act, got her grades up, got a scholarship to Duke. Now she had an engineering degree and worked for Johnny Melton, one of the premier engine builders in the business, while Justin was still just a good ol' boy driving race cars.

"You have a date? A real date? With a real woman, not a groupie?" she asked tilting her head just a bit to gauge his reaction.

"A date with a real woman." He'd had his share of dalliances with fans—most single drivers did—so he didn't resent his sister's question. But he'd been pretty exclusive over the past couple of years during his on-again, off-again relationship with Lucy Gunter.

"It's all over with Lucy, then?"

"Finito," he said. "Lucy broke up with me and I deserved it, but it was just a matter of time." He looked down at his arm, mostly healed now, the scars already losing their angry redness. "We had been sniping at each other since before we left for Daytona. Hell, almost since we got back together this last time."

"She's a nice woman. I kind of wished you two would make a go of it."

"She *is* nice," he agreed. He slouched down in his seat. "I don't think I have the settlin' down gene in my DNA." He ratcheted up the North Carolina drawl to add to the effect of the statement.

Rachel took the bait. "Don't be ridiculous," she said a little huffily. "All men have it. It just takes the right woman to trigger it."

"Lordy, now you sound like Kim," he said, pulling his hat down over his eyes to block the rays of the late-winter sun.

"Speaking of Kim, did you see her today when she stopped by the shop?" Rachel asked, glancing over at him to make sure she had his full attention. "I swear she's lost more weight."

Justin swiveled his head. "Are you sure? I was holed up in the conference room most of the day with Hugo, getting my pedigree read. I didn't see her."

Kim Murphy was Hugo's adopted daughter. Her mother, his uncle's ex-wife, had abandoned her. Hugo had taken both Rachel and Justin to raise after Troy Murphy's death and it was too much for Sylvie. Justin could see why the woman hadn't wanted anything to do with a toddler and an infant who weren't her own, but how could she abandon her own daughter? And her husband? Unless Hugo, like Troy, had treated his wife badly, too.

Justin always shied away from that conclusion when he thought about the past. After all, Hugo had adopted Kim and raised him and Rachel as his own. That had taken guts and hard work and sacrifice. Justin was pretty sure he wouldn't measure up if he was faced with the same situation his uncle had been. But something had happened all those years ago to cause Sylvie, Kim's mother, to leave town and never look back. And there was always one thing more that he wondered about from that long-ago time. What role had his father's death played in the collapse of his brother's marriage. A lot? A little? None at all?

He never asked and Hugo never explained.

"I'm worried about her," Rachel continued, her thoughts firmly centered in the here and now, not in the past. "And so is Uncle Hugo. Maybe we should talk to her? She's always been slender, but well, now she looks like...like she's starving to death."

"Do you think it's some kind of eating disorder?" Justin had dated a couple of supermodels in his day. They had strange eating habits. Or non-eating habits, to be more specific. And they were really, truly, skinny as hell. He'd never admit it to his fans, or even some of his friends, but personally he liked his women with a little more meat on their bones. And curves. Sophia had a great-looking body. He'd dreamed about her curves more than one night over the past week.

"Kim? Have an eating disorder? Are you kidding?" Rachel snorted, pulling into the parking lot of her apartment building out near I-77. "She's the most levelheaded woman I know. She hasn't got self-esteem issues, or depression, or whatever it is now they think causes eating disorders." Her voice tightened. "Honestly, Justin, I'm worried there's something wrong with her. Physically. I...I'm afraid she might be sick."

"Has she told you she's not feeling well?" Justin was getting uncomfortable. Was Rachel referring to one of those mysterious female problems afflicting wives and mothers and girlfriends the guys in the hauler mentioned, in hushed tones and cryptic references from time to time? They were way, way out of his league if she was.

"I'm not sure what it might be. But she isn't herself. She seems tired and out of sorts—" She drove slowly through the parking lot of her apartment building, wheeled the Impala into the space beside her truck and shifted into park. "Why don't you talk to her?" she asked, surprising him.

"Me? Why don't you ask her what's wrong? You're both women. It'll be easier for her to talk to you."

"She'll play the big-sister card with me: 'Don't worry, Rachel. I'm fine. Really I am. Thanks for being concerned but there's no reason to be,'" she mimicked Kim's serious, no-nonsense tone perfectly.

"You think she won't play the big-sister card with me, though?"

Rachel sighed. "She probably will. Of course, I'll talk to her if I get a chance. But I'm not kidding. I think she'll open up to you quicker."

"I'm not so sure." He loved Kim, she was the big sister to both of them, but like many siblings, their lives had been going along different lines since they became adults. It was great when they saw each other, but during the season, the time they had to spend together was short and fragmented. "The trouble is, when will I have time to see her? I told you I've got plans for tonight and I'm leaving for Vegas in less than twenty-four hours."

"Oh, I didn't forget. No way. Who is she?" Rachel teased, dangling the truck keys in front of his nose. "Anyone I know?"

Justin couldn't decide what to say. Could he get away with lying to his sister, making up a name and then laying rubber out of the parking lot? He looked at her pretty, clever face, her narrowed, fiercely intelligent eyes. Remembered the fact that when they were young she had never hesitated to put him in a headlock if she thought it would get him to tell her everything she wanted to know. Her current method of learning what she wanted to know might be less physical—but would be no less successful. "I'm taking Sophia Grosso out to dinner tonight."

Her mouth formed an O and nothing came out but a little gurgle of sound. The truck keys dropped from her fingers and he caught them in mid-air. Seconds passed. "Hey, sis, are you okay?" he asked working hard to keep a grin from breaking out on his face.

Rachel's mouth snapped shut then opened again on a torrent of words. "You are dating *who?*"

"Sophia Grosso."

"That's what I was afraid you said. Kent Grosso's sister?" She elaborated as though she couldn't quite believe her ears. "Dean Grosso's daughter?"

"Yes."

"Have you lost your senses? You can't date a *Grosso.*" He attempted to refute that statement but she never even slowed down. "Okay, okay. She patched you up after the fight at that bar. You owe her for that. But candy and flowers and a nice card would have done the trick. You don't have to start seeing her. What about Uncle Hugo? What about our father and Uncle Connor? Everyone in NASCAR thinks one Grosso or another killed them both."

"We don't know that. No one's ever been charged. Or even arrested."

"But who else could it be?"

"As far as our father was concerned, it could have been any of a dozen people. NASCAR guys he'd pissed off. Husbands he'd cuckolded. I don't know." He shrugged. "He was a good driver, but a pretty lousy guy, Rachel, you know that."

"No, I don't," she said, her hands fisted on the wheel. "Most of those stories probably got started after he died. We don't know what he was really like. We never got a chance to know him." Her teeth were clenched, he could see the tightness of her jaw.

Justin didn't want to argue with his sister. "Okay. Okay. But you and I and Sophia Grosso had nothing to do with what happened to our dad. Or what happened to Great-Uncle Conner."

"Well, I for one wouldn't be surprised if old Milo Grosso didn't kill both of them," Rachel said stubbornly. She reached out and touched the almost healed cut on his arm with gentle fingers. "Be careful, Justin. I don't like the idea of you getting involved with Sophia Grosso. I don't like it one little bit. And no one else in the family will either, when they find out about it."

CHAPTER SEVEN

"HI," HE SAID AS Sophia opened the door to her apartment.

"Hi, yourself." It wasn't a scintillating opening to their evening's conversation, but when she saw him standing there, one hand on the door frame, sunglasses dangling from his fingers, one hand in the front pocket of his tight-fitting jeans, her mouth grew dry and her breath stuck somewhere between her chest and her throat.

Justin Murphy was one good-looking man. His hair lay velvety smooth against his scalp, there was a shadow of evening beard darkening his chin, and his eyes were narrowed against the last rays of the setting sun. He wore a black leather jacket and a dark red golf shirt in a silky cotton blend that clung to the hard planes of his stomach and stretched across the muscles of his chest. He was smiling at her and she only had to tilt her head slightly to make contact with his peat-brown eyes.

She'd hoped the two weeks since she'd last seen him would have lessened his effect on her. She'd been wrong. She hadn't been this sexually dazzled by a man in a long time—maybe never.

"You got your coat back," she noted, just for something to say.

He shook his head. "It's a new one."

"I like it."

"Thanks. How did your inspection go?" he asked, staying on his side of the threshold.

"Fine. Perfect score. Full accreditation for the next two years. How did your testing at Hickory go?" She'd grown comfortable with the sound of his voice during their phone conversations of the past two weeks. It gave her enough confidence to face the devastatingly sexy actuality of him standing on her doorstep with something like aplomb.

His brows snapped together in a frown. "Fine," he said but didn't offer any more details. *Good heavens, he was even sexier when he frowned.*

"C'mon in," she offered, remembering her manners, corralling her lustful musings and pushing them into a small, secure corner of her mind. She stepped back inside her door, inviting him into her garden apartment. "Want something to drink? Wine? Beer? A soda?"

He stayed where he was. "Not unless you've been slaving over a hot microwave for the past hour," he said candidly. "I'm starving. Let's go eat."

She laughed, she couldn't help it. "Are you always this impatient?" she asked, reaching behind the door for her coat. It was March now, but spring hadn't yet arrived, although the days were growing warmer and here and there spring flowers were pushing their way up out of the ground in the beds she and Alicia had planted around their tiny patios.

"When I'm hungry, I surely am," he said shoving the sunglasses into the pocket of his jacket and resting his hand lightly on the small of her back as they walked to an old, but well-kept-up Chevy pickup parked at the curb. "I only had coffee and a bagel for breakfast and no lunch. It's nearly seven and my stomach's been growling like a wild boar for the last hour."

"Well, you're right about one thing—I haven't been slaving over a hot microwave. In fact I just got home from work myself. I would have scrounged up some cheese and crackers to go with your beer, but that's about it."

"We'll have cheese and crackers some other night. Now I want meat. Is it too much of a cliché if we have barbeque?" he asked, sounding at once both uncertain and hopeful. "I know this place where we can eat in peace."

"Barbque's fine," she said. She wasn't particularly interested in going anywhere fancy or well-known. It happened every time she tried to enjoy a meal with either her father or brother at the table. First would come the ripple of excited recognition, then the fans among the other diners would start looking and whispering. For a while, usually until just after the entrées were served, they'd keep their distance, but then some brave soul would venture over to their table with a piece of paper and a pen, maybe a napkin or a menu to be signed, and the onslaught would begin. "Eating in peace sounds wonderful. And as a true daughter of the South, I love barbeque."

"Great," he said, helping her up into the passenger side of the truck. "With your kin's following in this sport I doubt your family can have a meal anywhere this side of the Amazon rain forest without having to stop and sign autographs."

"Luckily my great-grandmother is one of the world's best cooks," she said fastening her seat belt as Justin turned the key in the ignition. She looked over at his profile as they pulled out into the quiet side street where she lived, and felt her breath catch again.

Heavens, he was good looking. No wonder his sponsors

all clamored for his likeness to sell their products. He was an authentic road warrior. A bad boy, the one good girls snuck out of their bedroom windows to meet so their parents wouldn't know they were seeing him. The rebel. The rake. The hot, sexy, summer fling you remembered all your life. If she'd never had one of those hot summer romances, she wondered if she'd be better able to think of something else.

She felt her skin grow warm and hoped the blush didn't reach her cheeks. Abruptly she shifted her thoughts to another topic, although it took more mental discipline than the time before. "Of course, I'd have a lot less trouble keeping from outgrowing my clothes if Nana didn't feed us so well. It's hard to say no to seconds, and I have to chain myself to my seat when she's baking cookies." There were definite feminine touches in the old pickup, she noticed, looking around her, as Justin merged onto one of the feeder roads leading to the Interstate toward Concord and the half-dozen other, smaller towns in the area where she'd grown up.

"Are we going to China Grove?" she asked recognizing a few familiar landmarks.

"You've been to Mikey's?" he asked swiveling his head to meet her gaze.

"Not for years and years. It was one of my favorite places when I was younger. I was crazy about their cherry-flavored soda."

"I keep forgetting you grew up not all that far away from me. I guess I always think of you as the NASCAR princess," he said, giving her that teasing, off-center grin that caused women of all ages to consider abandoning husbands and children and careers and running off to the ends of the earth with him. "Finishing school and ballet lessons and all that. Way different from growing up in Mooresville."

"I grew up in Concord," she said. "And you know it. I'll admit to the ballet lessons, but only for two years. And I got my nursing degree from North Carolina State. No finishing school in my résumé." She curled her fingers around her purse strap reaching inside for the courage to assert herself. "And if you call me NASCAR princess one more time I'm going to shove you out of this truck and you can walk back to Mooresville," she said tilting her head.

He laughed again, turning slightly in his seat, his attention evenly divided between her and the traffic he was passing at more than a few miles above the posted speed limit. "I believe you mean that," he said letting his words slow and soften into a drawl so thick you could spread it with a knife. "But aren't you supposed to threaten to get out and walk home, not throw me out?"

"That scenario went out with saddle shoes and poodle skirts," she informed him, not letting herself get drawn into that moonlight and magnolias trap quite so easily. "Just for the record I meant every word. I can do it, too," she said. "My brother taught me a couple of tricks if I ever get caught alone with a randy NASCAR driver."

"Do you mean ever get caught alone *again* with a randy NASCAR driver?" he asked, clearly referring to the numerous incidents in their past.

"You were not a NASCAR driver, then," she pointed out. "You were just a horny teenager."

"Ouch," he replied, still with that maddening, infectious grin. "I guess that puts me in my place." They were traveling the rolling back roads now, lined with landscaped brick ramblers and the occasional Tara-style mini-mansion with a barn and paddock of riding horses.

Sophia settled back in her seat and found herself thinking again that she was not the first woman to ever ride in this truck. There were engineering magazines in the console, yes, and a pair of steel-toed work boots poking out from behind the seat, but when she really looked at them Sophia noticed they were too small for a man's feet. The cup holders overflowed with hair scrunchies and even a tube of lipstick. There were moisturizing wipes in a dispenser by her feet, and a hair brush tucked in the pocket on the passenger side door. She sniffed the air and recognized the same light, floral scent that Alicia favored in the summer.

She sat a little straighter in her seat. How many women did Justin Murphy haul around in this truck?

"It's my sister's ride," he said, proving that his ability to read her thoughts that first night might not have been the race car driver's luck she had convinced herself it was. "She let me borrow it. My truck is two-thirds of the way to Las Vegas by now. My spotter and another guy are hauling my trailer with it."

Most of the drivers and their families referred to their baronial traveling quarters as motor homes, not trailers. And she'd once overheard her mother and Juliana remarking that not all the drivers were happy to see Justin's vintage trailer parked beside their units. But she was beginning to know him well enough to suspect Justin Murphy liked being thought of as one of NASCAR's bad boys, flaunting the rules, styling himself as a maverick, old guard, outwit-the-law-during-the-week, race-like-demons-on-Sundays driver—like her great-grandfather. Although, of course, Milo had not flaunted the law.

He *was* the law. And in the Grosso clan he still was.

"I'd give you a penny for your thoughts but if your

frown is anything to go by, they look way too deep to be worth so little," Justin said as they pulled into the small town of China Grove, turned left at the four-way stop and headed out by the Hardee's and across the railroad track back into the rolling countryside to the cinder-block building with the neon sign that had been home to Mikey's Bar-b-que and Drinks for six decades.

Sophia brought herself up short. She was not going to let her life be governed by events that happened so long ago. She was her own woman, and if she wanted to see Justin Murphy, eat barbeque with him, maybe kiss him again she would. Her father and her great-grandfather's quarrels with men long in their graves were not going to dictate the way she lived her life. "I wasn't thinking weighty thoughts," she lied with a straight face. "I was pondering whether to order the ribs or the pulled pork. I can never make up my mind."

"Well, if you don't care about getting your fingers dirty, I'd go for the ribs. They are damned good."

"All I know for certain at the moment is that I'm going to save room for the banana pudding." She hadn't eaten at the little out-of-the-way restaurant since she graduated from high school, but she was certain they still served the dessert they were famous for. That's what she liked about towns like China Grove and restaurants like Mikey's. They never changed. "You'll help me eat it, won't you?" Mikey's banana pudding came in half-pound servings—two ice cream scoops—with whole vanilla wafers and slices of banana *and* a mountain of whipped cream overflowing the dish.

"I'll split it with you," he said quietly, making no move to exit the truck. A little shiver skittered up and down her nerve endings, a sensation halfway between excitement and anxiety that pooled low in her stomach and made her want to squirm in her seat.

It had grown dark on the drive up from the outskirts of Charlotte. There was little moonlight, but the glow of a security light bathed the parking lot in a silvery wash. He reached out and touched her cheek with the tips of his fingers. "You might be thinking of banana pudding now, but you weren't a minute ago. Want to tell me what it was?" he asked, his tone low and coaxing, as beguiling as a sorcerer's spell.

She shook her head. "I wasn't thinking of anything except my dinner," she said stubbornly. Name. Rank. Serial number. Wasn't that all the information you were supposed to give out about yourself if you were captured by the enemy?

"Liar," he said softly, moving his leg so that it almost touched hers. He leaned closer. "Were you thinking about me? About us?"

Sophia took a deep breath. She wasn't going to be caught off guard by his kiss again. She would be ready when his lips touched hers. She wouldn't faint. She wouldn't flinch. She wouldn't pull away like a frightened little girl. No, most of all, she wouldn't pull away. "As a matter of fact I *was* thinking about us," she replied boldly.

He nodded once, his mouth just inches from hers. "*What* were you thinking about us? Were you wondering how good it would be between us?"

"A little," she admitted, closing her eyes as his features swam out of focus. "But mostly I was thinking it's a mis—"

"Hush." His lips brushed across hers. That was all—a touch, a taste, a testing, over too quickly. Then wrenching emptiness and a great longing for more of him sprang up inside her. She curled her fingers into her palms so that she wouldn't reach out and grab handfuls of his shirt to bring him even closer. He leaned back slightly and the cool air that swirled between them with his movement gave her back a small sense of herself.

"You didn't look as if you were waiting for me to kiss you. You looked as if you were carrying the weight of the world."

She leaned back, bracing herself against the truck door. "You're right. I was wondering why in heaven's name I was here at all. Justin, nothing good can come of our seeing each other, you know that. It was a mistake to agree to come out here with you tonight." They had crossed a line coming to this restaurant. Flirtatious phone calls were one thing. Taking the relationship to the next level, being seen in public together, was quite another. "What if someone sees us and tells my father, or your uncle, or worst of all, my great-grandfather?" It was no use to pretend there wouldn't be consequences from their continuing to see each other. It would be smarter, more expedient, to break this off now, before it had a chance to go further.

"I don't give a damn who doesn't like our seeing each other," he said, fisting one hand on the steering wheel. "I make my own decisions about who I want to see." He reached out and cupped his hand behind her head. "Who I want to be seen with. Who I want to kiss."

This time, when his lips came down on hers she didn't have the option of thinking of dandelions or butterflies or anything so greeting-card romantic. All she could think about was the man beside her. His mouth was hard, insistent. She opened her lips a little, just to get enough breath to keep her head from spinning. He took advantage of the invitation and pulled her closer. She struggled for just an instant, then she gave in to her own longing and kissed him back, giving and taking, learning his taste and scent and feel.

"Just look at us," he chuckled, laying his cheek against hers. His voice was husky with amusement—and something more? A bit of wonder, a lot of confusion? The same conflicting emotions she was feeling? She couldn't be sure, so she opened her eyes, but he had moved slightly and his face was cast in shadows. "We're doin' this all backward, Princess. I haven't bought you a drink or dinner or even tried any of my world-famous sweet talkin', and I'm already thinking of sneaking out to Lake Norman and crawlin' into the back of the truck with you."

He laughed a bit shakily. "Hell, I'm thinkin' why even drive out to the lake. Why not just make love to you here and now?" His hand was moving in small circles on the back of her neck, soothing and arousing all at the same time, but she felt the tremor in his strong fingertips and knew he was more affected than his teasing words revealed, so she didn't tell him to take his hand away.

"I'm not getting into the back of the truck with you," she whispered, and she meant it. "We can't let it go this far this fast. We have to think this through. We have to talk it out. Fifteen minutes before you showed up at my apartment, I was going to call you and back out. That would have been the smart thing to do."

"It would have been the wrong thing to do," he said with all the self-assurance and arrogance that made him what he was, a professional stock car driver, one of the best of the best. "This is just picking up where we left off thirteen years ago."

"Don't be silly," she said testily, but she couldn't keep from smiling. "You don't believe that. We were children then, or almost children, despite an overabundance of hormones. But I'm not denying there's something here and now." She waved her hand in the air between them. "Or I wouldn't be stirring up trouble for myself by seeing you."

He heard the uncertainty in her voice and grew serious. "Okay, let's back up and start over."

"What do you mean?"

"I mean no more talking about making love. We go back to square one— What's your sign? What's your favorite color? Do you like pepperoni or sausage on your pizza?"

"You just can't keep your mind off food, can you?" she asked, picking up her cue, trying to keep it light, stay away from the personal. What was his favorite color? His birthday? Did he like country or rock or hip hop? She could probably find the answers to all those questions on his website, or in his NASCAR bio. But what of all the more intimate details of his life? Did he want a home in the country? Or a town house in the city? Did he want children? How many? Two girls and two boys, the way she did? Dangerous questions and dangerously alluring if his goals in life were similar to her own.

He watched her intently for a moment. He probably had excellent night vision and could see every thought she had flit across her face. "Pepperoni *and* sausage *and* ham *and* bacon," he said finally. "Let's go get something to eat." The teasing lilt returned to his voice. He dialed back the charisma. She could almost feel it recede from the air around her. He gave her a charming, nonthreatening grin. "After that, we'll consider working our way into the bedroom."

"I'm not going to bed with you, so concentrate on your dinner. We won't be in there five minutes before someone recognizes you, you know."

"Or you?"

"It's possible. If they're really hard-core fans. Then we'll have something to worry about." She opened the door and dropped her foot onto the running board of the pickup.

"Hell's bells. It isn't even going to take five minutes," he said tightly, as a car pulled into the parking space directly across from them, its headlights filling the cab of the truck with harsh light.

"Someone you know already?" A model-thin woman got out of the car and stood for a moment with her hand resting on the top of the open door. She was a few years older than herself, Sophia guessed, and very pretty. Or would be if she didn't look so pale and drawn. But perhaps that was just a trick of the unflattering lighting.

"Justin? Is that you?" The woman tilted her head as though to bring them into focus. "I thought I recognized Rachel's truck, but I never expected to find you driving it. What are you doing way out here?"

"It's me, Kim," he said rounding the hood of the pickup. "I didn't expect to see you here, either." He enfolded the woman in a hug and Sophia experienced a pang of unexpected envy.

She clung to him for a moment. "What a coincidence. I didn't think I'd get a chance to see you before you left for Vegas."

"Me, either. What are you doing away from your computer and test tubes?"

"I'm getting some pulled pork for Dad—" She caught sight of Sophia as she closed the door of the truck and turned to smile at her. "You're not alone. I should have known you wouldn't be. Is it Lucy? I can't quite see." She lifted her hand to her eyes, and even in the poor light Sophia could see she was trembling.

"Lucy and I broke up," Justin said. "After Daytona. For good." His eyes narrowed slightly and his jaw tightened. "Kim, it's Sophia Grosso. Sophia, remember my cousin, Kim Murphy."

"Sophia Grosso? Oh, Justin no."

"Kim?" Real alarm arced through Justin's voice. "Are you okay?"

She shook her head, reaching out as though for something to hold on to. "No," she said weakly. "No, I'm not okay." And then she toppled forward into his arms.

CHAPTER EIGHT

"AND THEN SHE FAINTED dead away and she would have fallen flat on her face if Justin hadn't caught her." Sophia said to her great-grandmother as they sat side by side at a row of slot machines. "She only lost consciousness for a few moments, but it was frightening to see."

"I'm sure it was," Juliana replied, scowling at the screen of her machine when it failed to produce a winning combination. "What was wrong with her?"

Sophia shook her head, betting quarters instead of dollars—and much more slowly than Juliana. She really didn't like gambling. She almost never came out ahead and it invariably made her feel guilty spending money she could have used to buy something useful. "She blamed it on low blood sugar. But it seemed more serious to me than just having forgotten to eat lunch."

"Never had that problem myself," Juliana said. "Constitution of an ox. Runs in my family."

Sophia nodded, watching the third fiery seven that would have given her a win slip past the center line and drop out of sight. She pressed the play button and continued her story. "We took her to the E.R. in Concord and they ran some tests, but didn't admit her. I doubt if she would have stayed if they did."

"All the Murphys are stubborn as jackasses. Hugo's the worst of the lot." Juliana didn't bother to keep the animosity she felt toward the man from edging her words.

Not wanting to take the conversation in that direction, Sophia remained silent. Poor Justin, two women fainting in his arms in less than three weeks, but for vastly different reasons, Sophia was afraid. She pondered the possible conditions that might have caused Kim's momentary loss of consciousness as she watched triple bars line up on her great-grandmother's machine.

Juliana nodded in satisfaction and doubled her bet. "I remember Kim. She's a few years older than you and Kent. She's Hugo adopted daughter, isn't she?"

"Yes," Sophia said, returning her attention to the spinning reels of her machine as she spoke. "She's a research scientist, I believe. We really didn't spend much time chatting."

"Under the circumstances, I suppose not. Her mother ran off and left her with Hugo not very long after Troy Murphy was killed, as I remember," Juliana went on. Her grandmother didn't have a mean bone in her body, but she did love to gossip. "I don't care for the man at all, but I do have to admire him for raising those three children—not one of them his own, either."

"You raised my father and Uncle Larry," Sophia reminded the older woman.

"Of course I did, and love them like they were my own flesh and blood. But sometimes it wasn't easy, being the step-grandmother, the replacement for a woman that everyone liked and admired. That's why I give the man credit. Oohh! Look! A three-hundred-dollar jackpot! This must be my lucky day." Juliana's machine erupted in a cacophony of bells and whistles. Sophia's came up with blanks.

She laughed. "I'm out of money. Let's go have a drink to celebrate your good luck and then head back to the track. The traffic will be terrible in another hour."

Juliana regarded the flashing lights on her machine with satisfaction. "All right. My treat. But let's go to the Bellagio. I want to watch the fountains before we go back out into the desert."

"What time is it?"

"A little past two." It was the Friday before the Las Vegas race. They had flown to Nevada in the Cargill Racing corporate jet and were now comfortably settled into one of the race teams luxurious motor homes. Dean and Patsy were parked beside them and Kent's coach was on the other side, ensuring the elderly couple a buffer zone between them and some of the younger and more party-oriented drivers and owners. But looking through the big picture windows of the vehicle at her parents' and her brother's bedrooms on either side, Sophia felt uncomfortably like the pampered princess in the tower, who Justin so infuriatingly compared her to.

"Are you going to join me in Alan's suite to watch the race or are you going down to the pits with Milo and your mother?" Juliana inquired as they waited in line to cash in her voucher.

"I haven't made up my mind," Sophia hedged. Juliana would not be happy to learn that Sophia intended to stay in the motor home and watch the race from between her fingers as she almost always did. She wished Alicia had been able to come with them. She was the perfect filter for Sophia, watching the race while Sophia puttered in the kitchen, did laundry, paid bills, feeding her updates and informing her when it was okay to come and watch the

replays of her father and brother's various spin-outs and occasional crashes, and generally holding her hand throughout the race.

Now on top of the anxiety she always felt for her parent
and sibling, there was her growing involvement with, and
fear for, Justin's well-being to contend with on race day.
She wasn't sure she wouldn't betray herself if she forced
herself to view the race in the company of other people.

"We have just enough time to catch the next fountain
show and that drink. I'm cooking for your father's team
tonight," Juliana said, stuffing a fistful of crisp new twenty
dollar bills in her oversized purse. "Have to get back to the
track and start getting stuff ready."

"It's no wonder Dad's team hasn't had a turnover in
three seasons. They'd never jump to another car owner
because it would mean losing out on all the meals you and
Jesse cook for them." Jesse was her brother Kent's motor
home driver. The grizzled army veteran was almost as good
a cook as Juliana. Their friendly rivalry produced some of
the best meals Sophia had ever eaten.

"Exactly," Juliana said with a mischievous smile.
"You've figured out my scheme."

Sophia hooked her arm through her grandmother's, and
gave it a squeeze. "You are the smartest woman I know."

Juliana accepted the compliment with a gracious nod.
"Thank you. And before I go to meet my maker, I intend
to teach you and your mother every trick I know."

THE No. 448 CAR QUALIFIED well, but Justin wasn't sure how.
He'd had to wrestle the car around the track, fighting her every
inch of the way. He keyed his radio. "Hugo, this thing is a pig.
You guys have to do something with her before tomorrow."

"Your last lap was your best all afternoon," his sister's voice came back, sounding metallic and a little like a *Star Trek* alien. "What more do you want?"

"I want a car I'm not going to put in the wall," he growled. It had been a hell of a week.

"If you can't give me more details than that I'm not going to be able to do anything." *Star Trek* alien or not his sister was not going to let him run roughshod over her.

"The hits just keep on comin'," he said, keying off his radio switch. The last few days had been nerve-racking and he was having trouble keeping his temper in check. Kim's collapse had frightened him. The fact that she wouldn't let him tell anyone else preyed on his conscience, fraying his temper even more.

He had one thing to be grateful for, though. Through the whole episode, Sophia had been a brick. She'd urged Kim to join them at one of the wooden tables in the pine-paneled restaurant whose walls were hung with soft-drink and racing memorabilia when she kept insisting that all that was wrong with her was that she needed something to eat. She'd kept up a flow of small talk while his cousin dutifully worked away at a grilled-chicken salad and half a portion of banana pudding while he watched her as closely as he watched the tachometer on his car.

She even asked for seconds on her glass of cola, but the strain had never left her eyes, and her color remained pale and Justin knew he wasn't imagining the unhealthy gray cast underlying her normally creamy complexion.

When Kim stood up to leave, clutching a plastic container of barbeque she had insisted on ordering for Hugo, she swayed again and that's when Justin's patience ran out. Thirty minutes later, Kim was being examined by a doctor at the nearest hospital emergency room. The doctor hadn't found anything seriously wrong with her at the moment, except that her blood pressure was a bit high—but nothing to account for the fainting spell. He'd suggested more in-depth blood work, but Kim refused the tests, saying she would make an appointment with her own doctor to have them done.

The E.R. was busy and the young intern agreed, succumbing to Kim's smile and sincere expression, but Justin knew his cousin better than the doctor, and he figured she wouldn't take the medic's advice. And now it was Friday, and he hadn't heard anything from her about test results or doctor's visits even though she had promised him that she would follow through on the E.R. doc's recommendations.

At this point she wouldn't even answer her phone.

Should he go over her head and tell his uncle he suspected that Kim might be seriously ill, or was he getting bent out of shape over nothing? Maybe he could talk to Sophia later. She was a damned good nurse and he'd like to get her take on what had happened that night, and to apologize for dragging her into the middle of a family crisis and then leaving her on her doorstep with no more than a thank-you and a quick goodbye kiss.

The problem was, as usual, her family. She wasn't answering her cell phone and he suspected it was because she didn't want to let her relatives know he had her number, let alone talk to him in front of them. He had to figure out a way to get her alone, away from the mini-enclave of Grosso family motor homes where she was ensconced.

"Hey, Justin, are you going to bring that car into the

garage or just keep circling the track?" asked his sister's voice inside his helmet.

He'd been driving on autopilot again. Practice wasn't as intense as running the race itself, but it was no Sunday drive in the country, either. If Hugo found out his mind wasn't entirely in the game, he'd skin him alive, even if it *was* Kim's health that had distracted him. He let up on the throttle, downshifted and slowed for the exit to pit road, following Dean Grosso's No. 414 car into the garage area.

Grosso's garage stall was a long way from Justin's. Garage space and the hauler parking area spots were assigned according to the number of points each driver and team had accumulated, while the pit stalls were chosen by qualifying positions.

Dean had qualified on the outside pole and Kent eighth. Justin had wrestled his reluctant car around the track fast enough to take the fifteenth spot, solidly in the middle of the pack, only a fair performance by NASCAR Sprint Cup Series standards, but a heck of a lot better than at Fontana.

Rachel was waiting for him when he boosted himself out of the race car and took off his helmet. "Still hearing that noise?" she asked, shouting over the roar of an engine being tested two stalls down. Bart Branch's car Justin noted with the lately too-small portion of his brain that was permanently wired into driver's mode. Running rough. Maybe the carburetor? Bart and his identical twin brother, Will, were trust-fund babies whose multi-millionaire father had sponsored their NASCAR Sprint Cup Series cars and Justin didn't have a lot of respect for either of the playboy brothers.

"It's not a noise exactly," he replied, almost shouting to make himself heard. "More of a vibration. A feeling." This was one of those times when he most felt the gulf between their educations. Justin considered himself a fair shade-tree mechanic, as the old timers would say. But he wasn't an engine specialist with two degrees behind his name like his sister. He was a driver. He knew when the car didn't run right, didn't sound right, but he couldn't tell you what was wrong with it. That wasn't his job.

"Okay. A feeling. I'll get right on it." Rachel smiled. Oddly enough she wasn't laughing at him, though. Her eyes and the tone of her voice were serious, all business. "Tell me, does this feeling get worse when you stand on the accelerator, or when you let up?"

Justin thought a moment, replaying the practice run in his head. "It was worse coming out of Turns Three and Four," he said. "Kept feeling like it wanted to give up and die on me heading into the frontstretch."

Rachel was nodding, making notes on a clipboard she'd picked up off a toolbox. "Could be a problem with the fuel intake valve. I'll get the guys on it right away. I'll see if we can tweak the setup so you can be dialed in by final practice, Las Vegas was an afternoon race. The track conditions during the last practice before the race would be closer to the conditions at the actual start of the race than the morning practice session.

"Thanks, sis."

Bart Branch's team shut down his car. For a moment, silence reigned in their section of the garage, although Justin could hear the cars still on the track getting in a final few laps of practice time. Rachel turned to walk away. He put out his hand and stopped her. "Have you talked to Kim today?" he asked.

She shook her head. "No. Have you?"

"Not a word. Do you think that means her tests came

back okay?" He'd promised not to discuss Kim's collapse with anyone, but he'd made the promise under duress and did not feel honor bound to keep the information from Rachel, although he hadn't yet said anything to Hugo about the episode.

Rachel blew a breath out between her lips. "I think it's more likely she didn't go to the doctor the way she said she would."

"Yeah, that's what I'm afraid of, too." Justin ran his hand through his hair. It was wet with sweat. He jerked off the jacket of his uniform and tied the sleeves around his waist. "Should we talk to Hugo?"

Rachel's eyebrows pulled together in a frown. He could see her chewing on the inside of her cheek, a nervous gesture she'd had since childhood. "No," she responded at last. "Not yet. What can he do while we're out here two thousand miles from home, except worry about her even more than he already does?"

"I was thinking the same thing," he said, settling his helmet under his arm as he stared down at the toes of his driving boots. He lifted his eyes to his sister's once more. "If we rat her out, she's not going to confide in either of us again."

Rachel nodded. "You're right there. We're probably getting all worked up over nothing, anyway," she said hopefully, but her expression remained serious. "Maybe she's just anemic, or has mono or something like that. When we get back home we'll both go to work on her again. If we have to we can kidnap her over the Easter break and drag her into her doctor's office."

Justin reached out and ruffled her hair. "Great idea, Rayray." He hadn't used her childhood nickname in a long time, but then they hadn't had this kind of family problem to deal with in a long time, either. "That's why you've got all the letters piled up behind your name and all I do is drive the car."

"Don't pull that 'just a country boy out to make some Sunday money,'" she said, her eyes flashing. "This is serious."

Justin wiped the smile from his face. "I know it is, Rachel. I'll do everything I can to make sure Kim gets to the doctor. You have my word on it."

"Mine, too. Now you go get in the shower and let me take care of your race car."

"Deal," he said, feeling better for having made a plan to deal with Kim's illness. Now all he needed was a plan to deal with Sophia Grosso, but he was out of luck there if he expected any help from his sister. Or his uncle. He was on his own.

CHAPTER NINE

IT WAS LATE. AFTER 2 A.M. but just about time to wake up as far as Sophia's internal clock was concerned. Her body was still on Charlotte time and in no hurry to readjust, so she gave up trying to sleep. She was tired of lying in the narrow bunk bed going over all the things that had happened since they'd come to Vegas, the most upsetting of which was her mother's revelation that eleven years earlier her adored big brother had been expelled from college for cheating. Kent was the most honorable and honest man she knew, and that included her father. She just couldn't believe that he had been caught cheating on exams.

But he had, by his own admission. Even though it had been a long time ago, the knowledge that he wasn't quite as perfect as she remembered him to be was upsetting. Yesterday, Kent had given an interview and the revelation "slipped" out. Now everyone knew. She was proud of her brother for being honest, but she still worried about how he'd be treated in the future.

Sophia continued to stare into the darkness. Sleep refused to return. She sat up and slid her feet to the floor listening for sounds that Milo or Juliana might be awake, but all she heard from behind the sliding doors that separated the bedroom and bathroom of the motor home from the main living area were gentle snores.

She stood up and padded toward the kitchen. The bunk beds where she was sleeping could also be closed off from the main salon, creating a second seating area and computer workstation during the day and a bedroom at night. The kitchen, with its leaded-glass cupboards and granite counters was directly in front of her. She got a bottle of water from the fridge and sat down on the couch. Next door, her parents' unit was dark and still. It was older than the one that Milo and Juliana and she were staying in, but still very nice and with the added plus of lots of happy memories of college summers spent criss-crossing the country like gypsies. Kent's coach was on the other side, a custom-built model with all the bells and whistles, a gift he'd given himself after winning the NASCAR Sprint Cup Series championship the year before. She pushed aside one of the window blinds and looked outside. The entire compound was dark and quiet. But it wouldn't remain that way too much longer. Today was race day. And race day started early.

A gleam of light caught her eye and she realized not everyone in the Owners' and Drivers' lot was asleep. One of the hotshot young drivers had broken his ankle racing go-karts the day before and had to pull out of the race. His driver had packed up his motor home and headed out of the compound only an hour or two later, leaving Sophia with an unimpeded view of Justin Murphy's "trailer" parked in the row directly behind.

A smile curved her lips. It was a trailer, not a motor home. A post-war model that Milo had grudgingly admitted had been a top-of-the-line unit fifty years ago. Streamlined and shining silver in the desert moonlight, it was dwarfed on either side by diesel-powered coaches almost twice its size.

Still, it had character, it stood out from the crowd, and it suited the man who owned it. In many ways she thought of Justin the same way she viewed his home away from home, a man who was slightly out of sync with what his sport had become, a throwback to an earlier time, to a different way of driving. She believed he would be more at ease with the drivers of Milo's era than his own.

As she stared across the compound, thinking her sleepy middle-of-the-night thoughts, Justin Murphy appeared in the doorway of his trailer. She blinked to make sure her eyes weren't playing tricks on her, conjuring the man from her half-waking thoughts. She could just see him silhouetted by the light behind him. He was awake and so was she, and she hadn't spoken to him for five long days.

She found herself standing, slipping her arms into the sleeves of a long cotton sweater that fell below her hips, sliding her feet into a pair of canvas slippers Juliana had left by the door. She hoped the near-complete darkness of the sleeping motor home lot would hide the fact that beneath the sweater she was wearing only a tank top and her flannel jammie pants, which were covered in sleeping bunnies with little cartoon Zs floating all around them.

She opened the heavy metal door of the Cargill Motors coach and slipped outside, shutting the door behind her with all the stealth of a teenager slipping out of the house to meet the wild boy from the wrong side of the tracks. She crossed the "street" that separated two facing rows of motor homes and moved into the shadow of Rafael O'Bryan's unit, drawn toward the faint light of Justin's trailer.

"Sophia?" His voice came out of the darkness. Evidently, years of driving race cars with un-muffled engines hadn't yet damaged his hearing. She was trying her best not to make any sound.

"I saw you come out of your trailer. I...I couldn't sleep," she said, wrapping her arms around herself, as much to hide her trembling as to shield herself from the chill of the desert night. What if he wasn't alone? What if he had only come outside for a moment's fresh air and someone was inside the trailer waiting for him. Lucy Gunter? Perhaps they had reconciled? Or maybe it wasn't even Lucy, but another woman.

Las Vegas was the race all the Hollywood people attended. Starlets and supermodels—surgically enhanced and perfectly made up—paraded up and down pit road with their cell phone wielding handlers all day long. The overabundance of such beautiful, alluring creatures was enough to give even the most confident of women pause.

"I'm not disturbing you, am I?" she asked. She glanced at the trailer. She wondered what it was like inside. "I'm not interrupting anything?"

He moved into a pool of moonlight and reached out his hand. "Only me trying to figure out for the hundredth time what's wrong with the setup of my car." He was dressed much like she was, a white T-shirt over low-riding flannel pants, only his were plain black, no dozing bunnies in cartoon poses. The soft cotton clung to the muscles of his hips and thighs. She dragged her gaze up past the hard flatness of his stomach and the width of his chest to his eyes.

He was watching her, and the upward curve of the right side of his mouth informed her that he knew where her thoughts and her gaze had been lingering. She kept on talking, hiding her embarrassment as best she could. "My dad said it was running rough for you today."

"Yeah, real rough. My sister's been in the garage day and night trying to figure out the right setup. Wish I could help more than I have, but she's the engine specialist. I'm just the driver."

There was an edge to his voice, a thread of self-doubt he probably never would have revealed in the light of day, but there was something about the small, dark hours of the night that loosened tongues—and inhibitions. She shivered with a mixture of dread and delight as he put his hand under her elbow and guided her toward the narrow steps leading into his trailer.

"Not everyone's born to be an engineer," she said, wanting to do something to take away the uncharacteristic uncertainty she sensed in him. "You're the athlete, the talent, remember? Let others do what they're good at. You drive the race car."

He laughed and the doubt was erased from his voice. "You sound just like my sister. And my cousin. Rachel would say, 'Shut up and drive the car' without any sugar-coating, and Kim would back her up with a few choice comments of her own."

"I didn't mean it that way. My dad says they can run all the tests they want. Hook the engine up to every machine and computer known to mankind, stick it in a million-dollar wind tunnel, but the driver's still the only one who can tell them how it feels to drive the car."

"I'll remember that."

"How is Kim? I've been wondering." Her feet were moving her forward, even though her mind was urging her to stand still, not to enter his lair. And that was exactly what she thought of it at that moment, a lair, a place where he was lord and master and she would be entirely at his mercy.

"I don't know. She hasn't returned my calls, and I'm ashamed to say these last two days I've been too busy with the car to try again. Just like I've been too busy to try to find you alone and unattended."

Another delicious shiver skittered along her nerve endings, but she pretended not to have heard that last remark. "I'm sure she'll be fine." She tried very hard to keep her concerns hidden, but her nurse's experience told her there was more than fatigue or stress behind Kim Murphy's collapse.

"I hope so, too."

"What's keeping you awake?" he asked moving the subject in a new direction.

"Time change mostly," she said, which was partially true. She wondered if she should confide her fears for Kent to him and reluctantly decided against it. If they had just been Sophia and Justin, two friends from Charlotte, it would be okay. But they weren't. He was a NASCAR driver, and she was the sister and daughter of his two greatest rivals. She didn't for a moment believe that Justin would go running to the tabloids or anything like that, but he was her brother and father's competitor and any advantage he could gain on either of them, he might use.

After a few more moments of silence, he must have decided she wasn't going to elaborate on her statement, so he opened the door and reached out a hand to help her up the steps. "It's too cold to stand out here. Come inside."

Her feet stayed glued to the gravel. "I should be getting back. It's late. You need your sleep."

"This might be the only time we have alone together," he said quietly. "I've missed you." He let her hear the longing in his voice and she was lost.

She hesitated while reason made one last effort to convince her to leave, then she reached up, accepting his hand, tightening her stomach muscles so that he didn't feel her react to his touch. His warm fingers closed over hers, and the expected jolt of electric sensation pulsed through her, just as she'd feared it would.

Then she was through the door and her uncertainty was momentarily forgotten. She had stepped back in time at least half a century. She laughed delightedly as her eyes took in the red-and-gray color scheme, the blond wood and geometrically patterned floors, the retro-styled appliances and light fixtures. "I love it," she said, giving his hand a squeeze. "It looks exactly as though Lucy and Desi might appear out of thin air and join us for cocktails any moment."

He grinned back at her. "Thanks. That's the look I was going for."

"You did all this?" It surprised her a little, that he would be interested in returning the travel trailer to its original condition. She'd thought she might walk into an interior full of mirrored reflections and granite and teak, not blond wood and chrome fixtures and a feeling of having stepped back in time to a place where Milo and Juliana in their honeymoon days would have felt right at home.

"My renovation specialist did most of the interior restoration," he admitted. "But I did all the nuts-and-bolts work on her, plumbing, heating, electrical." He pointed to the plasma-screen TV recessed into an overhead cabinet. 'I draw the line at 'period appropriate' when it comes to my personal comfort."

"I can see why you wanted to bring her back."

"She was in pretty bad shape when I found her," he said proudly. "I take quite a ribbing from the rest of the drivers when we wheel her in beside these million-dollar rigs of theirs, though. Not all of it good-natured. There's one or two tracks grumbling pretty loudly about the lots not being trailer parks."

"I wouldn't listen to them if she were mine," Sophia said running her hand over the brick-red countertop edged with chrome. "I love that the kitchen is in the front. All these windows."

"The bedroom is in the back," he said softly.

She spun around. "I...I didn't come for—" Words failed her. What *had* she come for?

"Why are you here, Sophia?" he asked, still in the same soft, rough-edged voice that sent shivers of longing up and down her spine.

She took a deep breath. "I've missed you," she said. "I haven't had a chance to talk to you since we got here."

"I saw you at your brother's hauler yesterday. I saw you with your mother in your dad's garage stall. You never even glanced my way. You haven't returned my calls."

She lifted her chin. "I wasn't ignoring you," she said, trying to align her thoughts into a coherent explanation. "I—"

He moved to close the distance between them. "You were afraid there'd be a scene if you spoke to me in front of your kin?"

"There wouldn't have been a scene," she said jumping to her family's defense.

"I'm not so sure of that."

She sighed. "I'm not either. But it doesn't change the fact that I wanted to see you again. That I hoped you wanted to see me again." She gathered her courage and focused it all in one spot—somewhere very near to her heart, she realized with a pang. "Was I wrong?"

His arms came around her. He pulled her close to his chest and laid his chin on the top of her head. "You weren't wrong," he said. "I wanted to see you, too. So badly I can't sleep at night for thinking of you. And I wanted to do this." He reached down and lifted her chin slightly so that she was staring directly into his eyes. "Kiss me, Sophia."

"Is that an order?" she asked, daring herself as much as him.

"No," he said, moving her to the red couch, pushing her gently down onto the seat, leaning over her, both arms on the back, one knee braced on the cushion beside her hip. "I'm asking."

"Good," she said. "I wouldn't want to have to say no to prove a point."

"Please," he said, his voice low and rough with desire. "Pretty please." Desire coursed through her veins, stealing her voice, so that she could only reach up, thread her fingers through his hair and pull his head down to hers.

"Lord, woman, where'd you learn to kiss like that?" He asked a few moments—or was it hours?—later. "I thought I was supposed to be the randy one."

She smiled against his mouth, pleased to note he was as breathless as she was. "Surprised you, didn't I?" She wondered where she found the courage to speak so boldly. "I've had some practice since those days when we used to sneak off into the woods together."

He gathered her close against him. "I think we should see how good we'll be together if we take it to the next level."

Desire had been singing through her veins making her light-headed and tingly, urging her to follow his lead, but when he shifted her in his arms and began to press her down into the cushions, reality snapped back.

It was all happening too fast. They'd only spent a few private hours in each other's company. They were barely more than strangers. It would be foolish to go any farther down this dangerously intimate pathway. "I have to go," she said, putting both hands on his chest as he dipped his head to kiss her once more.

He looked down at her, his eyes darkened to obsidian by the low light, his breath coming as quick and hard as her own. She braced herself to hold him off, keep those wicked lips from hers, stop him from drugging her into forgetting herself and not caring what happened next. For a moment more he held her gaze, then moved slightly to put a little space between their bodies. He leaned his forehead against hers, took one shuddering breath, then another, reasserting his own control. "You're right. You should go. I should have never invited you in here."

Her heart twisted in her chest, longing and common sense at war within her. "I came because I wanted to," she whispered. "I'm leaving because I have to. Nana is a light sleeper. She might miss me. I don't want to have to explain where I've been." She hesitated just long enough to draw a shaky breath. "Or lie about what I've been doing."

HE ACHED WITH THE need to make love to Sophia but her last words had brought him back from going over the edge, and taking what he wanted so badly.

Sophia Grosso was a woman for a lifetime, not a one-night stand.

Justin surged to his feet. *Where had that realization come from?* From his heart? His soul? He couldn't say, only that it had risen from a place so deep inside him he hadn't been aware it existed until that very moment.

He was falling hard for her and it didn't much matter any more if he tried to deny it, even to himself. From that same newly discovered well of feelings inside him, he realized he'd known it since the night he'd taken her to Mikey's and she'd handled the emergency with Kim like a trooper. Although true to form, he'd told himself it was only the way any trained nurse would react. But that was only partly the truth. She wasn't fragile like his mother or Sylvie, Hugo's ex-wife, had been. She wouldn't turn tail and run away when life threw her a curve. She was her own woman, strong, intelligent and independent. The way he wanted his wife, the mother of his children, to be.

Wife. Was he really thinking of her in those terms? Thinking of happy-ever-after? He was getting ahead of himself. He had to take this one slow. Justin Murphy, husband and father. That would take some getting used to. Some major retooling of his thought processes. And even if he succeeded in rewiring his own brain, there was still the matter of the Grosso dragons to slay.

Metaphorically, of course. The last thing he needed was for his wooing of the NASCAR princess to come to a knock-down, drag-out, no-holds-barred battle with Dean and Kent Grosso—and for all he knew, old Milo, too.

Him, a dragonslayer. Who'd have figured? He felt as if he'd been gut-punched. He had to think about this some more. "Come on then. Let's get the princess back in her million-dollar tower before all the Grosso dragons wake up and find the ogre's stolen her away," he said, hoping she'd take it as a joke.

She didn't. "Why do you keep saying things like that, Justin? I'm here, aren't I?" He heard the hurt in her voice and it shamed him in his very soul. "I came of my own free will. Despite what you think. I'm leaving because I think it's best for me…and for you…not because I'm afraid of my family."

Her family. His family. It always came down to that between them, and it always would. "I'm sorry, Sophia." He ran his finger along the soft skin of her throat. "I shouldn't have put you in this position. I shouldn't have brought you in here at this time of night. It won't happen again. You have my word." He reached out his hand and helped her stand.

"Oh, don't be so melodramatic," she said, scowling up at him. "I told you, I came in here of my own free will. I'm leaving the same way." She stood up, ignoring his outstretched hand, opened the door of his trailer and marched out into the night.

He stood rooted to the spot long enough to watch her cute little fanny disappear down the steps, then he thrust his feet into his shoes and took off after her. She might be a princess, but she was her own woman. He had to remember that. She was just moving into the shadows of O'Bryan's behemoth motor home when he caught up to her. "You can't just take off like this."

"Of course I can," she said with dignity. "I don't see what reason there is for me to stay. I'm not making love with you and you're not communicating with me, so we might as well both get some sleep. Good night, Justin."

"Wait," he said, closing his fingers around her wrist. "I'll walk you home." He needed time to think, to come up with some answers for her. He hadn't sorted out his own feelings yet. How could he deal with hers? He'd never felt like this about any other woman, including Lucy, and he'd almost asked her to marry him. Was this love? He still had no idea what being in love actually felt like but it was something a hell of a lot more complicated than plain old lust. "We've got to talk."

"Fine. Talk." She spun around, directly underneath Rafael's bedroom window. Thank God the air conditioner was whirling away. He probably couldn't hear them.

"Not here," he said. Justin raked his hand through his hair. Damn it, what was it about this woman that caused him to revert to the angry outsider he'd felt all through his growing up years. Still felt himself to be when he was in the company of the top tier of drivers to which Dean Grosso and his son belonged. And Sophia was the biggest prize of all, bigger even than winning the NASCAR Sprint Cup Series championship. As much as she denied it, she was NASCAR royalty. Four generations on the inside, at the top of the leader board. And he was the son and great-nephew of men who had never played by the rules, had made enemies wherever they went, and had been despised enough that it was more than an even bet that they both had met death at the hands of those they'd wronged or betrayed. He was fooling himself if he thought the Grossos would let him steal their princess away. Not while Dean and Kent, and even the old man, Milo, were around to keep him away. He saw the moment she read his thoughts in his eyes and in the scowl he felt taking over his face.

"You're as fixated on the past as my family is," she said quietly, shaking her head. She started walking away again, all light and shadow—a rustle of soft material, a whisper of flowers and spice on the desert air. She crossed the paved street between the rows of motor homes and stopped at the edge of the awning that separated her great-grandparents' palatial coach from her brother's. He'd felt intimidated talking beneath O'Bryan's bedroom window. How in hell was he supposed to tell her how he felt when her entire family was sleeping within twenty feet of them? She laid her hand on his arm and he steeled himself against the longing that poured through him to reach out and take her in his arms and show her with his hands and lips and body the feelings he couldn't yet put into words.

She took one step closer. Her voice was a whisper on the cool night air. "I'm leaving because I want so badly to stay, Justin. I'm not used to getting in this deep so early in a relationship. It's scary for me. We have to work this out, think it through and come up with some kind of plan. Some way to get our families to see reason, so we can put it all behind us and move into the future."

Her words drifted off into silence. She dropped her eyes to her hand that still rested on his arm. Somewhere down the line of motor homes a dog began to bark; the sound of early arriving delivery trucks drifted over the night air from the track. The faintest wash of lighter gray drew a line just above the horizon.

Time was running out. Race day started early. Soon people would begin to stir and move about. He didn't want her subjected to the gossip that being seen together dressed as they were, would generate in this small, closed community. And the desert air was cold. He could feel her shivering. He needed to get her back inside. He turned then, so he could frame her face with his hands, make her look at him. She was so open, so honest, he could read her every emotion as they played out over her expressive features. "Why should they let go of the past, Sophia? Your father, your great-grandfather have held on to their hard feelings for almost fifty years. They've passed them on to your brother. He hates my guts. And it's not just on your side. My uncle's the same way. Why should they end it now?"

She locked her gaze with his. "So that we can be—"

Together? Was that the word she couldn't quite say? He took the risk, said it first. "Together?"

She hesitated a moment, then nodded. "Together."

"God, Sophia, do you mean that?" He could feel her tremble, knew what it cost her emotionally to open herself to him this way—to a man whose relationships with women had a habit of crashing and burning, and whose sexual exploits, both rumored and real, had been tabloid fodder since he won his first NASCAR Busch series race.

"I think so." She closed her eyes a moment as though searching inside herself. "Yes, that's what I mean." She smiled, and it hit him like a blow to the chest. He loved her smile, it changed her face from pretty to incandescent, her eyes from blue to sapphire. "I know exactly what I'm saying. What I need to know is if you feel the same way I do. Do you want to keep seeing me? Do you want us to take the risk of standing up to all the Grossos and Murphys and telling them we're a couple, or is it all you want that I keep sneaking out to see you in the middle of the night like I used to when I was young and silly?"

He was enchanted by that smile, mesmerized by the sound of her voice. At that moment he would have walked into the jaws of hell, the front door of the Grosso motor home—*to have her love him? Was he that far gone on her already? He'd never been in love before, but he had a sneaking suspicion he was more than halfway there over Sophia.*

"Sophia? I just walked you home. Will you do the same for me?"

She glanced over his shoulder at the Manor only a dozen

steps behind them. "I don't understand." Her smile was a little lopsided and he wanted to kiss it straight.

"Will you walk me to my car before the race?" He knew he was asking a lot. It would bring their relationship out in the open, make it public. Was she ready for that?

Before Sophia could answer, a figure moved out of the dark shadows beneath the canvas awning of Dean Grosso's motor home, breaking the spell of moonlight and intimacy that had cocooned them, yanking him back to reality. A woman, an inch or so shorter than Sophia and only slightly rounder of figure confronted them, hands on hips. Patsy Grosso. Justin had seen her many times, but had never spoken to her before. She stopped a few feet from them and fixed her gaze on him—a gaze as blue as Sophia's and laser-sharp, even in the darkness. "You know Sophia walking you to your car will cause no end of trouble in this family, Justin Murphy. And in yours too, I imagine."

"Yes, ma'am. I reckon it will." Justin used every ounce of willpower to keep Patsy Grosso from realizing how her presence had startled him.

"I certainly hope this is more than just another one of your tabloid romances. Taking up with you will most likely cause Sophia heartache and possibly destroy her relationship with her family. I'm warning you. You had better be dead serious about it."

CHAPTER TEN

WALK HIM TO HIS CAR? COULD she do that? Could she proclaim so publicly and so blatantly that she and Justin Murphy had something going on? Because there was no way the small world of stock car racing would think any differently.

Sophia nearly jumped out of her skin when she heard her mother's voice. She took a quick step backward and Justin let her go, but she saw his mouth harden and knew he felt her startled reaction. "Mom, what are you doing up at this hour of the night?"

"I could ask the same thing of you." Patsy Grosso said giving both of them the once-over. "Sophia, what are you thinking running around out here in your night clothes? It's freezing. You'll catch your death of cold."

"I couldn't sleep," she said trying to gather her scattered wits. "Justin couldn't either. We were just talking."

"In his trailer? In the middle of the night?" Patsy's eyebrows rose toward her hair line. "I saw you coming across the road when I looked out the window."

"Talking," Sophia repeated. *Mostly,* she added to herself.

"Your father and brother aren't going to like this."

"I'm twenty-eight years old, Mom. I pick my own friends."

"You're right, of course." Patsy nodded in grudging acceptance of that inarguable fact.

Justin had been standing quietly beside Sophia. Now her mother turned to him. "You didn't answer my question," she said, arms folded across her chest.

"I'm dead serious about two things, Ms. Grosso," he said, slow and deliberate. The honeysuckle-and-molasses drawl would cut no slack with her mother.

"And those two things are?"

"My driving. And my—" Sophia sucked in her breath. If he said his women she'd have to slap his face or kick him in the shins if she intended to hold up her head in front of her mother again. "And my friendships. I'm honored Sophia thinks of me as a friend, considering our families' past history." He turned his head a fraction of an inch and smiled, devastatingly sexy as always, but perhaps, just a little tentative? "If it comes to more than that in the fullness of time. Well, as your daughter said, she's twenty-eight years old. I guess it will be because she makes up her mind in that direction for herself. I'll ask you one more time, Sophia. Will you walk me to my car?"

"I—" Her cowardice won out. She didn't want to be at odds with her family. Not ever. What she was beginning to feel for Justin wasn't yet strong enough to make her brave enough to take such a risk.

She saw the quick flash of hurt in his eyes, gone as quickly as it had come, replaced with hard-edged, diamond-bright pride. "That's okay, Sophia, I can see your answer in your eyes. It's my fault for being presumptuous enough to ask." He inclined his head slightly. "My apologies, Ms. Grosso. Good night, ma'am. Good night, Sophia. See ya'll around."

"Justin."

But he'd turned on his heel and walked away without a backward glance.

Sophia turned on her mother. "Mom, what possessed you to be so snotty to him? All he did was walk me home."

"And kiss you right in front of me."

"He didn't know you were spying on us from the shadows." Sophia couldn't remember ever being so put out with her mother.

"I agree. That was sneaky of you, Patsy," came a second voice from the darkness.

"Nana? You've been eavesdropping, too?" Sophia's legs no longer wanted to support her weight. She sat down in a folding canvas armchair and stared open-mouthed at the dark bulk that was her great-grandmother.

"I've been trying to enjoy a smoke," Juliana returned unperturbed. "It's the only time I can sneak one without Milo catching me at it, but it seems everyone else in this family is out and about at this ungodly hour, too. I imagine it was you leaving the coach that woke me in the first place."

"I couldn't sleep," Sophia said. "I was worried about Kent."

"Your brother can take care of himself." Sophia could feel the older woman staring at her purloined shoes. She tucked her feet underneath the chair. "What were you up to with the Murphy boy?"

Sophia sighed. "Nothing, Nana. We were just talking."

"Did you say anything to him about Kent's cheating in college all those years ago?" Patsy asked.

"I wouldn't do that, Mama. Besides, it's common knowledge now."

Patsy sat down beside her with a sigh. "I'm sorry, honey. I know you wouldn't talk to him about it. The whole thing's thrown me off balance, that's all."

"It's okay, Mom. Nana's right. Kent can handle his own affairs. It's not like he robbed a bank. Granted it was foolish, but he was very young. His fans will understand. He's been a role model for NASCAR for almost ten years. It will all blow over. I'm sure it will."

"Your father said the same thing." Patsy returned to the subject that worried her most. "I still don't like the idea of you being alone with Justin Murphy. You know how easily gossip spreads in this place."

"I told you. Nothing happened. We just talked."

"Well, if he invited me into his trailer in the middle of the night wearing what he had on, you can believe I would have found something better to do than just talk."

"Nana!" Sophia was shocked.

"What? Just because I'm old doesn't mean I don't remember what it felt like to have hormones and not just hot flashes."

"Well, I'm not as old as you and I'm beginning to feel the same way," Patsy said candidly. Sophia wrapped her arms around her waist and hunched her shoulders. She didn't want to listen to her mother and great-grandmother discuss their hormones, even if it did deflect their attention from her.

"I'm not having a relationship with Justin Murphy," she insisted, aware of how unconvincing the words sounded.

"Well, you should be," Juliana remarked, flicking a disposable lighter and holding the flame to the end of her cigarette. "Or at least having one with someone who's not a Murphy."

The trouble was, she didn't want to have a relationship with anyone *but* Justin.

"Give me one of those," Patsy said, interrupting Juliana's tirade, and disappearing into the darker shadows where the older woman was seated, wrapped in a thick terrycloth robe that glowed faintly white in the darkness. Momentarily, a second glowing cigarette tip appeared beside the first one.

"Mom, you don't smoke." What other shock to her system was her mother going to deliver that night?

"I don't now. I used to though, before I married your father. I gave it up when I got pregnant with your brother."

Sophia did some quick math. Her mother had married her father one week after her high school graduation, one month shy of her eighteenth birthday. Kent had been born exactly nine months later. If her mother smoked it had been when she was sixteen or seventeen. Good Lord, what would Sophia's strait-laced, maternal grandmother, say if she knew that about her daughter?

"Milo's biggest sponsor was a cigarette distributor from Memphis. One season he got paid in cartons of cigarettes. Those were the days," Juliana reminisced, inhaling so deeply the tip of her cigarette glowed as red as a lava flow.

"Those days won't come again," Patsy observed.

"Nope. More's the pity."

"I think I'll go back to bed," Sophia said, rising for a quick getaway.

"Oh, no, you don't." Patsy stubbed out her cigarette. "We need to talk. How far has this thing between you and Justin Murphy progressed?"

"Just as far as you saw tonight." She was a little surprised how disappointed she was to say those words.

"He's going to break your heart, honey," Patsy said, but there was no scorn, no anger in her voice, just worry and apprehension.

"Causing heartbreak's bred in the bone with those Murphys," Juliana added.

"Justin's not like his father or his great-uncle." How

many times would she have to repeat that statement to get anyone in her family to believe it? Her mind shied away from having this conversation with any of the male Grossos. It was awkward enough with her mother and great-grandmother.

"You don't know that for sure. Troy Murphy made so many passes at me that your father threatened to beat the living daylights out of him in front of half a dozen other drivers. That's why the police came looking for Dean the night Troy was killed. He was the last man to warn him to stay away from his wife. But he wasn't the first. Not by a long shot."

"Thank the Good Lord, Dean had an alibi that night," Juliana said, blowing smoke out through her nose. "He was meeting with a potential sponsor. He wasn't even in the county."

"I can't believe that the police thought Dad might have been driving the truck that ran down Justin's dad. I always thought it was stolen from Grandpa's garage."

"It was," Patsy said emphatically. "We never discovered who took it. We didn't bother to lock stuff up in those days."

"And there wasn't any such thing as DNA testing and all that computer voodoo, either," Juliana inserted.

"But what about fingerprints?"

"The steering wheel and door handle had been wiped clean, even the dashboard. The truck had cloth seats, so those were the only places they could test for fingerprints."

"I think it was a woman who killed him though," Juliana said, stubbing her cigarette butt out with the toe of her slipper.

"Because of his reputation?"

"Because a man would have shot him or took a knife to his liver," she said with relish.

"Then do you think it was a woman who killed Connor

Murphy, too? He was run off the side of a mountain road while he was on his motorcycle, wasn't he?" Sophia asked. "I've always heard it wasn't an accident. He was too good a driver for that." She had discussed the similarities of the two deaths with her family before over the years but no one ever had the right answers.

Juliana stood up suddenly. "My arthritis is killing me. It's cold and it's almost dawn. This place will be waking up in another hour."

"Nana, you didn't answer me." Sophia glanced at her mother and could see Patsy's face more clearly than she had a few minutes before. It was nearly dawn, she realized. Her mother was frowning, shaking her head a little as though to warn Sophia off.

Juliana turned, her foot on the first step of the motor home. "I don't know." She sounded every one of her seventy-seven years, for almost the first time Sophia could recall. "Your great-grandfather knows something about that night. It was before we met. He's told me everything about his marriage to Dean and Larry's grandmother. About his career in the FBI. About the early days of NASCAR and the cheating Connor did to win himself the championship. He has never, ever, spoken of the night Connor Murphy died, but I know it haunts him to this day." She moved heavily up the steps. "It haunts us both."

Sophia and Patsy sat quietly for several minutes after the old woman had closed the door behind her, each busy with her own thoughts.

"What did she mean?" Sophia finally asked her mother. She really didn't want to know the answer. It was all well and good that she and Justin had decided between them that the Grosso and Murphy feud should be put to rest, buried like the bodies of Connor and Troy Murphy, ended and forgotten, but what of the others more closely tied to the actual events? Could they forgive and forget so easily? Obviously not. The realization weighed heavily on her spirit.

Patsy stood and the movement drew Sophia to her feet also. Her mother walked toward her and lifted her hand to stroke her hair as she had done so often when Sophia was little. "She means, you taking up with Justin Murphy isn't just a NASCAR version of Romeo and Juliet. Your great-grandfather and your father were both grievously wronged by Connor and Troy Murphy. Hugo's never believed that Milo and your father didn't have something to do with his kin's untimely deaths. Fair or not, ancient history or not, that's all standing between you two."

"But if we knew who had really killed Troy, and maybe even Connor, that would help," she said, knowing she sounded like a desperate child wanting to make everything right.

Patsy shook her head. "I'm not so sure. Discovering who was responsible for their deaths may create even more trouble for our family than turning your back on Justin and walking away."

I CAN'T SEE YOU AGAIN, Justin. I'm so, so sorry. It's all just too complicated. I wish you all the best in your career. In your life. I'd say we could just be friends but that's not going to work. We both know it.

She had been waiting for him when he came out of the drivers' meeting. She was wearing a cute little blue sundress with a short blue-and-white striped jacket. Most likely she was planning to watch the race from one of the luxury sky boxes atop the grandstand. Rarified atmosphere. Rarified company.

I'm so, so sorry. She'd repeated with tears in her voice. Then she'd kissed him on the cheek, turned and walked away.

"Justin. Can you hear me? Talk to me, JM."

It was Dennis, his spotter, and he'd been wandering again. Even if his thoughts had taken only a fraction of a second, it wasn't what you did going three-wide down the backstretch at a 160 miles an hour. Not if you intended to still be there at the end of the race.

"Got you, buddy. Radio button stuck."

Inside his helmet, the radio receiver crackled to life again. "The No. 414 and No. 427 cars are coming up on your backside like bats out of hell. Keep low. Keep low, or they'll both get by you."

"Can't. Running too rough in the low groove," Justin said, and toggled off his radio. He knew that millions of fans, the TV crew and announcers, and who knew how many other teams were listening in to his radio transmission. The car was so tight he was lucky he didn't go into the wall on every turn. He'd pitted three times in the first sixty laps of the five-hundred mile race so that the crew could work on correcting the problem. Nothing had helped.

And to make matters worse, he couldn't keep his mind off Sophia Grosso telling him she was breaking up with him before they even qualified as a real couple.

"Go low, J-man. Go low."

"If I could keep her low, I would," he growled into the radio. But if he was passed by both Grossos, he'd go a lap down, and he'd worked too hard to stay with the leaders to let that happen. His pride wouldn't stand for it. He stood on the accelerator, trying to find another couple horsepower, but it just wasn't there. And then it happened.

The Grossos had dropped back coming out of the turn,

but Will Branch came up on his high side disrupting the air flow around the race car. Justin's back end came loose, spinning him up the track. In less time than it took his brain to register the danger he was in, his body had already reacted, muscling the wheel, trying to correct the slide, struggling to keep the nose out of the wall. But it didn't work. The outside wall came up and smacked him on the back quarter panel, spinning him around in the opposite direction. The race car skidded down the steep-banked track, smoking, gathering other cars up in its wake.

But Justin almost didn't feel the subsequent impacts. The first one had knocked all the air from his lungs. He functioned on instinct alone, wrestling to keep the car from barrel-rolling into the infield. It was a losing battle. He spun onto the grass, smoke obscuring his vision. Kent Grosso's car spun past him.

Then the younger Grosso was gone, hitting his father's car, the duo sliding off together in a steel embrace. Justin's car took one more dervish spin, the g-forces increasing, compressing his laboring chest. The fence came nearer. He braced himself for the instantaneous deceleration that would more than likely send him airborne, but it never came. He skidded along the concrete barrier below the fence, and then the car began to slow and finally ground to a halt. It had seemed to take forever, but was over in less than a handful of seconds.

Dennis's voice came through his headphones, loud with apprehension. "Talk to me, J-man. Talk to me."

Justin fumbled for his radio switch, but his hand refused to obey his mind.

His spotter's commands were replaced by his crew chief's. "Justin. Son? We need to hear from you." Hugo's voice was flat and calm, no emotion allowed to seep through for all those listening ears to hear. "Get on the radio, boy. Let us know you're okay."

Justin struggled to respond. He reached up to let his window net down, let the fans and the emergency crew and his team know he was okay—or at least still conscious, but it was taking a lot longer than he planned to execute the simple maneuver.

"Justin. You have to get out of the car. The engine's smoking bad." It was Rachel's voice. Calm, also, but slightly too high-pitched to sound natural.

It was the spur he needed to shake off the disorientation the crash had produced. "I'm okay. Winded is all." Not exactly true, but close enough. He undid his safety harness, let down the net and gave a thumbs-up sign tot he crowd before he levered himself painfully out of the window. As he did so, his air hose and radio connection detached themselves. He unfastened the unwieldy HANS device that had most likely saved him from serious injury and dropped it beside the car. Smoke, acrid and thick, hung over the race track, filling his helmet. He jerked that off too, with fumbling fingers.

The car smelled of burned rubber, hot oil and spilled gasoline. It barely resembled an automobile anymore. The front and back ends had been damaged by contact with the track walls. The passenger side was flattened. He watched smoke roll out from under the hood and was thankful there hadn't been a fire. Justin had just long enough to process those observations before the emergency workers moved in on him. He took one last look around before the EMTs hustled him off to the back of the ambulance for the mandatory trip to the infield care center.

He'd never drive this car again.

Damn, he thought surveying the half dozen other mangled race cars that littered the track and the infield, their drivers milling about their wrecked rides or making their way to the emergency vehicles as he was. Thankfully, no one appeared to be seriously injured. "The Big One," Justin said to himself, his ears ringing so loudly he could barely hear his own disjointed thoughts. *And my fault. There'll be hell to pay for this one.*

CHAPTER ELEVEN

IT WAS THE SUDDEN cessation of high-decibel engine noise—after hours of assault on the eardrums and nerve endings—that always made Sophia's blood congeal with dread. The only reason for that ominous silence during the running of a race was because there had been a wreck. She was just making her way into the garage area, having changed from the blue sundress she'd worn for the pre-race ceremonies and the obligatory visit to her father and brother's owners' suites. She liked dressing up—what woman didn't?—but she felt more at home in her lightweight slacks and shirt and running shoes, security credentials dangling from a lanyard around her neck. She was scanning the figures in the Smoothtone Music pit looking for her mother when the earth-shaking roar and vibration of forty-three racing V-8s fell silent, leaving her with her heart in her throat and blood pounding in her ears.

She saw garage crews and pit-crew members drop what they were doing and begin to gather close to the TV screens that each team watched to keep up to date on the race. She averted her gaze, fighting the urge to put her hands over her eyes. Instead, she feigned calm as she made her way to the war wagon, the huge rolling toolbox that anchored the Cargill race team's pit area.

Atop it Milo was hunched in a folding chair, signature straw hat on his head, his gnarled hands wrapped around his cane as he listened to radio chatter between his grandson's spotter and crew chief through earphones that gave him something of the look of an ancient space traveler. Her mother was beside him, earphones in place, scribbling notes on her clipboard to keep Milo informed of what was going on in Kent's pit and car as she monitored his team's frequency.

Patsy was dressed in much the same outfit Sophia was wearing, her hair bundled up beneath a blue-and-white Smoothtone Music cap, the old-fashioned clipboard that she had used to keep Dean's lap times since Sophia was a little girl clenched between white-knuckled hands. Her face was a pleasant mask as a TV camera was aimed at her from below, but she steadfastly ignored the microphone thrust up at her.

"Six cars were involved in the wreck," the disembodied voice of the track announcer intoned. "Will Branch in the Branch Investment Alliance Ford, Shaky Paulson in the second Dixon Rogers's Chevrolet are making their way back to pit road. The No. 414 Smoothtone Music Dodge and the No. 427 Vittle Farms Chevy are being towed. Their drivers are out of their cars and appear to be unharmed, though."

Kent. Her father. Not both of them! Sophia had to grab onto the top of a stack of tires. Her eyes flew to her mother's face again. Surely nothing too terrible had happened to her father and brother or Patsy would be off the box and on her way to the infield medical facility. As if to reassure her, Patsy smiled and gave Milo a thumbs-up sign as she spoke into her microphone. Sophia's tightened nerves relaxed a fraction. Patsy wouldn't be smiling like that if both of them weren't okay.

Sophia moved a couple of steps farther into the pit and caught a glimpse of the small TV screen one of the shop dogs had fitted into a cubby of the huge toolbox. The camera panned across the wrecked and smoking race cars. Her dad's was a mess. Kent's car appeared slightly less damaged, salvageable at least, and then the camera stopped, focused on a familiar orange-and-brown Chevrolet. The Turn-Rite Tool car. Justin's car.

Sophia couldn't take her eyes from the TV screen. In the sudden, unaccustomed silence she was able to hear the voices of the TV announcers as they described the action on the screen. "One driver's still in his car. We're waiting for him to put down his net."

"Always a scary time," another announcer, a former driver, added.

"The worst. We sure hope Justin Murphy's all right. The No. 448 car's done for the day, though."

"So are about half a dozen others including both the Grossos. But thank the Good Lord they're out of their cars and making their way to the emergency vehicles."

Sophia watched as her father and brother walked together to the ambulance, helmets under their arms, looking so alike in their mannerisms and the way they held their bodies that she had to blink away tears.

But another part of her still waited in terror. Why didn't Justin lower his net, hoist himself out of the damaged race car and wave to the fans and emergency workers to show he was all right? Smoke rolled from under the hood. Had he been so badly injured he couldn't get out of the cockpit by himself?

She could feel her nails cutting half-moon grooves in the palms of her hands, but she thought of her mother and her great-grandmother and the strength they always showed in these situations. Drawing on those examples, she managed to keep her tears to herself and her urge to run out onto the infield under control.

Other drivers were emerging from their cars, heading toward the Turn-Rite Tool Chevrolet. The announcers fell silent as the emergency workers and three or four members of Justin's pit crew arrived at the wreck simultaneously. They mingled around the driver's side window for what seemed like forever, and then as if moved by a single hand they all stepped back and the window net went down, Justin's gloved hand, gave a thumbs-up sign to the silent crowd and moments later his helmeted head appeared outside, followed by the rest of him.

Cheers erupted from the grandstands, mingling with more than a few boos. After all, Justin had wrecked her father and brother and half a dozen other drivers, more than one of which was as big a crowd favorite as the Grossos. Race fans weren't shy about showing their dissatisfaction with drivers of rival cars—or their own drivers, if they didn't perform up to expectations.

Sophia didn't really take heed of any of that beyond a momentary acknowledgment of a resumption of noise. She was still too worried about Justin and the reason for his belated exit from his car. She continued watching the images on the screen, although she could no longer hear the announcers' voices as cars that had not been as seriously wrecked began to make their way back to the garages for repairs in hopes of finishing the race.

As she watched, the tow trucks began hooking up to the race cars unable to make it to the garages under their own power. The ambulance with Justin, her father and brother all in the back sped off to the Infield Care Center.

She had begun to breathe almost normally again when she saw Justin walk to the ambulance without assistance, but now she wondered what was going on in the vehicle. Her father and brother were usually calm and even-tempered on the race track, unlike a lot of drivers, but this was the second time Justin had wrecked at least one of them, and there was no telling how hot their Irish-Italian tempers would flare.

"Sophia?" Her mother stood beside her. She was still wearing the oversized headphones and radio receiver that were a necessity in the pit area if you wanted to make yourself heard at all. Sophia had been so focused on what was happening on the TV screen that she hadn't seen Patsy climb down from her perch on top of the war wagon. Patsy motioned to the sky boxes atop the grandstand, indicating that she thought Sophia was there with Juliana.

"I wanted to watch with you." She nearly had to shout to be heard as powerful racing engines roared past less than a hundred feet away.

"And you got here just in time for the big one." Patsy gave her a pat on the arm. "They're okay," she said, motioning for one of the pit crew to bring Sophia a set of headphones.

Sophia searched her mother's face. "All of them?"

Patsy watched her from eyes as blue as her own, but with far more serenity than she could summon at the moment. She nodded. "All three of them are in the care center at the same time." Her smile turned grim. "It's not that big a place. I don't think the rubbin' and bangin' is over by a long shot."

JUSTIN WALKED INTO THE small reception area of the care center after being examined and declared fit to race again—

except that he no longer had a car to race. He was enjoying a last few seconds of peace and quiet before he opened the door and faced the media swarm waiting outside. Looking around, he found he wasn't alone in the room.

Damn, the Grossos. Both of them. Waiting for him.

"Hold up there, Murphy. There's something I want to say to you." Kent Grosso made no effort to hide his anger. And contempt. The affable facade he showed the media and the fans was nowhere to be seen.

Every muscle in Justin's body ached. So did every bone they were attached to, but there was no way he was going to let either of the Grossos see that. "Look, I'm sorry you got caught up in that," he said, indicating the race track beyond the care center. "Glad you're both okay." He was thankful he'd already slipped on his mirrored sunglasses. It gave him just that one iota of extra swagger and confidence he needed to face two of the best-known and best-liked drivers in the sport, when inside his pride and ego were as bruised and battered as his body.

He had been driving like an amateur out there today. Worse than that, he'd been driving just plain bad, with less than every ounce of his ability and experience focused on his car and the track. Thank God no one had been badly injured—or worse. He'd never scrub that guilt off his conscience.

Kent took two long steps toward him, came close enough to let Justin know he had no respect for his personal space. In his uniform, helmet tucked under his arm, he had the presence of some Old West lawman getting ready to run the no-good gunslinger—that would be him—out of town. "You damned near took out half the field today. You don't belong on the race track driving like that. Clean up your act or get the hell out of NASCAR."

He didn't even give Justin the courtesy of waiting for his reply, but jerked open the door and waded into the phalanx of microphones and shoulder-held video cameras beyond. The door was steel, spring-loaded and slow to close. Justin didn't hear the question shouted from one of the waiting reporters, but he heard Kent's answer. "Justin Murphy's driving over his head this season. Maybe NASCAR should sit him out a couple of races, let him think about it some. Or maybe Dixon Rogers should get himself a real driver and send Murphy back to short tracks to learn some fundamentals from the young guns on their way to the Show."

The door latched shut on the last words. Justin was left with Dean Grosso staring at him from eyes that held over a quarter century of NASCAR Sprint Cup Series racing experience and twice that of life's wisdom. The older man needed no help from mirrored sunglasses to project the steely race car driver image his fans loved so well. He did it looking you dead in the eye. "He's right, son," he said in his slow, unmistakable drawl. "Better take heed of what he says. Ya'll got the grit to be a damned fine driver. If you learn to drive with your head and your hands, not your balls."

Justin bit back a retort. "Yes, sir," he said. "I intend to."

Dean gave a curt nod as if to say, *we'll see.* "And Murphy?"

"Yes, sir."

"While you're at it. Stay away from my little girl."

SOPHIA'S HEART WAS BEATING almost as fast as it had after the race, but for far different reasons. Did she dare cross the graveled driveway that separated the Cargill motor home from Justin's trailer? Did she have the nerve? The courage it would take to bridge the divide she'd opened between them that morning, and that Justin's subsequent wrecking of her father and brother's cars had widened to biblical proportions, seemed beyond what she could muster. But her feet kept moving her forward through the fast-emptying lot, closer to the man she had hoped to put out of her thoughts and her heart—but couldn't.

It was almost sunset, the late-winter day nearly ended. Brian Horning, a well-respected journeyman driver had won the race after Justin's spectacular wreck had taken out the frontrunners. She still heard the echoes of the crowd booing when Justin got out of his mangled car. She hadn't liked the sound of it. It made her angry. Made her want to track each and every one of them down and give them a piece of her mind.

She smiled at that ridiculous thought. There had been over one-hundred thousand spectators at the race today. It would take the rest of her natural life to confront them all. And she hated being confrontational. It was a measure of how far gone she really was when it came to Justin Murphy that she'd even fantasize such a scenario.

Her smile faded. She may have told him she didn't want to see him again that morning, but she hadn't meant it. Not by a long shot.

"Justin?"

The huge motor homes that had dwarfed his trailer on either side had already left the lot, heading east, on to the next race in Atlanta. He was hunkered down behind the big Chevy 4x4 pickup securing the ball hitch of the truck to the trailer axle. He rose, moving slowly, stiffly, without the effortless grace she was used to seeing from him. Even though he hadn't been seriously injured in the terrifying multi-car crash, she knew he must ache in every bone and muscle. And she wished there was something she could do for him to take his pain away.

He watched her from narrowed eyes. "I didn't expect to see you again, Sophia," he said, his voice as distant as his expression. "I thought you'd have left already with your family."

For a moment she had thought he looked glad to see her and her pulse rate shot up a few dozen beats a minute, but it must have been her imagination, a trick of the fading desert light, because now he sounded downright indifferent to her being there. She had known this wouldn't be easy, but she also knew if she didn't take the risk, she'd wake up with regret in her heart the next morning, and possibly every morning after that for the rest of her life. "My great-grandparents are flying back tomorrow morning," she said. "I'm going with them. Today was hard on my grandpa. He's too old for that kind of stress and excitement. He needs a good night's rest before such a long flight."

"Cargill sending his jet back for you?" She cringed at the ice in his voice.

"We're flying commercial," she said, giving him back stare for stare.

"Sorry," he muttered, patting his shirt pocket for his sunglasses, then evidently thinking better of shielding himself behind them. "Been a bad day."

She laced her hands together, then forced herself to let them hang naturally at her sides. Even though the lot was emptying fast, there were still people coming and going all around them. "That's one of the reasons I'm here," she said. "I came to apologize for saying what I did this morning."

"Because you didn't mean it?" he asked, still with that terrible distance in his voice and his eyes.

"No," she lied, trying to protect her most vulnerable

spots. "Because I know better than to pick a fight, or deliver bad news to a driver on the morning of a race. I'm apologizing because what I said might have contributed to your wrecking the race car today."

"I wrecked it because I had a bad setup and I couldn't keep control of it. No other reason." He didn't quite meet her eyes when he said it.

"That's not what you told the reporters. You said you had a good car. You said your head wasn't in the race."

"It's what they wanted to hear," he said, his voice hard and flat. "Look, thanks for coming by, but I have to get this trailer ready to roll."

"You're driving it back yourself?"

"Fulcrum Racing isn't Cargill Motors," he said. "We don't run cross-country shuttles. The team plane left two hours ago. The shock guy that usually spells my driver has a sick kid back home. I gave him my seat on the plane." The admission came reluctantly, as though he didn't want her to know there was a softer side to his bad-boy image. But it was too late. She had heard the sadness in his voice when he talked of the sick little boy, Wiley, and she had seen firsthand his concern for his cousin Kim.

He wasn't going to scare her off that easily. "You're not considering driving all night after the trauma you suffered today? That's a really stupid idea." Sophia felt her color rise. "I'm sorry. I didn't mean to sound like Nurse Ratched."

He shrugged. "The truth is I *don't* feel much like horsing this rig down the Interstate. I'm riding shotgun. Dennis is driving. He's in the trailer now trying to get a little sleep. We'll be leaving in an hour or so, soon as the traffic clears a little."

"Will I see you back home?" The words came out of nowhere, from some place of longing so deep inside her she hadn't known it existed until the pain of realizing she might never be alone with him again rose up from that darkness and threatened to escape as a sob.

"I know I got banged around pretty good today," he said coming closer, laying his arm along the back of the pickup, bending slightly toward her so that she could smell the tang of his aftershave and the even more evocative scent of his skin. There was a bruise on the side of his cheek, and one on the back of his wrist. There would be others that she couldn't see, where the safety harness had dug into his skin. She curled her hand into a fist so that she could resist the urge to reach up and soothe the hurt he couldn't completely vanquish from the stubborn set of his mouth. "But I swear I remember you in a really hot little blue dress, just this morning, telling me we shouldn't see each other again. Am I right?"

His voice and face were still serious, but a little of the icy distance she had felt between them was melting away, warming his brown eyes, or so she hoped and prayed. "Yes," she said, secretly pleased he'd noticed the blue dress.

"Why the change of heart?"

"I told you I wanted to apologize—" Here was where she had to do battle with her cowardice or slink away. She opened her mouth but no words came out. She swallowed hard and tried again. "Because I was lying when I said it." She fixed her gaze on the pulse she could see beating in his throat. Slow, steady beats that almost hypnotized her as she waited for him to respond.

"Let me get this straight. Eight hours ago you told me we couldn't see each other again because the situation was too complicated."

"Yes."

"Has something changed I don't know about? Because from the conversation I had with your father and brother a while back, I'd say it's still pretty damned complicated, all right."

She wondered what Kent and her father had said to him when they'd been together in the care center, the only possible place they could have had any privacy at all. "I'm sorry if they were hard on you."

"No harder than I've been on myself. They were right. I didn't have my head in the race today. It's just about the worst damned thing you can do, drive when you're mind's not focused like a laser on what you're doing. I'm never going to drive that way again, Sophia. Do you understand?"

Inwardly she cringed at the words. She, and the situation between their families, was the distraction he was talking about. This whole scene wasn't going as she'd hoped it would. Tears began to sting the backs of her eyes and she blinked hard to keep them away. "I understand," she said miserably. "But—" Why had she told him they couldn't be friends, salvage something of what they had together? "We could—"

He put a finger to her lips. "Don't tell me you changed your mind about being *just friends*," he said. "Because, Princess, you were right about that one. It just ain't gonna happen."

"Do you hate my family that much?"

"To hell with your family," he said angrily. "This is why we can't just be friends." He closed the distance between them so quickly she didn't have time to respond. He scooped her up in his arms and when she opened her mouth—to object? to agree?—he stopped her words with a kiss that sent her few remaining wits spinning off into the void. When he lifted his mouth from hers they were both breathing as though they had run a mile. "It just ain't gonna happen," he repeated as if to convince himself as well as her.

"Take your hands off my great-granddaughter." Sophia jerked out of Justin's embrace, coming back to a sense of time and place with a jolt that was physically painful. "You may not mind having everyone in the sport talking about you but I don't want Sophia's name mentioned in the same breath with yours."

"Grandpa." The single word was all she could manage. She felt her face grow hot with embarrassment. Milo was right. She shouldn't have been kissing Justin Murphy in such a public place. The Owners' and Drivers' lot of a race track was like a small village with the same proclivity to gossip and spy on your neighbors' comings and goings.

"So this is what all the whispering and eye rolling between my Juliana and your mother is about. I thought those rumors were false, but you're carrying on with this loser behind my back." Milo leaned on his cane, bending forward a little to catch his breath. He was a small man, made even smaller by the passing of time. His head was almost bald, covered as always with his battered old straw hat that was legendary in the racing community. His back was stooped by the weight of his ninety-plus years but his eyes were bright with intelligence—and at the moment, real and abiding anger.

"He's not a loser, Grandpa," Sophia said keeping her voice quiet, hiding her dismay at his unexpected appearance as best she could. She had feared this might happen. She should have taken him aside and told him everything as she had Juliana. Now it was too late, and Justin was going to bear the brunt of Milo's famous temper.

"He sure was today. Damned fool driving like some carjacker out of the big city."

"I agree it wasn't my best day, sir," Justin said, letting her go but not moving away from her side.

"You could have gotten my grandson and great-grandson killed out there. You could have killed yourself. You drive like your old man," Milo said, his lip curled with disgust.

Milo was accustomed to saying whatever he wanted, and she loved him, but Sophia wasn't going to let him talk to Justin that way. Especially not within earshot of the half-dozen motor homes still making preparations to leave the lot. "Justin lost his concentration for a moment, that's all. It happens to good drivers, too. I've heard Dad say so."

"Bah, no real driver would use that excuse."

Justin moved past her, closer to Milo, but not so close that Milo would have to lift his head to meet his gaze. Sophia thanked him in her heart for sparing her great-grandfather's dignity that way, even though at the moment she was so angry with him she could have cheerfully wrung his scrawny neck. "I admitted I drove a bad race today but that doesn't excuse what you just said. Don't ever bad mouth my father that way in front of me again, or I'll forget the respect due you for what you've done for this sport over the years. My father could have been one of the best if he'd had a ride and a sponsor that believed in him the way you believe in your kin. He might still be racing today if he hadn't died so young."

Milo's expression hardened to stone with Justin's last remark. "Are you accusing me of having something to do with your father's death?"

"No, sir. Not my father's death. That would be my great-uncle Connor you're thinking of," Justin said quietly.

"You son of—" Milo's sputtered to a halt, his face turning red then purple. Sophia put out her hand to steady him, momentarily fearful he might be suffering a stroke, instead of a fit of temper. "Connor Murphy was a cheat. He cost me the NASCAR championship. Damned near cost me my reputation in racin' and that's worth a damned sight more to me to this day. But I didn't kill him. I wanted to, yes sir, I'll stand right here and say it to your face. I wanted to but I didn't, do you hear? I did not kill Connor Murphy."

"I'm sorry, sir," Justin said his voice tight. "I was out of line."

Milo lifted his right hand and shook his fist in Justin's face. "You still are."

"Milo?" Juliana was standing beneath the canopy of the motor home, watching them. She started forward when she saw Milo's threatening gesture. "What's going on?" she asked, hurrying to her husband's side.

"This ungrateful child is consorting with this spawn of Satan behind our backs," Milo said dramatically. "It isn't enough he wrecks Dean and Kent. He's making a spectacle of Sophia in front of half the drivers on the circuit."

"That's enough," Justin said, still quietly, still with a respectful tone, but Sophia could sense the anger roiling beneath his surface calm. "I'm not making a spectacle of Sophia. We were talking."

"In my day what you were doing wasn't called a discussion. Not by a long shot."

"Grandpa—" Sophia was afraid she was going to cry. Why had she ever thought this would work? The animosity between the Murphys and Grossos might be half-understood, half-mythical happenings of a bygone day for her. But for her great-grandfather, and the rest of her family, they were still fresh wounds. And for Justin, who had grown up without his father, the hurt and shame was closer to the surface than he would ever admit, she realized with dismay. She had not taken all the dynamics of the past into consideration as she should have before she almost let her heart be stolen away.

"Come, old man. Come back inside. Sophia's a grown woman. She makes her own decisions about who she has for a friend. Or more than a friend." Juliana's eyes were sympathetic, but the corners of her mouth were turned down in a frown.

"Nana's right, Grandpa."

Milo stared at her and she gave him back look for look. "Humph," he said finally. "I thought I taught you better than that. You're right. I can't tell you who to see and who not to see. But don't ever bring this Murphy trash around my place or I'll fill his hide with birdshot—then call the cops."

"Milo. You've said enough." Juliana looped her arm through his and tugged him away. "I'm sorry," she mouthed over her shoulder.

Justin looked down at her. Sophia left off watching her great-grandparents' retreating figures and focused on his face. He might as well have been wearing a mask. She couldn't tell what he was thinking, what he was feeling.

"It's your call now, Princess." He searched her eyes, her face. His voice softened, lowered half an octave, sending shivers of need and wanting up and down her spine. "Your dad's warned me off. Your mother's warned me off. Your brother was too busy ripping me a new one to get his two cents' worth in this afternoon but I can guess what he'd say. Old Milo's made it pretty clear what he'd do if he sees us together again. But I'm still willing to take the risk. Are you?"

She waited just a fraction of a second too long to answer. She saw it in his eyes. He stepped back, taking all the warmth and light that was left in the desert sky with him, leaving her standing in cold shadows of her own making.

"Okay. I get the picture. I guess there's nothing more to say except see you around the track, Princess."

And she, poor fool, was so befuddled she had no idea if he meant that as a threat or a promise.

CHAPTER TWELVE

HUGO DROPPED HEAVILY INTO the seat beside Justin. The whine of the chartered jet's engines weren't completely muffled by the pressurized cabin, creating an undercurrent of sound that afforded them a measure of privacy. "Just got off the phone with Dixon," he said. His crew chief's voice pulled Justin out of the half doze he'd been drifting in. He lifted the bill of his ball cap and eyed his uncle from its shadow.

"And is our owner satisfied with my driving today?" He'd won at Atlanta, finishing a full two seconds ahead of Dean Grosso and the rest of the field. And he'd driven a clean race. The car had been great right off the hauler, which meant that his sister's marathon overhaul sessions all week at the garage had paid off. He owed her big time. He was going to offer to have a sauna put in the master bathroom of her house at the lake as soon as the season was over as a thank-you gift.

"He's pleased," Hugo responded dryly. "He's happy you didn't wreck yourself or anyone else. He's glad the race car's still in one piece and the engine didn't blow."

"He'd better thank Rachel for that. She's been at the garage almost 24/7." Justin glanced past his uncle at the sleeping figure of his sister seated across the aisle. She was clutching her clipboard to her chest like a baby. It would be loaded with lists, he knew. Things to do. Things to check. Probably her grocery list and a list of errands she needed to run before they were back on the road for the first Bristol race the next week. His sister was a list writer from way back. Even when she was a little kid she'd made lists and stuck them up all over the house with pieces of tape. He caught his uncle smiling and knew he was remembering those days, too.

"She's a damned good engine specialist. She'll be a damned good engine builder one day if she's got a mind to do it."

"Can't come soon enough for me," Justin said under his breath. "She's got Melton beat by a mile. Wish Dixon Rogers could see that."

"Johnny Melton's got a good reputation in the business."

"And he's good at taking the credit for someone else's hard work, too," Justin grumbled. If he decided to fight the Grosso males for the woman he just might be in love with, he needed steady employment. And to keep employed in NASCAR he needed to win races. Top racers came from top teams. From now on, he'd do his part to get Fulcrum Racing to that next level.

"Got plans for tomorrow?" his uncle asked.

Justin groaned. "Not another team meeting? I was planning to sleep in tomorrow." Turning over a new leaf was harder than it sounded.

"Don't worry. We won't need you at the garage until, oh, ten or so."

"No rest for the weary."

"Or the wicked," Hugo commented dryly.

Justin grunted but didn't respond.

"Dixon's coming down from New York. He wants to

take everyone out to dinner at The Pines tomorrow evening to celebrate your win."

Justin whistled. "The old skinflint must be happy with us. He never ponies up for a spread at a place like The Pines." The brand-new, exclusive golf and country club on Lake Norman was less than a fifteen-minute drive from the property he and Rachel had inherited from their parents. In fact they'd been approached by various developers about selling their land for the project, but they'd agreed between them never to give it up. It was the only legacy they had of the parents they had so few clear memories of.

Hugo's cell phone beeped. He glanced at the display. "It's a text message from Kim." He scanned the screen. "She's sending us her congratulations. Says it's the finest race you've driven."

Justin grinned. "That's high praise from her. Why don't you ask her to join us tomorrow night? Old Dixon's got a soft spot for Kim. He'll be glad to see her."

"I'll do that." Hugo punched in the message, his big fingers surprisingly agile on the tiny buttons.

Justin settled back against his seat, looking out at the distant sunset far to the west. Below them night had fallen. They'd gotten out of Atlanta in good time. He was going to sleep in his own bed tonight. And tomorrow, he would begin his quest to make amends with Sophia. He'd stayed away as he'd promised her he would. Six long days and nights and counting. No unannounced visits, no phone calls. It had been the hardest thing he'd ever done.

He missed seeing her. He missed hearing the sound of her voice. He missed talking to her, kissing her. Hell, he even missed arguing with her. She gave as good as she got and he'd realized he needed that in a woman. His woman.

His friend. Now he only needed to convince Sophia it's what she wanted too.

Hugo's phone beeped again interrupting his train of thought. "That didn't take long," Justin noted with a grin. "I knew Kim wouldn't turn down an invitation to The Pines."

Hugo snapped his phone shut and stuck it in his shirt pocket. "She's not coming," he said, a frown gouging two deep furrows between his eyebrows. "She says she's got a big day ahead of her tomorrow and she's just going to grab a bite on the way home and turn in early."

"That doesn't sound like her," Justin said, feeling his way through this conversational mine field.

"I'm worried about her," his uncle admitted. "She's losing weight. She's thinner every time I see her. Her excuse is always that she's under a lot of stress at work. I think there's more to it. I'm worried she's ill." He looked at Justin, waiting for him to reply.

"I—I haven't seen her since before the Vegas race, but yeah," he hedged. "I thought she looked tired. Rachel feels the same way."

"You've both noticed she's not herself, huh?"

Justin nodded.

"I've tried to get her to go to the doctor, get a check up. Maybe she's anemic, or run down or whatever they call it these days."

"Rachel and I tried to get her to do the same thing after that night at Mikey's."

"Mikey's? What happened at Mikey's?"

Damn, he was too tired and too distracted with his own problems to sidestep the question. Besides, he was worried about his cousin. She evidently wasn't getting any better. He decided to tell his uncle what had happened two weeks earlier. "I took Sophia Grosso to Mikey's one night for barbeque. Kim was there getting some take-out for you two. She was going to surprise you with it, I guess. She…she fainted is all. Nothing serious," he said holding up a hand to forestall his uncle's question. "We took her to the emergency room. The doc checked her out. Said they couldn't find anything wrong right then and there. Told her to go to get some tests. She said she would, but evidently she hasn't done it, right?"

"Right," Hugo said bluntly. "At least not that I know of. I'm going to have a serious talk with that young woman when we get home, make sure she gets an appointment with her doctor—if I have to frog-march her to the office door to make sure she gets there."

"Don't push her too hard," Justin warned the older man. "She's even more bullheaded than you are. Maybe we should let Rachel talk to her first. It…it might be some kind of female problem, you know," Justin finished uncomfortably.

Hugo's frown deepened. "Yeah, maybe that's a good idea." He glanced across the aisle, saw Rachel was still sleeping and turned back to Justin. "I'll talk to her about it first thing tomorrow."

Justin settled back against his seat. "If anyone can get her to listen to reason it's Rachel."

Hugo changed the subject. "And are *you* listening to reason?"

"What do you mean by that?" Justin gave up trying to sleep. It just wasn't going to happen.

"C'mon, Justin. You dodged a couple of bullets by driving back from Vegas with Dennis, but you have to know how fast word gets around. There are no restrictor plates when it comes to racing gossip. The plane had barely touched down last week before I heard about Milo Grosso catching you kissing his great-granddaughter in front of God and everyone left in the Owners' and Drivers' lot after the race."

"The old buzzard nearly had another stroke, he was so mad."

"Heard she left you standing there alone and went home with him and Juliana," Hugo continued, not looking at him now, staring at the back of the seats where Shaky Paulson and Justin's catch-can man were discussing the prospects for the upcoming fishing season. "Heard you haven't seen her since."

"Who told you that?" Justin narrowed his eyes.

"You didn't get back 'til Tuesday night. You were at the garage before me on Wednesday. We've been together damned near every minute since. Is it really over between you two?"

He was surprised how much someone else saying those words hurt. A sharp pain, right in the middle of his chest, right over his heart. "There wasn't much of anything to be over," Justin said flatly. "I'd think you'd be as happy as old Milo to know she's through with me."

Hugo's response was blunt. "I am," he said. "No good can come of you two together."

"Hell, you sound like we're Romeo and Juliet or something," Justin growled, pulling his hat down low on his forehead so Hugo couldn't see how his jab had hit home.

"As far as I'm concerned those Italians didn't have anything on the Grossos and the Murphys. Maybe Dean had an airtight alibi the night your dad was killed, but no one could ever prove Milo's whereabouts the night Uncle Connor was run off the side of that mountain."

"Do you think he had something to do with Connor's death?"

Hugo sighed. This time he was the one who pulled his ball cap low over his eyes hiding his thoughts just as Justin had tried to do. "I don't know," he said wearily. "It was a long time ago. I thought Connor was the greatest race car driver since Barney Oldfield. But as I grew up I heard the stories about him, too. He'd do anything to win. There were others besides Milo Grosso that he had turned against him."

"And my dad?" Justin had to make an effort not to grip the armrests so tight his knuckles turned white. Womanizer. Hell raiser. But was he a cheater, too?

Hugo didn't turn his head, didn't change the inflection of his voice, but Justin knew he was having as hard a time discussing the less savory elements of the family history as he was. "I loved your dad. He was my big brother. He was a driver, old school. But he wanted to win more than anything. Maybe too much. And there were the women. He wasn't good to your mother. He had a lot to answer for the way he treated her."

"And then he went and got himself killed."

"He wasn't the same after your mother died," Hugo said heavily. "I think the guilt started to get to him after a while. He'd look at you and Rachel, both of you still in diapers, and I could see the panic in his eyes. He started drinking more than was good for him. Started chasing women even worse than before. Started picking fights."

"And one night someone got fed up with him and stole a Grosso pickup and ran him down in the middle of the road and left him for dead."

"Stole?" Hugo muttered and then sighed. "Yeah, that about covers it. The police said it was an accident. I didn't have the money or the time to hire private detectives to prove them wrong."

"Because you had me and Rachel to take care of."

"And Kim," Hugo added gruffly.

"And Kim." Kim's mother, Hugo's wife, had run off and left her with Hugo only months after he had taken Justin and Rachel into his home. Justin knew better than to ask any more questions about Hugo's ex. Her name was never spoken in their home, not even by Kim, who had been four when she left and must have had a few memories of her. "Do you have any idea who was driving the pickup?" Justin had never asked his uncle so directly about the night his father died.

Hugo shook his head. "I wanted it to be Dean Grosso but it wasn't. He was in Richmond or somewhere, I forget just where, that night. But that doesn't mean it couldn't have been any one of his kin. As for Milo, there were some who wondered if he didn't get one of his old FBI buddies to find him a hit man." Hugo started ticking off points on his fingers. "Or maybe it was Alfonso?"

"Dean Grosso's father?" Justin had to stop and think a moment before he came up with the name of Milo Grosso's son by his first wife.

"Yeah. Alfonso. He had the makings of a good driver but he died young. Him and his wife were swept away in a flash flood while hiking the Blue Ridge. Left Milo to raise Larry and Dean. 'Course by then, he'd married Juliana. Now there's a formidable woman. Not like his first wife, Frances. She was one of those frail, Southern belle types. Died young. Cancer, I think." He was quiet a moment. "Not long after Connor died, if I got all the dates straight." He rubbed his forehead as if it hurt. "I was only a lad at the time. Your dad was a few years older. When our parents died young, too, used up from trying to make a go of a worn-out, hard-scrabble farm, we were the only ones of our branch of the family left. My dad always said, we couldn't forget. Troy and I couldn't give up trying to find who killed Connor."

"You haven't forgotten."

Hugo might have fallen asleep he was quiet for so long. "Nor forgiven," he said at last. "I want you to be happy, Justin. You're the son I never had. I couldn't love you more if you were, but I'm in no mood to forgive or forget what Milo Grosso and his kin did to our family. I'm sorry, boy, if you truly think that Sophia Grosso is the only woman for you. Because as things stand now, there's no way on earth I can welcome her into this family."

CHAPTER THIRTEEN

"SOPHIA, THERE'S A CALL FOR you on line two." Olivia Washington was fielding phone calls since Sophia's assistant Janice was out for the day. Olivia popped her head in the door of Sophia's office. "It's him again. I can see from the caller ID. Should I pick up or not?"

"Not," Sophia said. She rubbed her temple. "I do not want to talk to him."

Can not talk to him. Dare not talk to him, if she was completely honest with herself. She'd missed him so much. Too much for a man she'd known barely a month.

"Oh, come on. You've got to give him credit for persistence." The older woman's broad face was creased with a grin. "And he does have great taste in flowers." She pointed to the tiny crystal vase, expertly cut and polished to diamond brightness sitting on the shelf beneath the window behind Sophia's desk. It held one perfect, pale peach rose and a sprinkling of lilies of the valley.

If he'd sent an expensive, overblown bouquet of exotic flowers, orchids or birds of paradise, or whatever, she could have ignored it, have it placed in the day room or the foyer of the main lobby—out of sight, out of mind, so to speak—and never given it another thought.

But he hadn't. He'd sent the tiny exquisite vase, the single perfect rose, and the lilies of the valley, her favorite flower, and something one Justin Troy Murphy couldn't have known unless someone near and dear to Sophia had told him.

And then there was the accompanying note. Just two words and his initials: *Miss me? JTM.*

The trouble was the answer was *yes.* With all her heart and all her soul.

Sophia shook her head. "I can't talk to him, Olivia. Tell him I've left for the day."

"My kid will be real disappointed not getting Justin Murphy's autograph," Olivia murmured. "The youngest is a real fan."

"No," Sophia said more sharply. "I don't want to talk to him. Nothing's changed since last week. I…don't…want to see him."

Something in her voice, perhaps the quiver of sadness she couldn't quite filter out got through to her assistant. Olivia's smile faded. She looked at Sophia with concern in her large dark eyes. "I'll tell him you've gone for the day."

"Maybe you should tell him I've gone to Timbuktu or somewhere. He won't give up otherwise." She tried for a smile but didn't have to look in a mirror to know she'd failed.

"You could always call the police. Tell them he's harassing you," Olivia suggested.

Sophia glanced up from the pad where she'd been making doodles that looked suspiciously like broken hearts strung together. She scratched them out and folded her hands together in front of her. Olivia's face was solemn, but the stern expression didn't quite reach her eyes.

"No," she said, a little too quickly. A little too sharply. "I don't want to do that."

Olivia relaxed, a smile tugged at the corners of her

generous mouth. "Then why don't you talk to him? Hear what he's got to say?"

"You and Alicia have been discussing this behind my back, haven't you?" Alicia and Olivia were her best friends at Sunny Hills. They were the only two of her coworkers who knew about her involvement with Justin Murphy.

"Not behind your back. We'd do it right to your face if Alicia wasn't in Richmond taking care of her mother." Alicia's mother had fallen down the back steps of her house and broken her ankle a couple of days after Sophia returned from Las Vegas. Alicia had taken an emergency leave of absence to go to Virginia to be with her.

"Then what did you two decide 'not behind my back'?"

"That you should hear what he has to say. Romeo and Juliet made a great play, but it sucks in real life."

The repeated comparisons to Shakespeare's famous play were beginning to get on her nerves. "I'm figuring that out. But it doesn't change anything." She was so tired of saying those words, of hearing them repeating in her thoughts in the long, slow hours of the night.

"You deserve your own life."

"I have obligations to my family, too," she said.

"Family obligations, yes. Those I understand. But you have no obligation to keep old hatreds alive. And most definitely not at the expense of your future happiness." Sophia didn't have a reply for that. Not for her friend. Not for herself. The phone had stopped ringing five minutes ago, but Sophia knew he would try again. After waiting for a few more seconds for her to respond, Olivia thinned her lips and said, "If he calls again I'll tell him. But I wish you'd change your mind."

"I'll think about it."

Olivia's smile returned. "Good," she said. "That's a start." And backed out the door.

Sophia swiveled her chair so that she could look out the window. It was a beautiful late-March day. Blue sky, white clouds and the sun was warm on her face. Several of the residents were sitting at tables and benches on the sheltered quadrangle between the skilled-care facility and the rehabilitation complex, where her office was located. The third side of the quadrangle supported the assisted-living facility, and beyond the stone wall that looked out over the gently rolling and landscaped grounds, the independent living condos were grouped among groves of oaks and maples.

Sunny Hills was a beautiful place, the staff attentive, the food excellent, and the atmosphere as close to home-like as humanly possible. If Milo and Juliana could no longer remain at the farm at some point in the future, she hoped they would consider coming to Sunny Hills to live. She watched the comings and goings of the residents and patients and tried not to think about the lonely, empty feeling in her center that wouldn't go away. In fact, with every day that passed without her seeing Justin or hearing his voice, it seemed to be growing larger, threatening to crowd out all the warmth and happiness inside her. A little sigh escaped her and she blinked, appalled to find she was close to tears.

A sudden stir of excitement rippled through the knots of sunning patients and their caregivers beyond the glass. Books, needlework and hands of cards were abandoned as people half stood from their chairs to get a better look at something—or someone—beyond Sophia's view. She thrust aside her melancholy thoughts and stood up, hurrying toward the French doors that led from her office onto the quad. Had someone fallen? Had a heart attack? Tumbled into the ornamental pond at the bottom of the sloping, manicured lawn?

She pushed open the door and rushed outside, half expecting the pager affixed to the waistband of her skirt to begin the coded beeping that indicated an emergency situation somewhere in the facility, but it remained silent. And then she saw what was causing all the excitement.

A man had walked onto the patio. He was dressed in a familiar orange-and-brown racing uniform, a shining helmet positioned under his arm, baseball cap on his head shadowing his face, mirrored sunglasses hiding velvet-brown eyes. A NASCAR driver in full race regalia. It took a stronger woman than Sophia to keep her pulse from kicking into high gear when confronted with a racing knight in his high-tech armor. Especially this driver. This man who filled her thoughts and dreams and fantasies almost to the exclusion of all else.

"Justin," she said so softly it came out a mere whisper of sound. What was he doing here? How had he gotten past security at the gate? She glanced past him and saw what appeared to be the No. 448 Turn-Rite Tool Chevrolet parked in the sweeping turn of the front drive. "Impossible," she said and this time she didn't whisper. There was no way on God's green earth he could have driven a stock car with a 400 horsepower performance V-8 engine under the hood onto the grounds without her hearing it. Then reality clicked in. It wasn't a race car. Or a show car, which was usually a retired race car. This was an imposter, a look-alike. A *replicar*, they were called. An actual street-legal vehicle painted to exactly resemble it's more powerful cousin.

And the smiling man shaking hands, signing autographs on note pads and the dust covers of books, and even pages of the newspaper, was he an imposter too? Like the car he'd driven onto the grounds, past the unforgivably lax guards? She narrowed her eyes giving him one last assessing glance. He was just too far away to be absolutely certain it was Justin; therefore, she couldn't take any chances with her patients' safety and well-being.

Sophia spun on her heel, making a beeline back into her office to dial 9-1-1 and set off the silent alarm to alert the staff that an intruder was on the grounds. She was so intent on her mission, the steps of the emergency plan she'd helped formulate reeling off in her head, she almost ran into her assistant director standing squarely in the doorway to her office.

"Move, Olivia," she said breathlessly. "That man. I don't think he's who he seems."

Olivia's black eyes widened, then caught the light as the smile that curved her lips spread up and out to encompass her entire face. "Oh, honey. Look again. He is exactly who he appears to be."

Sophia spun back toward the brown-and-orange garbed figure. He turned his head toward her, eyes still hidden by the sunglasses, and smiled. She blinked, then blinked again. Her pulse slammed against her wrist, her heart hammered in her chest. No imposter's smile could affect her like that. She swung her head back to Olivia. "You knew he was going to do this."

Olivia nodded. "I told him you were gone for the day, just like you told me to. He said, well, I won't repeat what he said. He was calling from across the street and your car was still parked in your spot. I couldn't lie to the man, now could I? It wouldn't be Christian. So I told him the truth. I said you didn't want to see him. He said fine. But what about our patients? Would they like to see him? Meet the NASCAR driver who'd just won in Atlanta?"

"And, of course, being the good Christian woman you are, you told him we would all be thrilled to have him visit," Sophia inserted dryly.

"Exactly," Olivia agreed. "I imagine he drove the fake car because he didn't want to upset any of our more fragile residents by driving a real race car up the driveway."

Sophia opened her mouth and closed it again without making a sound. It was no use ragging on her friend. Olivia and Alicia were both incurable romantics, and also thick-skinned. Her scolding would just roll off them like water off a duck's back.

"You don't mind, do you?" Olivia asked, all innocence and concern. "It's such a nice day and such a treat for the residents—"

"Yes, I mind," Sophia said gathering her wits and her pride around her like a shield. "But the damage's done now. No use getting into an argument over it."

"I thought you'd see it that way," Olivia said with satisfaction. "Oh, look, here he comes."

Sophia wanted to push her friend aside, run straight through her office and out the other side of the building and not stop until she was locked safely inside her apartment. All the long week since Las Vegas, she'd told herself over and over she could deal with seeing Justin Murphy when their paths crossed, as they invariably would. She could handle it, she kept telling herself. She could see him and not feel as if her heart was breaking, that she was making the biggest mistake of her life by walking away from, instead of into, his arms. But she was lying and, in her heart of hearts, she knew it.

"I don't want to see him, and you know full well I can't go out there and order security to get rid of the man. And he knows it, too."

"I admit it's a pretty clever scheme." Olivia looked over her shoulder. "He's attracting quite a crowd, but I can see one or two faces out there turned this way, wondering why you're standing here with your back to him instead of going out there to welcome the man to Sunny Hills."

"You will pay for this," Sophia said between clenched teeth.

"I'm quaking in my shoes." Olivia linked her arm through Sophia's. "Come on. I'll walk with you. Give you some extra courage."

Sophia sighed. Extra courage. That was exactly what she needed and not just for the moment but for, oh, the next fifty or sixty years or so. She had made the wise decision, the logical one. She must listen to her intellect and not to her heart. Justin Murphy was not good for her. She was no better for him. She had chosen the wisest path in not seeing him again, but if it was the wisest decision, then why did she feel as if her heart was ready to break?

"Sophia! Sophia, come over here and meet this handsome young buck." The imperious voice summoning her belonged to Marvin Marsden, one of the center's oldest residents. A contemporary of Milo's, he'd come to stay in the assisted-living unit after the death of his wife of sixty years. He was a great race fan and the smile that creased his weathered face spread from ear to ear.

"Mr. Murphy and I already know each other, Marv," she said giving the old man's arm a gentle squeeze.

"I should have known that," the old man slapped his hand to his forehead. "Pretty girl like you. Your dad and brother bein' drivers, too, and all."

"It's a small world, all right." Sophia agreed. "Hello, Justin," she said pleased with the nothing-out-of-the-ordinary tone of her voice.

"Hello, Sophia." His voice wasn't ordinary at all. It was a low, sexy growl that sent little shivers up and down her spine. "How have you been?"

"Well," she said. She lifted her chin a little and dared to look him in the eyes, even though his were hidden behind the damned mirrored sunglasses. "Very well."

"Good."

"This guy won the race at Atlanta yesterday," Marv broke in. He was almost deaf and she doubted he could pick up on the weighted undertones in their conversation.

"I know. Congratulations, Justin. You drove a great race."

"'Course you know that, too. Beat out your brother and daddy for the win, didn't he?"

"Yes, he did."

"Did you watch?" Justin asked. "Since you stayed in Charlotte and didn't come to the track?" He took off the sunglasses and the full force of those brown eyes nearly knocked her off her feet.

She didn't panic though, just took a quick shallow breath, swallowed hard and answered after only a very short hesitation. "Yes, I did. I was doing laundry and cleaning my apartment, but I managed to watch most of the race."

"Your dad and brother stayed with me. Made me work for the win."

"Takes some of the sting out of the DNF at Las Vegas?" she couldn't help asking.

He had the grace to flush, a dark stain spreading along the line of his high cheekbones. "Winning usually does."

"What are you doing here today?" she asked. There was a lull in the number of people milling around in the quadrangle and for the moment they were alone.

"I came to visit the residents."

"It wasn't on the events calendar."

"It's an event all right, though," Marvin chimed in having heard that particular exchange loud and clear.

"It was a spur-of-the-moment thing," Justin told him.

"NASCAR drivers don't make spur-of-the-moment public appearances." Her brother and her father's schedules were so busy they were broken down into fifteen-minute segments on most days.

He slid the sunglasses back on his face, widened his stance, bending forward slightly from the waist. "I do," he said.

"Damned glad he did, too." Marvin was blissfully oblivious of the tension between Sophia and Justin. "Got myself an autograph and Justin promised to autograph hero cards for my youngest twin great-grandsons' birthdays. They're fifteen, or will be next week. Car crazy. They'll love 'em."

"Mr. Murphy is a very busy man. He might forget to send the cards." She didn't believe that at all, but she could give as good as she got.

Justin shook his head. "Oh no, I won't. I have their names and their address right here in my pocket." He put his hand on his heart, indicating the information was in the slit pocket of his uniform where he usually kept his sunglasses. "I always keep my promises," he said, his voice soft but challenging. "Always."

"Pictures, everyone," Olivia sang out, stepping onto the patio with a digital camera in her hand. "Mr. Murphy is a busy man. He can only stay a few more minutes. Come on, everyone gather round."

It took more than a minute or two to arrange twenty or so seniors, several in wheelchairs or with walkers, into a manageable group, but Justin was amiable and friendly throughout the entire process. After the pictures were taken and everyone was promised a print or two or three, he suffered the equally long goodbye, bear hugs and kisses on the cheeks, handshakes and slaps on the back, with unfailing good grace.

"And now, ladies and gentlemen," he said raising his voice a notch or two to make himself heard. "I made a promise to Miss Sophia that I'd give her a ride in my race car. But since NASCAR Sprint Cup Series cars don't have a passenger seat we'll have to make do with this replicar. Is it all right if I whisk her away for a couple of laps?"

Sophia opened her mouth to decline the dare disguised as an invitation, but she never had a chance. Applause and laughter and whoops of glee broke out all around her. "Go, Sophia. Go with him," one of her nurses hollered.

"Have him take you for a turn out by the lake," another voice suggested.

"And don't hurry back," Marv added with a wink and a wave of his cane.

More laughter and applause followed the last remark.

"I'll hold down the fort," Olivia assured her. "Go. Enjoy yourself."

"My chariot awaits," Justin said, making a sweeping bow, that didn't look nearly as ridiculous as it should have.

"I…where are we going?" Sophia managed to ask as he escorted her to the orange-and-brown replicar, the paint scheme identical in every detail to the race car he drove each week. Justin opened the passenger side door, where even the door handle had been painted over to make it more closely resemble the doorless stock car it mimicked.

"Just for a ride," he said.

"Someone will recognize you. We'll draw a crowd. It will turn into a mob," she cautioned as she pulled the folds of her skirt from the door and reached over to fasten her seat belt.

Justin leaned his head in the doorway. "Then we'll take a ride in the country. I'm hell on wheels on a country road. Nothing can catch me—" His face was close. His teeth white in his tanned face, his eyes still hidden by the sunglasses she was beginning to hate with every fiber of her being because they prevented her from any ability to read his thoughts. "Unless I want them to," he said and slammed the door, cutting off any reply she might have made—if she could have thought of something, anything, to say.

CHAPTER FOURTEEN

"WHERE DID YOU GET this car anyway? Who does it belong to?"

"To the guy who designed my Web site. He let me borrow it if I promise to get him tickets to Bristol this week. I have a sneaking suspicion he's really a Dean Grosso fan, but I pay his salary so he tricked out his car to look like mine instead of your father's."

"Humph." She wasn't buying that one, Justin figured. Trouble was he was telling the truth. His IT guy was a closet Dean Grosso fan.

"What if someone recognizes you? You'll cause an accident. Someone will run a red light staring at you, or run up onto the curb, hit a little old lady walking her dog, and then where will we be?"

"Boy, you *are* a pessimist, aren't you?" He didn't care if she was still on her high horse. At least she was in his car, beside him, close enough to smell her perfume and feel the warmth of her skin. She was wearing blue again as she had been the morning of the Las Vegas race. But this time it wasn't a slinky little sundress. It was a long skirt in some soft, floaty material and a lacy sweater set in a deeper shade that almost matched her eyes. Gold earrings with little bobbles on the end of a tiny length of chain dangled from her earlobes and danced in the sunlight whenever she turned her head.

He'd asked if she missed him on the card he'd sent with the rose but in truth he was the one who had missed her. It had been the longest week of his life, not seeing her or talking to her—or kissing her.

"Aren't you going to take off your uniform?" she demanded.

"Here? Now?" He looked over at her and grinned, wiggling his eyebrows lasciviously. "I will if you want me to. Next red light. I promise."

She gave him a look that made him think, a little nervously, of old Milo. "Very funny," she said, her tone dripping icicles.

"What are you doing?" Her voice rose a couple of notches and she scooted around in the seat to face him head on when she heard the sound of a zipper. "You are not taking off your clothes?"

"Just pulling down the jacket," he said, tugging down the zipper and wrestling his right arm out of the sleeve before the light changed to green. "Contrary to what you think I don't want to attract a crowd or start a riot. Although riot's probably overstating the size of my fan base." He was wearing a plain white T-shirt underneath the uniform. He then exchanged his signature mirrored sunglasses for a pair of drug-store ones, and turned his ball cap around backward. He looked over at Sophia and grinned. "Do I look like a NASCAR driver now? Or just a fan with a lot of time and disposable income to spend working on his wheels?"

"You." She waved her hand in a little gesture of disbelief. "You don't look like you at all."

"Good, that's just what I want to hear."

"You look like someone's little brother."

He scowled over at her. "You sure know how to take the wind out of my sails."

She gave him a snotty look and a sassy grin. "I'd have to resign my position at Sunny Hills. Keeping you humble would be a full-time job."

"Do you want to apply for it?"

Her eyes darkened momentarily. "Justin. I—"

"Sorry. I didn't mean to make you uncomfortable. It's just that I've missed you. I'm damned glad you're sitting here beside me."

"So am I." She smiled. "So am I."

God, that was all it took. A smile and he was lost. He was falling hard. So close to being in love with her it didn't much matter any more if he tried to deny it, even to himself. He'd known it since Vegas. Today he'd quit fooling himself that he could still walk away. Admitted it the moment he stepped onto the quadrangle of Sunny Hills and saw her standing there, ready to put herself in harm's way for her patients, fierce and protective. He replayed in his mind the exact moment she recognized it was him and her eyes went soft and wistful for a couple of seconds until she got hold of herself and put on her prissy face again.

He was getting ahead of himself. He had to take this one slowly. Had to say all the right things, make all the right moves, because she was as certain as he was becoming that they belonged together no matter what obstacles there were to overcome.

But his instincts told him she was close. *Very close.* And if his luck held, he was going to steal the princess away from her guardian dragons and make her his own.

She was quiet for a while, sitting bolt upright in the passenger seat, eyeing the people who came alongside them, some waving, some staring with their mouths open, puzzled looks on their faces. Was it? Or wasn't it? He simply ignored them, kept driving as though this was the car he drove to work every morning and home every night, and oddly enough they seemed to believe it, too, and eventually lost interest. Besides, he had the sneaking suspicion most of the male drivers weren't as interested in the replica of the No. 448 car, or its look-alike driver, as they were in the pretty girl sitting beside him.

Once they left the last of the Charlotte sprawl behind and headed deep into Mecklenburg County, he put the pedal to the floor and let the car open up. He'd driven it before, knew his computer geek was also a pretty good mechanic, and had it tuned to a fine pitch. Sophia didn't seem unduly alarmed by his breaking the speed limit by more than a few miles an hour, or that he once or twice took a curve on less than the requisite four wheels. Speed and the love of fast driving was bred in her bones even if she refused to own up to it.

"Where are you taking me?" she asked finally as they turned onto a feeder road that followed the shore of Lake Norman, formed fifty years earlier when the Catawba River had been damned by the Duke Power Company. It used to be ringed by woods and farmland and summer fishing cabins. Now it was trendy, so there were golf courses and condominium developments, and a number of high-profile drivers and crew members had year-round homes there.

"My place," he said.

"You live here?" She was looking out over the lake at some of the palatial homes on the far shore of the bay they were paralleling.

"My family's had land here for a long time," he said suddenly wondering if he'd made a mistake bringing her to this place that was so special to him. After all, she had a lot more in common with the people who lived in the big houses across the bay than she did with the blue-collar background he came from. He shoved the self-defeating thoughts aside. "I lived here when I was a baby. Before my parents died."

"You say that very matter-of-factly." The earrings swung as she gave him her full attention.

"It was a long time ago. I barely remember my father, my mother not at all. I was only a few months old when she killed herself."

"I'm so sorry," Sophia said in a soft, regretful voice. "I'd forgotten how she died. I shouldn't have pried."

"That's okay. Like I said, it was a long time ago."

"I don't think you ever completely get over losing someone you love, especially in such a tragic way."

He didn't answer right away, then decided to tell her the truth, to give her access to some of his most private thoughts. It was another measure of his growing involvement with her. He never talked about his mother. Never. "You're right. You don't get over it. There are always those times when you stop and wonder how it might have been. And there are always the questions that will never be answered about why she did what she did."

"She must have been very troubled to abandon her babies. I'm so sorry there was no one for her to turn to for help."

"So am I." He would always be sorry. Always regret her loss.

"My father's parents died very young, too. Did you know that? They were swept away by a flash flood while they were hiking in the Blue Ridge. My dad and my uncle Larry were very small, like you and Rachel."

"Yes," he said. "I know all about the Grossos."

"Of course. Hugo probably told you." He nodded. She hesitated then spoke again, quietly, thoughtfully. "There are so many things about them I'll never know. Kent and I had Milo and Juliana, and my mother's parents growing up, of course, but there are always those moments when you wonder how altered your life might have been with them there, even if it was only in small ways."

He hadn't intended for the conversation to veer into deep waters so early on, but that's the way it was with Sophia. She spoke from her heart and like a siren he followed her lead. He wanted to confide in her. He wanted to tell her the plans he had for this place, those nebulous dreams of a future where he could share the peninsula's natural beauty with kids who were growing up parentless as he would have done if it hadn't been for Hugo. But not yet. He wasn't quite ready yet.

They'd arrived at the gate that marked the boundary to the forty or so acres he owned with Rachel. The land jutted out into the lake, an old ridgeline left high and dry after the lake was formed. "There's Rachel's house," he said. The landscaping was looking good. He'd helped his sister clear away all the old underbrush and dead shrubs from around the foundation the winter before. What remained was just coming into leaf and bloom. Now the house was beginning to look as it had when he was little and Hugo would bring them all out to the lake to swim.

"I like the house," she said. "Looks good and solid."

"It is. My dad had built it for my mother with the prize money from his first season of racing. They were practically giving away lake lots in those days. Too far out in the boonies for most people back then. One of the only smart things he did in his life, buying this land," he added, aware that she would probably pick up on the lingering bitterness he just couldn't scrub out of his voice.

"It's a beautiful location," she said. "The sunrises must be spectacular out over the lake."

"And the sunsets are just as fantastic on my side of the point." He felt his spirits rise as they always did when he came to the fork in the red dirt road that marked the unofficial boundary of his side of the small peninsula. "My place isn't much more than a cottage, though," he said. "It was moved up here by the original owner before they flooded the valley. It's cedar and native pine. Too good to let be taken by the lake waters, I guess. It's not much, but it suits me for now." Once started he couldn't seem to stop. He wanted her to love this place, too. To love him.

"I'm going to build out here someday," he said, not letting his thoughts go further into a future he couldn't see. "But so far, I haven't had the time or the money to do much more than put on a new roof and upgrade the wiring and the septic system. Oops, I probably shouldn't have said that." He looked over at her and grinned. "Septic systems are not subjects for polite conversation."

"I'm a nurse. I appreciate the value of a reliable septic system," she said primly but her blue eyes were filled with light and more than a hint of laughter.

"What I'm gonna appreciate is the eight-person hot tub I'm putting in when I replace the deck" he said, wheeling the car into the graveled area behind his cabin. "I can't think of anything better than to come out here and soak away the aches and pains of a hard day's racing."

In an earlier incarnation, the building had been a garage. It had old-fashioned, heavy wooden folding doors facing the lake, and a wide outside staircase that led up to the two bedroom apartment above it. "Rachel calls it the boathouse and since I keep my bass boat here, the name's kind of stuck."

"I like it," she replied. "It suits the place."

He tried to see the building through her eyes. The cedar shingles had aged to a silvery-gray over the years. He'd re-glazed the many-paned windows on the lower level and painted the trim on the double-hung ones on the upper story a piney-green that had enough gray in it to blend in with the weathered wood and not stand out like a sore thumb. Over the winter months, he'd concentrated on infrastructure repairs, hiring local contractors to do wiring and plumbing and the stonework of the fireplace and chimney.

He'd been looking forward to a fire in his own fireplace. He hoped this evening might be the night. "Would you like to see the inside?" he asked pulling the replicar up to the foot of the staircase.

"Sure," she said. "But I can't stay long. I…I have things to do before I leave."

"Leave? For where? Paris? Cairo? Brussels? Or maybe just to Bristol?"

She didn't quite meet his gaze. "I…yes. I'm thinking about attending the race. But not until Friday. I can't take any more days off work this month."

"Yeah, that can get to be a hassle."

"I like my job," she said opening her door before he could get around to doing it for her.

"What does a director of nursing do anyway?" he asked, reaching into the backseat for the cooler he'd brought along—just in case.

"Sunny Hills has over two hundred patients and residents. There are almost that many employees. The nursing staff is my responsibility. About seventy-five men and women. I make sure the duty rosters are made out. That all the nurses keep their continuing education credits up to date. I teach safety and emergency classes. I do professional evaluations and mediate disputes. I also do a fair share of hand holding and even a little family counseling, and if someone's work is sub-par or putting patients at risk, I fire them. In a word I administrate."

"Kind of like a crew chief," he said.

She thought it over a moment. "I never thought of it that way, but I guess you could say that." She eyed the cooler. "What's that for?"

"I thought maybe you'd have dinner with me. The last time I tried to take you somewhere it didn't quite work out the way I hoped it would. Here, there won't be any interruptions."

"Barbeque?" she asked tilting her head a little to one side.

"Nope. Thai."

That surprised a laugh out of her. "Thai? That doesn't fit your image at all."

"What *does* fit my image?" he asked, indicating that she follow him up the recently reinforced staircase to the upper level.

"The note that came with my flowers," she said unexpectedly.

"Hey," he said. "Someone might have read it besides you. Have to keep the NASCAR bad-boy persona intact."

"You succeeded," she said.

"But you did miss me, right?" he dared.

She sighed and her answer and the expression in her deep water-blue eyes was serious, and instantly sent his heart rate into overdrive. "Yes, Justin. I did miss you."

CHAPTER FIFTEEN

WHY HAD SHE GONE and admitted she missed him? Why couldn't she just get through the next couple of hours, say goodbye and then go home and have a good cry into her pillow? Why couldn't she shield herself from telling him whatever came into her thoughts and into her heart?

Because she was falling in love with him. That's what she had learned in the days since she'd walked away from him in Las Vegas. It didn't matter that they hadn't spent that much time together. Love didn't always follow a time-table. She didn't know exactly when it had happened. In bits and pieces, she guessed. His concern for the sick child in the hospital might have been the first mark on the chart. The knee-weakening relief that the sight of him crawling from the wrecked race car had produced in the very center of her. The dignity with which he'd treated her great-grand-father even as the older man taunted and insulted him and his family. His smile, his laughter, his kisses. All small things alone, but taken together they were forging an un-breakable chain around her heart. She'd accepted the in-evitability of it the moment she'd looked out her office window and seen him stride onto the patio of Sunny Hills and smile for her alone. She was falling in love and it was too late for her to turn back now.

"So nursing administrators don't actually do any nursing. They don't take care of people who are sick, right?" He was about four steps above her when he turned back to speak.

"That's correct," she said hoping she hadn't lost the thread of the conversation, or that he had read her thoughts as he seemed to do from time to time. "A crew chief doesn't drive the car. I don't do patient care. I oversee the people who do take care of the patients. I did the Florence Nightingale thing," she confessed. "And now I've moved to the next step for me."

He'd kept on climbing while she babbled on, reaching the top of the stairs ahead of her. "I'd say you're good at the Florence Nightingale thing," he stuck out his arm and she saw that the cut from the beer bottle had faded to a thin, almost invisible line. "You did a pretty good job of patching me up. But I also remember you did drop like a stone when you saw my blood."

"If you tell anyone what happened that night I—"

"You'll what?" he asked.

"I don't know," she said narrowing her eyes. "But I'll think of something. I always do. You can ask my brother. I always get even. It's a family trait."

He didn't respond for a moment and she wanted to kick herself for saying anything remotely relatable to the family feud. "I'll remember that," he said finally. "But I don't think I'll ask your brother for confirmation, okay? At least not yet." He held out his hand and grinned. "Welcome to my home at the lake." She placed her hand in his and felt the warmth of his strong, tanned fingers close over hers, triggering the familiar jolt of pure sensual delight that passed through her nervous system and almost buckled her knees.

Oh yeah, she'd passed the point of no return all right. She was well on her way to head-over-heels.

They'd arrived at a door whose top half contained an inset of stained glass in a scene that depicted a sunset over the lake. Sophia turned her head looking out over the narrow deck to the trees and water beyond. The view from where she was standing matched the picture in the door exactly. She studied the stained glass more closely. It was beautifully done, the colors bright and clear, the artistry considerable.

"It's lovely," she said. "And it's a very good likeness."

"Thanks," he said, standing aside to let her enter first. "A friend told me about the artist. He's got a studio on the other side of the lake. I'll take you there sometime during the off-season."

"What off-season?" she asked sarcastically. The Chase for the NASCAR Sprint Cup ended in November but with the Championship festivities in New York and test runs at various tracks and preseason practices most drivers found themselves with only a few short weeks of downtime over the holidays.

"I'll find the time," he said, and then added in that low, seductive tone that never failed to take her breath away. "I always find time for what I want to do."

The visions his velvet-and-whiskey tone engendered left her breathless with longing. Hurriedly, Sophia stepped across the threshold into a surprisingly light and open great room, paneled in a warm, yellow-brown cedar that rose in alternating patterns to a high ceiling that lay directly beneath the roofline. A fieldstone fireplace dominated the wall in front of her, the stones blackened by time and thousands of nights of warming fires. An intricate wrought-iron chandelier hung from the highest point of the ceiling, and a stuffed deer head with satiny brown eyes and an enormous rack of antlers held pride of place above the rustic mantel. Two big leather couches were placed parallel to the fireplace and between them what appeared to be an old wagon seat did duty as a coffee table. Floor lamps that matched the chandelier in design stood sentinel on either end of the couches.

She turned her head to the left and saw why the big room was so filled with light. Windows, double-hung below, with fixed panes of glass above them shaped to follow the peak of the roof, flanked a set of French doors. Beyond them was a narrow deck and beyond that her eye was drawn down the steep slope of the tree-shaded lawn to the lake.

A hallway bisected the cabin's remaining space and Sophia assumed the bedroom and bathroom lay beyond the plank wall that held a glass case filled with trophies. Not the elaborate metal and crystal and glass trophies given out to NASCAR winners, but small ones, plastic and gold-colored metal on wooden bases, with crossed flags or go-kart models projecting from their tops, or affixed to their middle sections. Justin's trophies from his boyhood racing days.

"It's a great space, Justin. I see why you love it so. I'm glad you have this legacy from your parents." Justin's boat-house, while far more modest than those homes she could see across the water through the bank of windows, was also more appealing to her. Like her great-grandparents' farm, it had character, a history of its own. She felt welcome here.

"That's the way I feel, too," Justin said, carrying the cooler into the galley kitchen that was separated from the living area by a pass-through bar along which tall wooden stools had been arranged. "My parents must have been happy sometime in their marriage. I like to think it was here. I have a house in Mooresville but all I do is sleep there when I'm too tired to make the trip out here." He set the cooler down and changed the subject so abruptly Sophia was caught off guard. "You said you like Thai. I have satay and spring rolls and drunken noodles. But if you were just being polite, I picked up a veggie sub with vinegar and oil dressing and three kinds of fruit yogurt. Or—" he pointed to the freezer portion of the stainless-steel refrigerator behind him "—I always keep a stash of Mikey's barbeque in case I get hungry."

Sophia laughed. She couldn't help it. He was trying so hard. "I really do like Thai," she assured him. "But I've never had drunken noodles."

"You'll like them," he assured her. "These are made with chicken and glass noodles, coconut milk and lemon grass, some heat, but not too spicy. Is that okay?"

"Fine. But who will eat the veggie sub?" If he didn't want to talk about his parents anymore, she would take the hint. That he could be closer to their spirits in this place pleased her, but to linger on the subject wasn't a good idea. Sooner or later, it would wind itself around to the connection with her own family and then on to past tragedy and remind her there were valid and unavoidable reasons she might never find happiness with him.

"I'll eat that, too. If you want to freshen up, the bathroom's down the hall," he said, as he unpacked the take-out containers, and emptied the contents onto paper plates he'd taken from a shelf above the stove. She settled herself on a stool at the bar.

"I'm fine," she said studying the kitchen over his shoulder. One of her guilty pleasures was watching DIY shows. She was addicted to them. She let her imagination run free while he was looking for napkins and silverware. The cupboards were old, painted pine—cream-colored once, now turning a less-attractive yellow. They needed to be freshened up, maybe re-hung with leaded glass doors since he already knew a talented artist in the medium, and filled with colorful earthenware plates and cups. The countertops were Formica, stained and outdated. Granite would be nice, she mused. No, quarry tile would be more in keeping with the age of the building. She wondered if that was the kind of renovation he had in mind considering what he'd done with the old Manor travel trailer?

Once more he might have read her mind. "Did I tell you one of those high-falutin' lifestyle TV shows wants to do a segment on my trailer?" he asked, his drawl slowing and thickening as it always did when he was making fun of himself. He looked over at her as he pulled a state-of-the-art corkscrew from a drawer and dealt with the cork in a bottle of red wine. A very nice bottle of red wine, she noticed, from a pricey California boutique vineyard. As she had suspected all along, there was more depth to his good-ol'-boy image than he projected to the world at large.

"Are you going to let them?" she asked, watching him pour the wine into two disposable plastic glasses. He caught her watching him and grinned. "My cleaning lady's not scheduled to come until next week and I hate to do dishes. Haven't got the wiring for a dishwasher in here yet. Sorry, I hope it doesn't spoil the bouquet for you. It's a pretty decent wine. Stands up to plastic glasses pretty well."

Sophia giggled and shook her head. "I hate doing dishes, too. You're not losing any points with me if you don't drag out the Sevres and the Sunday silver."

"I don't have china or silver but thanks for being such a good sport about it. Ready to eat?"

"Starving. I missed lunch, but you didn't answer my question," she pressed as he brought loaded plates—he'd appropriated the veggie sub for himself and placed it alongside heaping portions of Thai take-out. "Are you going to let them film a segment on your travel trailer?"

He set the plates on the old wagon seat and then pulled two oversized woven throw cushions off the leather couch and laid them on the wide-planked pine floor—which was in desperate need of refinishing, the repressed DIYer in Sophia noticed. He carried the wine glasses while she settled herself on one of the cushions. He knelt beside her. "Yeah, they're coming out to film over the Mother's Day break. Can't have 'em doin' it at a race. I'd never hear the end of it. Guys would start to question my masculinity, ya' know." He dialed up his North Carolina drawl 'til it peaked the meter. "It's for a segment on celebrities and their offbeat hideaways or some such silliness."

"I like your trailer. It has character, just like this house."

"Thanks," he said. "But I'll probably have to park her after this season. She's not in the best shape. Besides much as I like her, she's too small. Nice to know she'll go out with a bang. And I've got a great spot to park her out here. Give her a second career as a guest house. Besides, I owe it to my PR rep. That woman works herself half to death trying to keep some of my stupider stunts out of the tabloids, and me out of the woodshed with NASCAR, and still get me noticed where it counts. So if I can make her job easier once in a while, I try to do it."

"How noble," she said and touched the edge of her glass to his in a silent toast.

"That's me, Sir NASCAR Trueheart.

"Do you want seconds," he asked a moment later, "or can I finish off the noodles?"

"Be my guest," she said, as he wielded his chopsticks with the kind of skill you'd expect from a man whose hand-eye coordination rivaled that of a fighter pilot. They ate in silence, but it was the comfortable, companionable silence of friends and Sophia enjoyed every moment of the meal. Clean up consisted of sweeping the cartons and plastic utensils into a trash container, which she also enjoyed.

"Would you like to watch the sunset from the deck?"

"I'd love to."

He refilled the plastic cups with more wine and snagged a hoodie, emblazoned with the logo of his old NASCAR Busch Series sponsor off a hook by the door and held it out to her. "It gets downright chilly on the water this time of year when the sun goes down."

"Thanks." She slipped on the hoodie, velvet soft from countless washings, and was once more swept off into a momentary erotic fantasy when the scent of his soap and his skin filled her nostrils. She stood as unmoving as one of Milo's pasture fence posts, staring at nothing, lost in her thoughts.

"I'm saving that wall for my big-screen plasma TV and home projection system," he said, thankfully misreading her mind for once. "I'm buying one first chance I get. No use winnin' a Cup race if you don't do a little somethin' nice for yourself."

"It will look good there," she said scolding herself for her lapse. If she got this spacey over wearing his old hoodie, how would she respond if he actually put his hands on her? For the first time since she'd given in to the impulse to climb into the replicar, she began to allow herself to contemplate where the evening might lead. Why hadn't she remembered sooner how fast the attraction between them had kindled into sexual fire the last time they were alone together?

Because you didn't want to, her incurably honest conscience replied.

"Go on ahead. I'll light the fire, and when we get back inside, you can warm up before I drive you home."

So much for worrying—or was it wishing?—that the evening would end in a seduction, Sophia thought, as she let herself out onto the narrow deck. He certainly wasn't sending out any signals that he wanted to keep her with him any longer than necessary. Despite her common sense telling her that was for the best, she was more than a little disappointed.

Five minutes later, he joined her. She had thought she'd used the time to good advantage, bringing her sensual daydreams under control. But the moment he came to stand beside her at the waist-high railing, her hard-won self-control evaporated as though the heat of his body had turned her rational thought processes to dust.

"This is the best part of the day," he said his eyes fixed on the sunset. "I don't care what season of the year it is, I try never to miss this moment when I'm out here."

The clouds had layered themselves above and below the sun's fiery orange disc. The lake water was the same shade as Justin's eyes when he kissed her, the tree-blanketed western shore a line of charcoal with serrated edges on which the sun seemed to catch and hang suspended for a long moment. The colors in the sky shaded from tangerine to coral to lavender and smoke. Sun streaks radiated out in all directions. A flock of geese arrowed past searching for an inland sanctuary in which to spend the night. Their movement seemed to break the inertia of the lowering sun and within moments it was gone, leaving behind only a blaze of golden light that faded quickly into dusk, as the night shadows, released from their chains, crept toward them over the glassy surface of the lake.

"Wow," Justin muttered, turning his head. "That's the best one I've seen in a long time. I hope you enjoyed the show." His eyes were indeed the same color as the deep water beyond the shore, and she would sink as easily dropped into their depths.

"It was beautiful. Thank you for letting me share it with you."

"A sunset isn't the only thing I want to share with you, Sophia." His head came close and she realized she'd been right. She was going to drown in his eyes.

His kiss was soft, slow, tantalizing. Only their lips touched, tasted, teased. He kissed her chin, her cheek, her eyelids, the tip of her nose before returning to her mouth, running his tongue along the seam of her lips, inviting her to open to him.

She stiffened slightly. All the problems between them hadn't blown away like a puff of dandelion seeds on the wind. They were still there. Would always be there. She should back away, break off the kiss. It would be easy enough to do. One step and she would be free.

But she stayed where she was, let him wrap her in his arms, take the kiss to another level of intimacy and longing. *She loved him.* And even though she was far too much of a coward to say the words aloud, she tried to show him with her mouth and her hands and her body. She swayed against him, curled her arms around his neck and held on as if she would never let him go.

"Don't be afraid, Sophia. I'll never ask you to do anything you're not ready for."

"I'm not afraid," she managed to whisper. "Not of you. Make love to me, Justin. Please." She closed her eyes and leaned into his kiss.

He scooped her into his arms and carried her into the lake house, laid her down among the cushions in front of the fireplace, then lowered himself beside her. She let herself revel in the give and take of a man and woman who wanted what each could give the other. She refused to think beyond the moment. She lay beside him and touched him and caressed him and let him love her. When it was over, she lay curled against him, sated and complete and let herself drift off in a rosy daydream of happily ever after.

Justin lay so quietly that she thought he had fallen asleep. When he spoke it was more a rough whisper of sound that she felt as much as heard. "I know you're not ready for this, Sophia, but I am. I've done a lot of thinking, hell, even some soul-searching since Las Vegas. I've got a good idea who I am now. What I can be in this life. I'm ready to settle down and make something good and lasting of myself. But I don't want to do it alone. I can't do it alone. I want you with me, Sophia."

"Romeo and Juliet," she said, rolling toward him once more, curling her arms around his neck, hoping he would stop talking and make love to her again. She could handle that. She could show him with her body what she didn't have the courage to say aloud. "We're like Romeo and Juliet. That story doesn't have a happy ending."

He reached up and unwrapped her arms from his neck, curled his fingers around her wrists and held them on either side of her head. Manacling her so that she was forced to look directly at him. "We're not Romeo and Juliet. For one thing we're twice their age," he said with that damnably sexy grin that always got past her defenses no matter how zealously she guarded them. The one that dared her not to take herself so seriously, to let go and live in the moment, instead of straining ahead to try and decipher the future and avoid the pain that might lurk there.

"That's true," she murmured almost smiling in return.

"So we're in no danger of becoming helpless pawns caught up in a battle of wills between powerful families."

She lifted an eyebrow. "You've read Shakespeare?"

"Hell no," he grinned again. "I rented *Shakespeare in Love.* Quit trying to change the subject by the way. We're going to settle this once and for all."

Panic returned as quickly as it had retreated. "Justin—"

"Shh. I told you I'm not rushing you. I meant it. But I'm not afraid to tell you what I'm feeling, Sophia. I love you. I think I've always been a little bit in love with you. I want to marry you. I want you to be the mother of my children. I want to be the best husband to you I can possibly be. I'm telling you this, but all I'm asking of you in return is that Saturday at Bristol, in front of God and every Grosso on earth, you walk me to my car."

CHAPTER SIXTEEN

"SOPHIA, YOU WASH THE greens for the salad while I set out the antipasto," Juliana ordered moving around the kitchen of Kent's motor home as smoothly and efficiently as she worked in her kitchen at home. And why shouldn't she? Sophia thought. This one was nearly as big and well-equipped.

She was exaggerating, of course, it wasn't as big as the kitchen at the farm, but it had every gadget money could buy, and all the appliances were top-of-the-line. Sub-Zero refrigerator, dishwasher, convection oven—you name it, Kent had it. Juliana and Jesse, Kent's driver and a good cook in his own right, had seen to that. But on this trip Juliana was in complete charge of the kitchen as Jesse was in Florida attending a reunion of his old army buddies.

"Be sure you tear the lettuce, don't cut it—" Juliana commanded over her shoulder "—and make sure the stems of the spinach aren't woody."

"I'll be careful," Sophia responded, rinsing the greens in the deep, double sink and laying them on the granite counter to dry on paper towels while she chopped green onions and red and yellow bell peppers and sliced tomatoes, fresh from the vine.

"The dressing is in the refrigerator. I made it when we got here last night," Juliana chatted on. She was in her element in a kitchen, any kitchen, and today was no exception. She was fixing Saturday night supper for Kent's and Dean's crews, as she often did the night before a race. Italian food. Pasta and antipasto and tiramisu to die for. Lots of carbs to build energy and stamina to last through a long, grueling race. Good-luck food.

Sophia had arrived by car late the night before, battling traffic, regretting she hadn't accepted Kent's invitation to fly up in his plane today with Tanya. But she'd wanted some time to think, so after she left Sunny Hills, she'd headed north on her own—except for the entire flock of butterflies swirling around in her stomach.

They were still there and had been since she woke that morning, and she wondered how she would even be able to eat, no matter how mouthwatering the kitchen smelled.

"I'm so happy you came for the race," Juliana rambled on. "I don't recall the last time you came to Bristol. My goodness, wasn't it three years ago? The year after your father won here the last time?" She stopped stirring the big pot of marinara sauce bubbling gently on the range and bent to check the oversize casserole of lasagna browning in the oven. "Or was it the year before that when you broke up with that jackass of a fiancé of yours?"

"It was the year I broke my engagement to Evan," Sophia confirmed, not contradicting her great-grandmother's assessment of Evan's character. It was dead-on and she was well rid of the roving-eyed pediatrician. She patted the spinach dry and inspected each leaf for stems that were too long or too thick, snipping them off with a paring knife. "I watched Dad win on TV because that was the spring I took the job at Sunny Hills and couldn't get away for the race."

"Goodness, have you worked there that long? Time flies, doesn't it? Well anyway, I'm glad you joined us. Today, you can watch in person as your father or your brother wins, God willing. How do you like staying here in Kent's motor home?" she tacked on.

"It's heavenly. Decadent, almost." The custom-built motor home carried a shockingly high price tag, but NASCAR Sprint Cup Series drivers and their families and crews spent nearly nine months a year on the road during the season. Kent often said he felt more at home in his motor home than he did in his apartment in Concord. Besides, she had the sneaking suspicion he'd also invested in it as a symbol of his arrival in the top tier of competitors.

But she also couldn't help comparing her brother's exclusive motor home with Justin's one-of-a-kind vintage trailer. She could see why some track owners and even other drivers might resent its presence among their status symbol homes-away-from-home, but she could also see why he clung to it so stubbornly. It was a throwback, the way he himself was, a nostalgic reminder of a simpler time and a simpler approach to the sport he loved so much. He would conform to the demands of the world-wide phenomenon that NASCAR had become, but in his heart he would always be kindred spirits with the good-old-boy legends of days gone by.

"I agree," Juliana said, interrupting her thoughts. "I've never been in such a nice kitchen in a motor home before. I can feed eight people in this place and not be crowded."

"I counted twelve for breakfast," Sophia reminded her. She'd awakened to a boisterous group of drivers' wives and children eating at the kitchen table and on the couch and overstuffed recliners and even on the floor. The kids chowing down on pancakes and waffles, the wives content-ing themselves with fresh fruit and yogurt. It was always like this when her great-grandmother attended a race. Nonstop friends and family. Sophia wanted to continue to be a part of it, but she might be exiled forever if she com-mitted herself to Justin, heart and soul. The butterflies took flight again and her stomach churned.

"I'm planning for twenty to twenty-five, this evening," Juliana said, breaking into her reverie. "We'll serve buffet and I'll have your father and brother set out tables under the awning. We'll have candles and it will be nice. As long as it doesn't storm."

Sophia looked out the window above the sink and frowned at the dark clouds that scudded across the blue, late-March sky. It was an unusually warm weekend for the first Bristol race of the season, with scattered thundershow-ers in the forecast before an approaching cold front. "Do you think it will rain enough to cancel the race?" Juliana's ar-thritis was often more accurate than the weather forecasts.

Her great-grandmother shook her head. "Can't tell. My elbow's a little stiff, but not too painful. If my elbow bothers me a lot, I know it will rain in the next twenty-four hours. I'll make sure we pray for good weather before we eat and maybe it will hold off until after the race."

Sophia closed her eyes and said a little prayer right then and there for blue skies and sunshine until after the race. She was so nervous already her hands were trembling. She didn't think her nerves could take a long rain delay, or even worse, a cancellation. She hadn't worked out how she was going to tell her family she was walking Justin Murphy to his car tomorrow afternoon. But she had to find the words and soon. Although some of the single drivers used the opportunity to show off their latest supermodel dates, or give a thrill to a casual girlfriend, for the married drivers it was a far more meaningful ritual. Many couples prayed as they stood together before the start of a race. All of them knew the possibility of injury might come in the next few hours and they treated the occasion with the respect it deserved.

To her family, it would be tantamount to announcing she was in love with Justin Murphy, archenemy of the entire clan.

And she had no doubt Justin's sister and uncle would view it the same way.

Sophia finished drying the salad greens and layered them into a big mixing bowl. As she worked, she listened to Juliana's running commentary on the food she was preparing and her observations on what was going on in the compound around them, catching Sophia up on neighborhood gossip, you might call it, since they all spent so much time together.

But most of Sophia's thoughts were centered on the emotional commitment she would be making if she walked Justin Murphy to his car and what it might do to alter her relationship with her family. She wanted to believe it would be something of a spring storm—sound and fury, and over as quickly as it blew up. But deep in her heart, she knew it would be more serious than that. The bad blood between the Grossos and Murphys dated back half a century. It wouldn't evaporate and disappear like raindrops when the sun came out again. It would always be there as long as there were questions about the deaths of Connor and Troy Murphy.

She loved Justin. She wanted to be with him. She wanted to be able to say the things that were in her heart as he had told her what was in his. But as always, she was afraid. She was afraid what she was going to do tomorrow would forever distance her from the people she loved. She was afraid that her great-grandfather, especially, would never forgive her for going over to the enemy. She might have very little time left with him. Milo was a vigorous man, but he was ninety-two. He wouldn't live forever. She would never forgive herself if he died with hard feelings between them.

But if she didn't go to Justin, and soon, she would never forgive herself.

She just had to trust that the love her parents and brother and great-grandparents had for her would be enough to overcome the bitterness of old enmities. Because if it didn't, her heart would surely break in two and then she would never be whole and happy again no matter which side she chose.

She got up, dried her hands and left the kitchen area. She could hear Kent moving around in the bedroom, the sound of water running in the shower. She thought of his easy and loving relationship with his fiancée, Tanya, who would be flying in to join them in an hour or so, and how happy she was for the two of them. How she wanted that same kind of happiness for herself.

"Nana?" she asked, wrapping her arms around herself as she stared out the window at the comings and goings in the Owners' and Drivers' lot. "Have you ever done anything that you knew before you did it was going to change your life so much you could never quite go back to being who you were before?"

"Two times," Juliana answered promptly covering Sophia's salad with plastic wrap and setting it in the big refrigerator. "Once, when I left home to go to Nashville to be a singer. And then ten years later, when I married Milo. But by then, my folks had toughened up pretty good and they were just thankful to see me married and out of show business. I never quite made it to the big time in Nashville or anywhere else, but I enjoyed singing and I was a regular at some pretty classy places. I even made it onto the Opry show a few times."

"I know, Nana, I love to hear you sing. I wish you did it more these days."

"Too many years and too many cigarettes," the old lady said candidly. "I only sing in the shower these days. And I was good," she said, wagging a wooden spoon in the air. "Don't ever think otherwise. But when I met Milo, it didn't matter any more. All I wanted was to marry him, and I did, even though everyone thought he was too old for me. He was only three years younger than my father! A grandfather already when we married! My dad hated that." Juliana had been the oldest of seven children, only two others had lived to adulthood. She was the only girl—the apple of her daddy's eye, Sophia had always suspected.

"And then there were the boys. After Milo's son and daughter-in-law were killed I was suddenly a mother taking on the raising of two heartbroken little boys that weren't my own. That was even more terrifying." She shook the spoon in Sophia's direction for emphasis. "I've never regretted what I did. Not for one minute. Poor Momma, she never had a day's fun in her life. Always so worried about doing the proper thing. About following all the rules. I vowed never to live like that and I've kept my word."

"You must have made the right choice. You and Grandpa are still married."

"Well, of course I did. But let me tell you it hasn't always been easy. I didn't only marry Milo. I took on the raising of his two grandsons. I was terrified but I didn't let it stop me."

Startled, Sophia looked across the granite-topped divide at her great-grandmother and saw her smiling a little dreamily at nothing, and realized she was reliving some of those early times of her marriage. But it was her confession that she had been terrified of what the future might bring when she married Milo that hit Sophia the hardest. Terrified, but she had done it anyway, without hesitation, and without lasting regret.

Sophia looked back to the scene outside. A steady parade of golf carts rolled by, filled with wives and children off to the play area, or perhaps to the Motor Racing Outreach coach that provided spiritual guidance and support for the drivers and their families, as well as expert day care for the children traveling the circuit. Somewhere nearby, she heard a dog barking and remembered Juliana telling her there were two extra motor homes on the lot this weekend, one set up as a spa staffed by a local salon, and the other manned by employees of a local dog-grooming service. "Can you imagine? A dog spa," she had asked Sophia, rolling her eyes. "Why, back in the day…"

Sophia smiled and then returned her thoughts to what Juliana had just said. It was the first time she'd ever heard her formidable great-grandmother admit to being afraid of anything. Maybe Sophia wasn't such a coward after all. Had her mother, Patsy, a teenage bride and mother with her own disapproving parents, and a young husband who faced danger and the possibility of serious injury or worse every time he strapped himself into a race car, battled those same inner terrors? She probably had, too. But the difference between Sophia and the other Grosso women was that she had let the fear shape her response to life.

Now she had the chance to break the pattern she'd

allowed herself to fall into, and she was going to do her best not to fail. As these thoughts played themselves out in the echo chamber of her mind another golf cart came into view beyond the window. This one wasn't filled with women and kids and dogs. It held a solitary man. Her heartbeat sped up as it always did when she recognized who was driving it.

Justin.

She hadn't expected to see him before the start of the race. She would meet him in front of his hauler before the pre-race introductions. It was what they'd agreed on when he dropped her off at her car that was in the parking lot at Sunny Hills after they had made love at the lake. He'd followed her to her apartment, making sure she made it home safely, but he didn't go inside. It was the time he had given her to make her decision. To walk him to his car. Or to walk out of his life. She dropped onto the sofa and peered through the narrow slats of the window blinds.

True to form, Juliana's radar picked up on something in her stance or on her face. "Who's out there? A friend?" she asked, narrowing her eyes and giving Sophia a questioning look. "Open the door. Give a shout. Invite them to dinner. There's more than enough."

"I don't know if I should do that," Sophia said, the butterflies in her stomach accelerating as though they'd suddenly become jet-powered. Beyond her great-grandmother's considerable bulk, her tall, handsome brother, wearing sweats and a T-shirt, had appeared from the back of the motor home, toweling his hair dry. The No. 414 car had been fastest at practice that afternoon. His beautiful fiancée was only minutes away from being at his side. He was a happy man.

"Why not ask them in, sis? I bought this thing so I'd have

plenty of room to entertain," Kent assured her waving his hand at the salon area. Her brother had inherited his olive skin and Roman profile from their Italian ancestors, and his height from Patsy's family. His blue eyes also came from their mother, a trait the three of them shared. "Who's out there? You've made yourself so scarce on the circuit the last couple of years I didn't know you'd kept up many friendships from the old days." He bent slightly to look out the window.

"It's not an old friend. It's a new one," she said hurriedly, springing up from the couch, hoping Justin's cart was already out of sight. "But I don't think I'm quite brave enough to ask him to eat with us yet."

"Why not? We don't bite," Kent replied, obviously thinking she was making a joke. She wasn't, of course, but neither was she going to chicken out and tell him to forget what she'd just said. She wanted to be like Juliana, with no regrets, not Juliana's mother who must have died a bitter and unhappy woman.

"It's Justin Murphy," she said squaring her shoulders.

"You're kidding, right?" Her brother didn't look happy any more. In fact he was scowling just like Milo.

"I'm not kidding."

"Sophia. Have you lost your mind?"

Sophia glanced at her great-grandmother, caught her eye and smiled. "I know exactly what I'm doing. And since I've told you, I might as well get this over with and go next door to tell Mom and Dad. And Grandpa when he gets back from the media center." Sophia didn't give herself a chance to pause and lose her nerve. "As a matter of fact, Justin's more than a friend. I'm almost positive I've fallen in love with him."

CHAPTER SEVENTEEN

"MURPHY, I WANT TO SEE you. Now." A rumble of thunder above the distant hills added unnecessary emphasis to Dean Grosso's low but distinct command. Bristol's nickname was Thunder Valley but today it was Mother Nature, not race cars, supplying the sound effects. Justin had been expecting some kind of confrontation with Sophia's father, or brother, or both, but not in so public a place as outside the building where the mandatory pre-race drivers' meeting had just been held.

With a quick inclination of his head Dean Grosso began to walk toward the fleet of colorful haulers parked with laser precision on the speedway's concrete infield. The track, a half-mile oval, was so small there were no garages. The teams worked on the cars on the pavement in front of their haulers, giving it something of a feel of what races had been like in the dirt-track days. Without a word, Justin fell in beside the older man. He'd be damned if he stayed a respectful step behind. Grosso's No. 414 car had qualified fourth, two rows ahead of him, but he'd beat Sophia's brother, Kent, by two one-thousandths of a second to take the number-seven starting position on the inside of the fourth row. That made them damned near equals—at least for today. And kept him from the added disadvantage of pitting on the backstretch. Another idiosyncrasy of the Bristol track, it was the only one on the circuit with two pit roads. A bad day qualifying doomed you to the backstretch pits that made it damned near impossible to win the race.

He could see men from other teams elbowing each other, turning to watch them as they passed, figuring the blow-up they'd expected over the Las Vegas incident was finally coming to a head. That wasn't going to happen; not unless Grosso started it. Rachel had worked like a slave on the engine setup for this week's race and no matter what kind of turmoil his heart was in, Justin wasn't going to let her down by allowing it to affect his driving. Besides, he knew it wasn't the Vegas wreck Dean Grosso wanted to talk to him about. It was Sophia that was on his mind.

The problem was finding any kind of privacy. The track seated 160,000 fans in grandstands that seemed to climb into the heavens. It was like standing at the bottom of a bowl when you looked up at the midday sun. In the summer, it beat down on you, the asphalt that covered the entire infield magnifying the heat. But the spring race was more often than not cold and dreary. However, today it was warm and humid and thundershowers threatened.

Bristol was Justin's favorite race venue. Short track, lots of rubbin' and bangin'. Hard on the gas. He wanted to win here more than just about anything else. The man beside him had won here more than once. So had his son. No Murphy ever had. He intended to be the first.

Early arrivals were already starting to file into their seats, but most fans were still outside the gates, tailgating, attending church services, strolling through the rows of souvenir trailers, or hanging around the chain-link fence that separated them from the drivers as they walked back and forth from the track to their motor homes over an elevated walkway.

Most drivers compared racing here to trying to fly a jet fighter in a toilet bowl, or maybe to racing cars in a blender. Justin didn't know what he compared it to, but wrestling 3400 pounds of sheet metal and high-performance horsepower around the steeply-banked concrete oval with forty-two other equally powerful competitors, was to him, the essence of stock car racing.

A couple of pit reporters, credentials dangling from straps around their necks, picking up the scent of a story, or at least a sidebar, moved in on them but Grosso waved them off. "Later, guys," he said, and such was his stature in the sport that they did as he asked. Justin was impressed in spite of himself. Dean Grosso was an inch or so shorter than Justin. Five-eight or five-nine at the most and slight of build, with thick brown hair and skin tanned and etched by the sun and wind. He'd been driving NASCAR Sprint Cup Series cars for thirty years but had never won a NASCAR Sprint Cup Series championship, although he'd won races at every track on the circuit, and had been voted "Driver of the Year" more times than Justin could count.

The deaths of Justin's great-uncle and father were now many years in the past, but some remembered. And whenever there was an incident like the wreck at Las Vegas, one enterprising reporter or another filled his word quota with a rehash of the old scandal. For that reason, if no other, Justin Murphy and the Grossos, father and son, were almost never seen together, unless mandated to do so by race-day protocols or NASCAR commitments.

The other reason was because they just plain didn't like each other.

When they reached the Smoothtone Music hauler, Dean jerked his thumb at the two men sitting on camp chairs outside the trailer, shaded from the hazy late-morning sun by the raised back panel of the semi-trailer that acted as a kind of porch roof above what amounted to a makeshift patio complete with a monster gas grill and coolers filled with cold drinks.

"Anyone inside?" Dean asked.

"Perry's in the lounge with the pit crew," one of the men replied, giving Justin the once-over. Both men wore short-sleeved blue-and-white shirts with Smoothtone Music's distinctive logo embroidered across their chests in darker blue with touches of gold. They were big and burly and towered over Dean and Justin, but jumped to their feet as soon as their driver opened his mouth.

"Thanks," Grosso said. He turned his attention back to Justin. "We don't need to have this discussion in front of everyone, but since my crew chief's using the lounge, we'll talk here." He indicated the narrow, low-ceilinged hallway that ran between built-in storage cabinets that likely held extra crew uniforms and cleaning supplies behind their closed doors, and the small kitchenette that served crew members' needs. The ceiling was low because the No. 414 car and its backup were stored in a bay directly overhead. Beyond them were work benches and tool boxes, computer consoles and engine storage compartments, and at the front end of the huge semi-trailer was the lounge where Dean's crew chief, Perry Noble, was meeting with his pit crew.

Justin stopped just out of earshot of the crewmen outside in their chairs. He pulled off his mirrored shades and shoved them in his shirt pocket. "What have you got to say to me, sir? I think you made yourself pretty clear at Vegas what you thought about me and Sophia seeing each other."

Grosso didn't even blink. "Good. No beating around the bush. No bullcrap speeches pretending to wonder what I want to talk to you about. Sophia told her mother and me this morning that she's been seeing you pretty steadily since Daytona."

"Yes, sir. Not as steadily or as often as I'd like but I'm working on improving that."

Dean's eyes narrowed to gunfighter slits and Justin's nerves tightened despite his determination to stay cool and in control. "If she walks you to your car this afternoon like she's considering doing, it's going to get some attention. And not just from me and her brother," Dean said, as nonchalantly as if they were discussing the chance of rain postponing the start of the race. "It's going to be noticed. It's going to be talked about. And then someone's bound to bring up what happened back in the day."

"Maybe that's not such a bad thing," Justin said thoughtfully. "Maybe it's finally time to track down who killed my dad. And figure out what really happened the night my great-uncle went head-first off the side of that mountain."

Dean never raised his voice but his expression hardened. "No one knows what happened the night Connor went through that guardrail and off the mountain, probably we never will. But get this straight. None of me or mine had anything to do with your father's death." He shifted his weight, shaving an inch or two from the small distance that separated them in the narrow confines of the hauler. "But we both know there were plenty of others who might have."

Justin came away from the wall. Now they were standing toe to toe. "Don't push me, sir," he warned.

"Don't threaten me, son," he replied, without moving a muscle. "I'm speaking truth here and you're going to listen. Troy Murphy was a damned fine driver. But he was a hell of a lousy human being. He had a reputation for womanizing that wasn't all exaggeration and bragging. Most of it was fact. I don't intend for my daughter to be subjected to the same humiliations your mother was. Is that clear, boy?"

Justin's ears rang with the force of angry blood pumping through his veins. Grosso was goading him and it was working. He wanted to punch the older man in the mouth just to shut him up. He stared down at his hands, balled them into fists, imagined how good it would feel to land that first blow. But another voice also made itself heard over the adrenaline rush buzzing in his ears. How did he defend a dead man when all the accusations Grosso was making were true?

"Go on," Dean taunted. "Take a swing at me. Prove me right."

Justin's head came up. "You are right," he said tightly, uncurling his clenched hands, making himself relax. His dad would have taken a swing at his opponent. Justin wasn't going to. "Can't defend the indefensible," he said, his jaw muscles so tight his teeth were clenched. "But let me tell you something, sir. I'm not my father. I'm not the SOB he was. I've made mistakes. I've done stupid things but falling in love with your daughter isn't one of them. I love her. I believe she loves me."

"Well, I'm not so sure," Dean said. "She's back in our motor home, crying her eyes out. Women who are happily in love don't do that. Don't count on her being there to walk you to your car this afternoon, Murphy. I'm hoping like hell she doesn't leave the lot. That she stays right where she is now."

Justin felt his anger rekindle and knew he had to get out of the hauler before he said or did something that would ruin whatever small chance he still had of winning Sophia's father's respect. Was the older man telling the truth? Was Sophia so unhappy she'd broken into tears just admitting she had feelings for him? How would she ever choose to defy her family and marry him if she was so unhappy already? Maybe he was like his dad. Maybe just falling in love with a Murphy was jinx enough to doom a relationship and eventually drive the woman he loved to take her own life.

He pulled the sunglasses back out of his pocket and shoved them in place, turned on his heel and launched himself out of the hauler—straight into the path of Kent Grosso. He was already dressed in his blue and red Vittle Farms uniform, helmet tucked under his arm. The reigning NASCAR Sprint Cup Series champion. A superhero. The most popular driver on the circuit. On his way to a meet-and-greet, or media interview, or maybe just to get his turn bashing the upstart who had dared to trifle with his sister. "Hey, what gives?" He widened his stance to keep from being bowled over by Justin's sudden emergence from the relative darkness of the hauler interior. "What the hell are you doing here, Murphy?"

"Out of my way, Grosso," Justin growled. "Just because I didn't take a swing at your dad doesn't mean I won't take a swing at you."

Forty-five minutes later, Justin was suited up, standing in the lounge of his hauler, cell phone to his ear. "Diane. It's me, Justin. Yeah, I'm at the hauler. Look, I told you I had someone I wanted to walk me to the car, right? Well, she broke our date. Can you still get your hands on the Miss Whatever-she-was you wanted me to escort? Yeah, track her down and get her over to the pit. We've got about five minutes for pictures before the pre-race ceremonies start."

He flipped the phone shut and closed his fist around it, wondering what would happen if he heaved it against the wall. His uncle swiveled away from the built-in console where he was making some last minute notations on the computer screen, and gave him the once-over. "You look like someone shot your dog. And what did you do to your hand?"

Justin looked down at his scratched and bruised knuckles. "Nothing. Just banged it on the closet door is all."

Hugo grunted. "Looks like you tried to punch its lights out and lost. What was that call all about? I thought Sophia Grosso was walking you to your car, 'whether I liked the idea or not,' was the way I remember you put it."

Justin felt worse than if someone had shot his dog. He felt like he'd been shot himself. Right through the heart, and the wound was self-inflicted. "Yeah, well you just heard me tell Diane she isn't."

"So she came to her senses and decided she didn't want to be seen publicly with the son of a man someone in her family just might have killed?"

Justin felt his color rise and pulled air in through his nose to keep from letting go with a string of four-letter words. He had had about all he could take for one day, and Hugo's jabs were the final straw. He held onto his temper with the last vestiges of his self-control. He knew Hugo was in as bad a place as he was. Kim was too sick to even make the race, and still she refused to see a doctor.

"No, she didn't break the date. I just told Diane that. Let it seem like the lady's the one who came to her senses and called it off. Isn't that what a gentleman's supposed to do? If you want to know the truth, I'm the one who changed my mind. I just stopped by the Grosso motor homes and told her I'd made a mistake. That I wasn't ready to settle down, give up the good life, the starlets, and the Miss Whatevers. Seems like when you get right down to it, I'm more my father's son than I thought I was."

"Oh, Justin, you didn't really say those things?" Rachel entered the lounge, carrying a handful of computer printouts covered with scrawled lists on half a dozen different colors of sticky notes, in time to hear what he said. "I mean, I wasn't happy when you told us you two were getting serious. Not because I don't want you to be happy. But because there's just so much..." She threw up her hands as she searched for the word she wanted.

"History? Baggage? Bad blood?" Justin said with a sneer.

Rachel blinked at his sharp retort, then sat down on the black-leather banquette that did double duty as dining and conference table and propped her chin in her hand. When she spoke, her expression was so sincere, her words so filled with pain for his unhappiness that he felt ashamed for lashing out at her. "Oh, Justin, I'm sorry, but maybe it's for the best. I mean, she's not one of us. She's...a Grosso."

He raked his hand through his hair then reached out and gave her a light clip on the shoulder. "Yeah, Rayray." She mustered a smile. "That about says it all, don't you think? Anyway, it's not a problem anymore. She didn't even put up a fuss when I told her *adios*."

That's what hurt the most, he realized. She'd just stood there looking at him with those big, blue eyes, her nose red from crying. *Over him, for God's sake. Her dad had been telling the truth.* She didn't say anything for the longest time, while he struggled not to take her in his arms and tell her to forget everything he'd said, to just run off with him and leave both their families and all the bitterness behind. But of course that was the root of the problem. He couldn't do that and neither could she. NASCAR was his life and it was in her blood, too.

Their love couldn't survive cut off from the small world of professional stock car racing and they both knew it. Finally, she'd nodded her head, whispered goodbye and hurried into Kent Grosso's motor home, never even looking back. There'd been nothing else for him to do then but get back in his golf cart and amble off like some old duffer playing eighteen holes at the local country club. He shut himself inside the Manor, sandwiched between the dog grooming motor home and the fence—a sign of the track management's disapproval—and put his fist through the closet door.

His cell beeped again and he flipped it open. "Diane. Yeah. You found her. Good. Five minutes? I'll be there." He grabbed his helmet from the table and hooked it under his arm, then picked up his sunglasses and slid them on. "Diane found Miss What's-her-name," he said unnecessarily. "Got to move. Diane says it looks like rain."

"I STILL CAN'T BELIEVE what happened," Sophia said, sniffing back a little sob that had snuck up on her after she thought she'd cried all the tears she could squeeze out. "When we were at his place at the lake he told me it was my decision. He promised he would wait for me to make up my mind." She was careful with her words, aware that her great-grandfather, ensconced in a big over-stuffed recliner in the salon, could hear every word she said, and admitting to spending the night with Justin would only make matters worse as far as the old man was concerned.

"Well, obviously you took too long." Tanya Wells, Kent's girlfriend—no, fiancée, Sophia had to keep reminding herself—replied. She poured herself a mug of tea and settled on the stool beside Sophia's. She was petite and pretty with a softly rounded figure, but when you looked in her eyes you saw confidence and resolve and realized she was a woman who knew her own mind and spoke it.

She could afford to, of course. Not only was she engaged to the reigning NASCAR Sprint Cup Series champion, but she was also a successful businesswoman, a wedding/special events photographer whose clientele included millionaires, debutantes and superstar country singers. "Men are real stinkers when they put their minds to it. At least he came by and told you in person. I mean, he could have sent you a text message, or even let you show up at his pit stall—dressed to the nines and ready for him to slip a diamond ring on your finger—and BOOM! You come face to face with some other woman hanging on his arm."

"The boy wouldn't do that," Juliana interrupted from the other side of the granite-topped divider where she was making sandwiches for Milo to take with him to Kent's pit where he'd chosen to watch this week's race.

"Don't see how you come to that conclusion, knowing the whelp's reputation. Hell, even I've heard of some of his shenanigans," Milo grunted, his scrawny neck coming up out of the collar of his shirt like a curious turtle. Her great-grandfather was a wizened little gnome of a man now that the decades had taken their toll. But when he was younger, he had been well-built and handsome. She especially liked the picture of him in his three-piece suit and snap-brim fedora that had been taken when he joined the FBI so long ago, but there were others she cherished equally as much. One of him with his army buddies from WW2 and others when he was racing stock cars after the war.

"Justin doesn't have much of a track record where relationships are concerned," Tanya said bluntly.

"Lucy Gunter. I'd forgotten," Sophia murmured. Daytona seemed so long ago. She felt her color rising. She had let herself forget Justin and Lucy had ended their romance the same night they'd met.

"To be completely honest, they hadn't been getting along for weeks before Justin met you. I'm surprised they lasted as long as they did. They really weren't suited to each other."

"Justin told me that. He never had a bad word to say about Lucy. Only that they weren't right for each other." Sophia perked up a little. He hadn't been lying. She wasn't wrong in believing she knew him well enough to tell if he wasn't being truthful.

"Lucy said the same. She's moved on with her life. I guess Justin has, too."

"Three days ago, he said he loved me," Sophia said, softly, remembering the hours they'd spent together in front of the fireplace. "He meant it, too. I'm sure he did."

"Did you say you loved him back?" Tanya asked, and behind her Juliana stopped what she was doing and listened, too.

"I...I couldn't. I was afraid," Sophia admitted.

"You weren't afraid. You were smart," Milo intoned from the depths of his chair.

"Be quiet, Milo," Juliana warned. "Keep your opinions to yourself."

"He said he would know I loved him if I showed up today to walk him to his car. He said that would be enough.

He could wait for the rest. I bought this damned outfit, got my highlights touched up, had a manicure, everything, so he would know I was making a real commitment when I showed up. And now this happens." She smoothed her hands over the copper-colored linen pants suit with the ivory silk camisole she hoped would knock his socks off. As it turned out, he'd stared right through her from behind those damnable mirrored sunglasses of his and knocked her for a loop instead.

Thunder rumbled beyond the motor home walls. At the same moment something connected in Sophia's brain. For a second, she felt as if she might have been hit by lightning, the shock of the revelation was so strong it was an actual physical jolt that set her nerves tingling. "He was lying," she said, slapping her hand on the counter. "He was lying when he said he didn't love me."

"How do you know?" Tanya asked. She was a very straightforward woman. Sophia doubted she spent a lot of time acting on hunches.

"Oh, why didn't I realize this before? He didn't look at me," she said, grinning like a fool. "He didn't take off those damned sunglasses of his. He wouldn't let me see his eyes because he knew I could see he wasn't telling me the truth. His eyes always give him away."

Tanya turned her head to look at Juliana who was smiling almost as broadly as Sophia. "Yes," she said, turning the smile on her scowling husband. "You can always see the love in their eyes." Sophia glanced at the older woman and knew what she said was true. When she looked at Milo she didn't see the ravages time had wrought on the handsome G-man and race car driver she'd married. She saw him as he'd been and always would be for her.

Sophia looked inward and brought forward an image of Justin's face that night by the fire.

You could see it in his eyes.

"But why did he come here today? Why did he say those things?"

"I think I might have an idea why," Tanya said. She gestured to what was happening beyond the big window opposite where they sat.

Sophia's breath hissed between her teeth. "Of course," she whispered. "I should have guessed right away."

Her father and brother stood between the two motor homes in full racing gear, her mother with them. Banners flying, helmeted and visored like knights of old, except for those damned mirrored sunglasses. Hiding their thoughts, their emotions, hiding their lies.

She bolted up off the stool and out the door and into the middle of an altercation between her parents.

"You shouldn't have interfered, Dean," Patsy said, her voice slightly brittle, on edge. "She's not a child. Sophia is capable of making all her own decisions. If Justin Murphy is the man she wants, then you can't do anything about it."

"I already have," Dean replied. Both of them looked tense and unhappy. Her father's forehead was furrowed and her mother's lips were drawn into a straight, uncompromising line.

Sophia crossed the small space that separated the two motor homes aware the others had followed her and were gathering around. "Dad, you talked to Justin, didn't you? What did you say to him?"

"Go on, Dean, tell her. We've never interfered in her love life before. Why start now?"

"He made you cry. How do you expect me to believe

you'll be happy with him when you were crying while you told us you loved him?" he asked sounding bewildered.

"Because I was afraid," Sophia confessed. "I'm always afraid on race day. I'm afraid for both of you. Now I'm afraid for three of you. It makes me emotional."

"Honey, you don't have to be afraid. Your mom and Juliana aren't afraid."

"Speak for yourself," Juliana snorted. "My butt cheeks are clenched from the time the pace car heads off the track 'til the checkered flag."

Patsy reached out and put her arm around Sophia. "You learn to deal with it, baby, but you never get used to it."

Sophia hugged her mother back and gave Juliana's hand a squeeze. "I'm figuring that out."

Dean was staring at his wife. "You never told me."

"I'm telling you now," she said and tossed her head. "We'll discuss it later. Now we have to come up with a plan to get Justin and Sophia back together."

"No," her father said. "Leopards don't change their spots overnight. He's—"

"Still a Murphy," Sophia interrupted. This time she wasn't going to let her reasoning overrule her feelings. This argument was too important. It might decide how she spent the rest of her life.

"Hell, yes, it's because he's a Murphy." It wasn't Dean who answered but Milo. "Worthless. The lot of them."

"That's not true," Sophia said firmly, but respectfully. She didn't want to argue with her great-grandfather but she would if she had to. "He's a good man and a good driver, Grandpa. He's not like his father or his great-uncle. You can't keep measuring the rest of the family by that same old template. Hasn't this gone on long enough?

There are no clues. No suspects. No reason to keep the bad feelings alive."

"Our honor," Milo rasped, leaning heavily on his cane. "My honor."

"Your honor's been vindicated a hundred times over. You're respected by everyone in the sport. Connor Murphy is fifty years in his grave and all but forgotten. That should be vindication enough."

"I'll always love you, you're my only great-grand-daughter, but I won't be in the same room with that young scoundrel."

"Grandpa, you of all of us should understand how I feel. You told me yourself everyone was against you marrying Nana, but you did it anyway."

"It's not the same. It was because of the difference in our ages. It's not the same," he repeated.

This is what Sophia feared most, a rift in her family. "Don't make my happiness hostage to the past. Let it go, Grandpa, please."

"I can't," he said his voice frail but unwavering. "I can't." He turned and shuffled back into Kent's place, shutting the door behind him.

"I'll talk to him," Juliana promised, coming forward to give Sophia a hug. She smiled and patted her shoulder. "Go to your Justin," she said. "I'll get my husband to come around eventually. I always do." She looked past Sophia to Dean and Patsy. She pointed her finger at Sophia's father. "And you. Remember before you come face-to-face with Sophia's young man again, that you weren't Patsy's parents' first choice for their daughter, either. Not by a long shot." She climbed the steps to the motor home and shut herself inside with her husband.

Her parents and brother and his fiancée remained, staring at Sophia, waiting for her to make the next move. A roar went up from the crowd both inside and outside the track. They all looked skyward and saw the skydivers, a Bristol tradition, silhouetted against towering thunderheads, spiraling down from high above the bowl, trailing giant American flags. "We'd better get a move on or we'll miss the driver introductions," Kent said. "I'm not starting at the back of the pack just so you can make up with Justin Murphy."

Sophia made up her mind. "I'm coming with you. I have to talk to Justin. Find out if he really meant what he said to me. Now. Before I lose my nerve."

CHAPTER EIGHTEEN

MISS EASTERN TENNESSEE AZALEA Queen was a wannabe actress and aspiring country singer. She also was about as dumb as a box of rocks. She had a handler, a formidable-looking woman with steel-gray hair, a darker gray power suit and four-inch stiletto heels that looked lethal enough to be registered as deadly weapons. She was there to see her charge got maximum attention and exposure—and not just for her surgically enhanced bosom, which Justin had to admit, being a man and not blind, was spectacular. Justin may not be the pole-sitter for the race but he was in the top five rows, that meant her Miss Azalea just might get some TV time when she walked him to the car. For that, she simpered and smiled and posed for pictures with every guy on the team, and a couple who weren't.

That was fine with Justin. He wasn't in the mood to make conversation anyway. He was trying to concentrate on the upcoming race, and he had been doing a pretty good job of it too, even with the distraction of the beauty queen and her handler, until he caught a glimpse of a sun-streaked blond in a coppery-brown pant suit in Kent Grosso's pit area just next door.

Sophia?

He hadn't expected her to come to the pits.

He hadn't expected to have to face her again so soon.

He hadn't expected that just catching sight of her would squeeze his heart like a vise.

And why hadn't he remembered before he went and did the oh-so-noble Sir Trueheart gig, that not only did Kent Grosso have the pit stall next to his, but that he'd also have to make a slow, uncomfortable loop around the track with him in a flag-decked pickup, smiling and waving to fans like he didn't have a worry in the world except to win the race, while the guy beside him, his friendly competitor, reigning NASCAR Sprint Cup Series champion, in most everyone else's opinion an all round great guy, was in reality ready to take him down in a flying tackle and wring his neck.

But oddly enough, Grosso hadn't said a word as they wound their way back to pit road to the ringing cheers, and occasional boos, of the crowd. They both jumped out of the back of the pickup and made their way to their pits, side by side, while around them, photographers pushed lenses in their faces, and TV commentators, on the lookout for a quick sound bite or bit of color commentary, followed every move of the VIP fans and family members, waiting for the invocation and the national anthem, all of them within earshot of anything they said.

That's when he'd spotted Sophia and stopped like he'd been welded to the pavement. Kent Grosso followed the direction of his gaze, then he'd turned to him pretended to adjust his cap, shielding his face somewhat from the sharp eyes and ears nearby. "My sister wants to talk to you. I suggest you get the Azalea Queen out of sight so she can have her say."

"I didn't think she'd want to see me again," Justin said, once more moving forward so that they weren't accosted by one of the more aggressive female pit reporters he could see coming at them from the corner of his eye.

"Well, she does. Why she's even bothering, I don't know. But she wants to talk to you, so I'll take the bimbo and her guard witch off your hands for five minutes," Kent offered. "And Murphy?"

"Yeah?" Justin replied wary again at the dark undertone in his words.

"I'm doing this because she asked me to. But if you make her cry again, I'll hunt you down and make you sorry you were ever born. Understand?" Then he walked away, a path clearing before him as though he had cleaved it with a knife. Thirty seconds later, Miss Azalea and her bulldog guardian had been whisked away to the Vittle Farms pit for the publicity op of a lifetime, one-on-one face time with the NASCAR Sprint Cup Series champion.

Justin just stood there, dumbstruck, feeling suddenly isolated in the maelstrom of sound and color that swirled around him. A moment later, Sophia was by his side. Already the teams and drivers were beginning to line up beside the cars, the signal that time was short.

"That's who you dumped me for? The Eastern Tennessee Collagen Queen?" she asked unexpectedly.

He was thrown even further off balance. He'd pictured her heartbroken and forlorn, the way he'd left her, the image that scoured his heart with shame, not looking like this, gorgeous and sophisticated and putting his second-string beauty pageant winner to shame. He narrowed his eyes. She certainly didn't look as if she'd been crying again. Her nose was a little pink, maybe, but that just made him want to lean down and give it a kiss. And her lips were pink, too, rosy and luscious— "What?" It was the only thing he could think of to say as he dragged his scattered wits into line.

"You'd rather that poster child for multiple cosmetic surgeries walk you to your car than me?" She put her hands on her hips.

"No," he said, realizing that more and more eyes were swiveling in their direction. His heart began to hammer in his chest, and not only with pre-race jitters, but with hope. "Hell, no. I just thought—"

"That's our problem, Justin," she said, and her lips curved into the slightest of smiles, but her eyes were almost the same dark blue of the clouds that seemed to be clinging to the top of the bowl waiting to drop their load of rain and wreak havoc with the race schedule. "We've been thinking too much."

He shook his head to clear the ringing in his ears. She was here. She had come just as she'd promised she would, despite his trying to brush her off. He had to know why. "C'mon. There's got to be someplace around here with a little bit of privacy."

The public-address announcer was calling the crowd to order, asking them to take off their hats, stand for the presentation of the colors and the invocation. Justin hopped over the pit wall, reached around and lifted Sophia over, too. She felt light as a feather in his arms, so right, as he let her slide against his body for just a moment.

He found a tiny space against a toolbox and the tarp the team had hung from the tent pole that held up the pit roof in anticipation of rain.

"I want an explanation for the things you said to me back in the lot," Sophia demanded. "I want you to take off those damnable sunglasses and look me in the eye and tell me you don't love me. If you can, I'll leave and never look back. If you can't then—" She took a quick, shaky breath. In fact, she was shaking like a leaf all over.

He wanted to pull her close and hold her tight until she was calm again, but he just stood there, waiting. "You'll what?" he prompted.

"Then I'll never leave you." Slowly she raised her hands to his face and slipped the heavy, dark glasses from his eyes. "Say it. Say you don't love me. I dare you. I double-dog dare you."

He blinked to clear his vision. Her face was solemn. She was clutching his sunglasses so tightly that her knuckles were white. He reached out and took her by the arms. "I made you cry, Sophia. I never want to make you cry again."

She tilted her head and frowned, then her crazy, wonderful smile broke forth. "I always cry, Justin. Dad knows that. I cry when I'm sad. I cry when I'm happy. I cry when I'm afraid."

"What are you afraid of?"

"Sometimes everything," she said her smile turning a little rueful. "But mostly for you. For us." She blinked very hard but one crystal tear escaped and rolled down her cheek. She brushed it impatiently away. "See. I'm a crier."

"And a fainter. But you've been doing a pretty good job not crying in front of me," he said.

"It's been hard. Really hard." She looked down at his sunglasses and then back up into his eyes, nearly dazzling him with her beauty. "I should have told you sooner. There just hasn't been time. Everything for us has happened so fast." She opened her eyes wide. They were blue as cornflowers, blue as the sky. True blue, loving eyes. "I don't care what you said back at the motor home. I'm telling you now. I love you, Justin Murphy. I love you with all my heart."

He continued staring into her eyes, looking into the very heart and soul of her, and no longer tried to hide any part of himself in return. "I love you, Sophia Grosso. I lied when I said I didn't. Your whole family thinks I'm not good enough for you and for a little while there I let myself believe it, too."

"Don't talk like that," she said, and if she'd been Miss Azalea Queen, he figured she'd have stomped her foot. "You don't have anything to be embarrassed about. Well, no more than any of the other drivers. Soon you're going to be just as successful as my dad and my brother. I won't let you be any less."

He laughed. He couldn't help himself. This was the Sophia he loved, feisty and stubborn. A match for his moods. For his temper, for his love.

She was on a roll. She couldn't seem to stop talking. "You'll make the Chase every season. You'll win the NASCAR Sprint Cup Series championship. We'll have a private jet and a million-dollar motor home. No one will park us up against the fence beside the dog-grooming salon. I promise."

He pulled her into a hug that left her breathless. "Then I can't fail to win The Cup. You won't stand for it, right?"

"Exactly."

He brushed the tips of his fingers across her mouth. "I think some part of me has loved you ever since I stole your first kiss back there behind the pool cabana. Now it's not just a part of me that loves you. It's all of me. Heart and soul."

"Oh, Justin. I love you, too. I was coming here today to tell you so, just as I promised, but when you appeared out of nowhere this morning and—"

"I thought I was being noble. Sir NASCAR Trueheart at his best. I thought I was giving you a way out. This isn't going to be easy, Sophia. Your dad and brother are probably hatching up plans to punt me up the track and put me in the wall right this minute."

"They'll come around. Kent's in love himself. He'll be on our side, I know he will." Justin wasn't sure of that at all, but he smiled because he wanted to see her smile in return.

"And what about Milo? I don't see him feeling soft-hearted over the course of true love." *Love?* How many times had he said that word in the last five minutes? More than in his entire life before today.

Sophia's smiled faded away. "I don't know. He said he wouldn't even be in the same room with you."

"Hell, see what I mean—"

"I don't care," she said, her mouth firming into a straight line but the shadows didn't completely recede from her eyes. "I love you."

"Sometimes love isn't enough." He thought of his parents. Surely they had loved each other at one time, before everything went wrong for them.

"Yes, it is," she said fiercely. She took both his hands in hers, aware as he was that they had only the illusion of privacy, not the real thing. "We love each other. That makes us strong. We'll make it all come out right in the end. I promise."

"And if it doesn't? If we can't get at least one of our families to accept our getting married then what will we do?"

"I'm going to marry you," she said fiercely. "Nothing will change my mind. I promise."

"Ladies and gentlemen, our national anthem," the loud-speakers boomed.

"I have to go." He leaned down and kissed her quick and hard. "You win, Sophia. I'll marry you, but only if our families come around. Do you think you can get the Almighty Grossos to change their minds?"

"Yes. Do you think you can get the stubborn Murphys to change their minds?"

"Yes," he said, sliding the concealing sunglasses back on his face so that she didn't pick up on the uncertainty he couldn't totally banish. "Leave it to me. By the Homestead race we'll have every last Murphy and Grosso professing undying friendship, all in one room, at one time, drinking iced tea and making wedding plans. I guarantee it." By the time he'd finished the speech he'd almost convinced himself. He picked her up and swung her around until she was breathless and laughing, and the shadows had fled from her eyes, then he set her gently on her feet and took her hand in his, pulling the sunglasses off once more and letting them dangle from his fingertips. "Now, Mrs. Murphy-to-be. Walk me to my car."

EPILOGUE

"WHAT ARE YOU MUTTERING about?" Juliana asked, coming to perch gingerly on the wide arm of Milo's recliner. Or more properly, Kent's recliner. She looked around her, awed as always by the luxury of this miniature traveling mansion. She was very proud of Milo's great-grandson. *Her* great-grandson. She didn't think after all these years that Milo's first wife would begrudge her thinking of Milo's grandsons and great-grandchildren as her own.

"Nothing," he muttered sinking his chin into the open collar of his shirt. "Just watching that no-good Murphy trash whoop it up in Victory Lane."

"He ran a good race. Best race of the season so far," she said, watching Justin Murphy being sprayed with champagne by his celebrating team members in Victory Lane. "Good, clean race." The hat dance started as they watched, photograph after photograph, high fives and victory signs, and each and every one taken with the driver and his team wearing a different sponsor's hat.

And Sophia, smiling and happy, standing at Justin's side in each and every one of them.

The only person in the group that didn't look like they'd just won their first Bristol was Justin's crew chief, his Uncle Hugo. She glanced at her husband, still scowling at the screen.

No, the Murphys weren't any happier about this romance than the Grossos were.

Milo grunted again, mumbling a curse, then flipping the channel from the network broadcast to the closed-circuit TV feed that the track provided for the drivers and their families. "Too many laps run under yellow to suit me," he groused.

"That's Bristol," Juliana said rising a little stiffly to her feet. "How about a cup of tea?" She was glad they'd decided to ride home in the motor home with Kent's temporary driver the next morning instead of flying. If they hadn't, she'd be rushing herself and her cranky husband to the helicopter pad for the flight back to Charlotte, instead of padding across the plush carpet to fix herself a cup of tea. She was seventy-seven years old and would never admit it to a living soul, but she loved barreling down the highway in what amounted to a very high-end doll's house. "Did you hear me, Milo?" she repeated, looking over her shoulder. "Do you want some tea?"

"Bah, tea's for women. I want a highball. You make great highballs, Juliana love, let's have one together."

She could never resist that smile. Not in forty-seven years.

"Just one. Remember what the doctor said about mixing alcohol with your blood-pressure meds."

"I like living dangerously. Don't be stingy with the gin."

She switched on lights as she moved into the kitchen. Twilight had fallen early, causing the rain-delayed race to finish under the lights. Milo had slept through the hour's delay while the huge jet blowers dried the track, but she had stayed awake, watching the human-interest spots and driver interviews that filled the time, enjoying seeing Dean and Kent on TV as she always did, watching closely as

Justin Murphy handled the questions thrown at him with almost as much aplomb as her men did. Secretly, she hoped for a glimpse of Sophia on his pit box and was rewarded with a close-up shot of her great-granddaughter smiling into the camera.

"She'll do fine," she had said aloud to herself. "They'll both do just fine."

But deep down inside, she wasn't so sure. She had promised Sophia to bring Milo around, but could she accomplish that feat? He was so set in his ways now, the bitterness of those long-ago incidents was so ingrained that it had seeped into his bones and she didn't know if any amount of arguing or pleading could make him change his mind at this late date.

And did she really want to bring it all to the forefront again, even for the sake of Sophia's happiness? Because there were so many things she still didn't know about the nights, separated by so many years, that Connor Murphy and his nephew died. Juliana sighed as she took two glasses from the cupboard. Even after forty-seven years of marriage, there were secrets Milo guarded so zealously he wouldn't reveal them even to her.

She poured a generous splash of gin and tonic into the glasses and added ice. She believed her husband when he said he didn't know a thing about the night Troy Murphy had been run down and left for dead by the side of the road, even though it had been a Grosso Racing truck that killed him.

But she had never had that certainty about the circumstances surrounding Connor Murphy's death. She hadn't even met Milo back then, let alone married him, but over the years she'd absorbed his memories, in bits and pieces, osmosis maybe, or just the familiarity of having him toss and turn, caught in nightmares he wouldn't share, night after night.

But of one thing Juliana was convinced. Milo knew who had forced Connor Murphy's motorcycle off the side of the mountain all those years ago, and just as surely, he intended to take that knowledge with him to his grave.

* * * * *

*For more thrill-a-minute romances set against the
exciting backdrop of the NASCAR world, don't miss:
TRUTH AND CONSEQUENCES
by Bethany Campbell
FULLY ENGAGED by Abby Gaines
Available in March 2008
And for a sneak preview of
TRUTH AND CONSEQUENCES,
just turn the page....*

"How much of your money's invested in BMT? Still over half?" Craig asked.

Penny turned away, feeling slightly sick. He'd always warned her to diversify her investments. After marriage she had. But she'd only sold half the holdings she had in BMT. She'd thought to sell more would hurt her father's feelings. Penny said nothing. Craig had been right. Wasn't he always? He was a model of strength, morality and good sense. Not like her.

"I see," he said with resignation. "And your mother?"

She stared at the cream-colored carpet. Maeve had a trust fund from her father, but Hilton had talked her into investing most of it in BMT. Penny set her teeth and said, "She'll still have her trust coming in every month."

"How much?"

Craig leaned nearer, and she had to fight back a shiver. She took a deep breath. "About four thousand a month, I think. It seemed like a lot of money, twenty years ago, when she started getting it, but…"

"Inflation. I know. Penny, I don't want to be presumptuous. But there are things she needs to do. And do quickly. I made some note cards with some actions you'll probably have to take. Some names that might help. Hold out your hand."

Reluctantly, she obeyed, fighting not to tremble.

He laid a blue card on her palm. "Check the mortgage. If Hilton didn't take out a second mortgage on the house, Texas protects the homestead from even criminal penalties. Then Maeve can stay here if she can afford the upkeep. If she can't do this yet, you'll need to help arrange it. Pronto. Got it?"

She nodded, even though she was bewildered. She swallowed and said, "Could he have taken out a second mortgage without my mother knowing?"

"He could have if he tricked her into signing it or forged her name. He didn't do it through BMT. I checked. But, yes, he might have."

Craig placed a second card, a green one atop the first. "She's going to need the best family lawyer she can find. This is a complicated case. Here are a couple of names that were recommended."

His fingertips brushed hers this time, but again she nodded numbly.

He added a third card, a white one, and once more his hand touched hers. *Don't do that to me,* she thought. *Don't.*

"Here are the names of the best two divorce attorneys in Dallas," Craig said, his voice tight. "I know she won't want to—"

Penny's gaze met his in anger and disbelief. "Divorce? She'd never do such a thing! Never!"

His eyes fastened on hers. He said, "She has to for her own good. It'll protect her. Once divorce is filed for, the judge issues a restraining order to freeze all assets except what's needed to cover reasonable expenses."

He gave her more cards. A detective to help investigate Hilton's spending and accounts. A therapist.

"Thank you," she said, humbled by all he'd done to try

to help. She paused, her chin trembling. "Would you do one more thing? Don't let this be revealed publicly—until Mom can—until we can put some kind of coping strategy into place. Too much is hitting her at once—you've seen that. So if you could just hold off a little while…"

"It's too late," Craig said, shaking his head. His expression was regretful. "Like I said, I had to call the auditor. And then have a meeting with the board of directors. We had to call the F.B.I. There's no choice. Agents may be here to question Maeve and you. They'll be questioning the boys, too. Maybe as soon as tomorrow."

Penny's humility vanished in a blaze of anger. Her shakiness fled, driven out by an outraged sense of betrayal. She took a step back from him, looking him up and down with flashing eyes.

"How could you?" she demanded. "You kept sending word that you love me. How could you plunge us all into this pit of crime and debt and shame with no warning? None at all! Is this your sick revenge because I told you we're through? Then you come over here pretending to be Mr. Helpful? Mr. Sympathetic? Mr. Faithful Family Friend?"

She brandished the cards in his face, close to tears of fury.

He set his jaw. "I said there was no choice. To stall would be a criminal violation. And we're still not divorced, Penny. If I held back because of you and your family, we could be accused of collusion. It would make things that much worse."

Penny, anguished and resentful, couldn't accept this. "You're not a part of this family, and we won't be married much longer," she said from between her teeth. "I'm filing for divorce as fast as I can. Tomorrow, in fact."

"Penny, the last thing I'd ever want is to hurt you. Or

your family. I love you, but I'm tired of trying to make you love me back. But if any of you need me, I'll be here."

"Please just go," she said. "Please. You only make things worse."

"Seems you're right," he said, his face hardening. He squared his wide shoulders, took a long and rueful look at her. Then he turned and his long-legged stride took him out the door. It shut behind him with a click of finality.

As soon as he was gone, she flung herself into a chair, covered her face and dissolved into tears. Part of her anger toward Craig was that he was such an old-fashioned, upright sort that it would never occur to him to slow the investigation of her father.

She wept because he was honest, and she was not. She had secrets, terrible secrets. And although she still loved him, she was not as good as he was. How could he love her if he knew the truth?

//// NASCAR

Ladies, start your engines!

Pulse-accelerating dramas centered on four NASCAR families and the racing season that will test them all!

After money scandals and sponsorship issues cause image problems for Gordon Taney's racing team, he looks to PR agent Sandra Jacobs for help. But the only way to save his team is to ally with the man who once destroyed Sandra's family. Can Gordon and Sandra's newfound love and trust survive the devastation of his secret?

FULLY ENGAGED
Abby Gaines

Available March

Visit www.GetYourHeartRacing.com
for all of the latest details.

NASCAR21787R2